"How do you feel, Steve?" Nan asked. "How do *I* feel?"

"Like we have to make love," Dr. Steve Winstead answered. "Like I'll explode if I can't hold you against me, if I can't touch you. And I think you feel like that, too."

Nan lifted her face for his kiss. Her mouth was open to the probing of his tongue, to the demands of his lips, to the moist heat of his need. Their bodies braced against each other. Nan could feel the flames leaping, at her breasts, at her groin, in her thighs. Her whole body felt soft and ripe with expectation. She dropped her hands from his waist to the hardness of his buttocks, pressing him against her.

"Oh, God," he breathed against her hair. "Would you be too cold without your clothes?"

It was a question that he didn't have to ask and that she didn't have to answer. Nan backed slightly away from him, and began to unbutton her blouse. . . .

Ⓢ SIGNET   **Ⓞ ONYX**

MEDICAL DRAMA FROM ELIZABETH NEFF WALKER

- ☐ **FEVER PITCH** Beautiful neurologist Dr. Nan LeBaron and emergency room chief Dr. Steven P. Winstead, III, are fighting for their medical lives. They are co-defendants in a malpractice suit after their best efforts failed to save a patient's life. Neither of them can deny the physical chemistry that flares between them ... or pull back from a steamy affair that makes it achingly hard to tell if it is love or just lust that fuels their fever. (404726—$4.99)

- ☐ **THE HEALING TOUCH** When Rachel Weis became ethics consultant at San Francisco's prestigious Fielding Medical Center, she knew she could depend on Dr. Jerry Stoner for support—until Jerry began to play a growing part in her personal life, leading Rachel to feel vulnerable ... again. (404734—$4.99)

- ☐ **HEART CONDITIONS** Dr. Angel Crawford and Dr. Carl Lenzini generated a different kind of heat when they came together after hospital hours. But how could Angel keep going back to Carl's arms when he persisted in patronizing her as a person? Angel had no answer until she discovered the real man behind Dr. Carl Lenzini's surgical mask ... and what it was she so deeply hungered for. (404718—$4.99)

*Prices slightly higher in Canada

Buy them at your local bookstore or use this convenient coupon for ordering.

PENGUIN USA
P.O. Box 999 — Dept. #17109
Bergenfield, New Jersey 07621

Please send me the books I have checked above.
I am enclosing $_____ (please add $2.00 to cover postage and handling). Send check or money order (no cash or C.O.D.'s) or charge by Mastercard or VISA (with a $15.00 minimum). Prices and numbers are subject to change without notice.

Card #_____ Exp. Date _____
Signature_____
Name_____
Address_____
City _____ State _____ Zip Code _____

For faster service when ordering by credit card call **1-800-253-6476**

Allow a minimum of 4-6 weeks for delivery. This offer is subject to change without notice.

FEVER PITCH

Elizabeth Neff Walker

A SIGNET BOOK

To Paul with love
and Janna with thanks.

SIGNET
Published by the Penguin Group
Penguin Books USA Inc., 375 Hudson Street,
New York, New York 10014, U.S.A.
Penguin Books Ltd, 27 Wrights Lane,
London W8 5TZ, England
Penguin Books Australia Ltd, Ringwood,
Victoria, Australia
Penguin Books Canada Ltd, 10 Alcorn Avenue,
Toronto, Ontario, Canada M4V 3B2
Penguin Books (N.Z.) Ltd, 182–190 Wairau Road,
Auckland 10, New Zealand

Penguin Books Ltd, Registered Offices:
Harmondsworth, Middlesex, England

First published by Signet, an imprint of Dutton Signet,
a division of Penguin Books USA Inc.

First Printing, August, 1995
10 9 8 7 6 5 4 3 2 1

Copyright © Elizabeth Rotter, 1995
All rights reserved

 REGISTERED TRADEMARK—MARCA REGISTRADA

Printed in the United States of America

Without limiting the rights under copyright reserved above, no part of this publication may be reproduced, stored in or introduced into a retrieval system, or transmitted, in any form, or by any means (electronic, mechanical, photocopying, recording, or otherwise), without the prior written permission of both the copyright owner and the above publisher of this book.

PUBLISHER'S NOTE
This is a work of fiction. Names, characters, places, and incidents either are the product of the author's imagination or are used fictitiously, and any resemblance to actual persons, living or dead, events, or locales is entirely coincidental.

BOOKS ARE AVAILABLE AT QUANTITY DISCOUNTS WHEN USED TO PROMOTE PRODUCTS OR SERVICES. FOR INFORMATION PLEASE WRITE TO PREMIUM MARKETING DIVISION, PENGUIN BOOKS USA INC., 375 HUDSON STREET, NEW YORK, NEW YORK 10014.

If you purchased this book without a cover you should be aware that this book is stolen property. It was reported as "unsold and destroyed" to the publisher and neither the author nor the publisher has received any payment for this "stripped book."

Chapter One

"What the hell took you so long?"

Nan LeBaron glanced up at the clock on the stark white wall of the emergency room. It showed 8:55. She raised an amused brow at the emergency physician. "I said I'd be here by nine."

"Well, we've been waiting for you," replied the impatient Dr. Winstead. He scribbled rapidly in a chart and signed his name with an illegible flourish. Without looking up at her, he grabbed another chart where he entered the time and added a note to his previous scratchings. Then he shoved the charts aside, straightened his lanky body, and frowned at her. "That second-year neurology resident is going to have to be a little more outspoken if he's going to get anywhere."

"I'll tell him to use you as a role model." Though her voice was tart, Nan smiled kindly at him, her hazel eyes rich with humor. Nan had only finished as chief resident in the summer, and the one-year fellowship she was serving had strengthened her resolve to take very little of this kind of professional advice from other doctors as seriously as most of her contemporaries would have done.

Dr. Winstead's frown deepened. "The patient's in a coma, Dr. LeBaron, and your resident dithered around about whether to get another scan or not."

"Hey, I'm not chief resident anymore, but I'll speak with him." And I'm sure I'll find a good reason why he didn't, Nan thought. She knew the second-year resident to be a perfectly capable doctor. "Shall we have a look at the patient?"

"Whenever you're ready," he said with exaggerated politeness.

Must have been a long night, Nan thought. But then Steven Winstead did not have a reputation for suffering fools gladly, or even tolerating them. She had had her own difficulties with him, but found for the most part that his virtues far outweighed his vices. He was a brilliant diagnostician, an efficient organizer, and a man with seemingly boundless energy. She had yet to see him look tired at the end of a twelve-hour, or even a double, shift. Emergency physicians got an adrenaline rush from their work, and it seemed to serve Dr. Winstead well. So he was short-tempered occasionally. Nan had seen worse.

FEVER PITCH

The second-year resident had been called to evaluate another patient. Nan found herself alone with Winstead, a nurse she didn't know, and the patient—a male in his thirties lying on the examining table with no obvious injuries to explain the cause of his unconsciousness. She read quickly through the notes in his chart. Found in this condition, with no identification on him and no one to offer any explanation. She grimaced. That always made things more difficult. Setting aside the notes, she approached the patient to begin the physical examination: level of consciousness, size and reactivity of pupils, ocular position and movement, motor response, pattern of respiration. It was all familiar ground.

"The ambulance crew gave D50 and Narcan, without response. His labs are normal. CBC is okay. Blood alcohol level is 0. Tox screen is negative." Winstead shrugged his shoulders. "Seemed likely it was a central nervous system problem. That's why I wanted the scan."

"What did it show?"

"Nothing. Even with contrast. It's on the board."

Nan turned to examine the CAT scan results. Though it was true there were no obvious anomalies, her brow wrinkled in studying it. "Tell me, Dr. Winstead, do we have any idea why he didn't have identification on him?"

"He was in a jogging outfit. People don't expect to need their wallets."

She nodded and turned from the films on the light board. "Fresh blood can look like fresh brain tissue. It's been long enough now for it to become old blood, and maybe with another scan we can pick up a subdural hematoma."

Winstead nodded. "Exactly what I suggested to your neurology resident."

"And he didn't agree?"

"He dithered." Dr. Winstead for the first time cracked a smile. "It seems to me second-year residents shouldn't be intimidated by me."

"Who could help but be intimidated by you?"

There was a moment when their eyes met, and they both remembered the day a year ago when Nan had disagreed with Dr. Winstead about a stroke victim. Had it been intimidation that had kept her from insisting on her viewpoint carrying the day then? Or simply her own knowledge that his experience was greater than hers, that it was a toss of the coin about which of them was right? If the patient hadn't died, it wouldn't have mattered.

"You've never been intimidated by me," he said, and nodded his head toward the nurse. "Carol hasn't either, have you, Carol?"

Carol gave him a cheeky grin and said, "No, Doctor. But you do have a tendency to snap at people."

FEVER PITCH

"Only at idiots," he insisted as he reached for the doorknob. "You going to take him for the scan, Dr. LeBaron?"

"Yes. I'd like to see it cleared up."

"Right." And he was gone with a flapping of his lab coat.

Carol, a short, dark-haired dynamo, helped Nan strap the John Doe to a gurney, chatting as she worked. "I hear he's rich, you know? Dr. Winstead. Comes from a wealthy old San Francisco family. Now, why would someone like that go into emergency medicine?"

"Beats me." Nan wasn't paying a great deal of attention because she was adding her own notes to the patient's chart. "I guess he wanted to do something useful."

"Yeah, but he could have been a cardiologist, or a neurosurgeon. Something kind of elite. Here there's trauma, and often the dregs of the earth. All those addicts and nut cases. You kind of picture him in a quiet office, you know? Looking dignified behind a big oak desk. He'd toss back that hunk of blond hair, and blink those blue eyes, and his women patients would swoon over him."

Nan laughed and tucked the folder under her arm. "You have quite an imagination. Write fiction on the side, do you?"

"No, ma'am." The nurse grinned at her. "But I read it, and Dr. Winstead just doesn't fit right where he is. Emergency medicine is fly by the seat of your pants stuff. Heady rush when everything is happening at the same time. It's the semi-wild guys who like it, and the women who especially like taking charge. Don't you think?"

"I hadn't given a lot of thought to it. Is that why you do it?"

"Well, I'm a nurse, but, sure, I like the excitement. I like having people expect me to react quickly and expertly. I've always been able to stay calm in an emergency. It's the one thing I'm really good at."

Nan regarded her thoughtfully as they pushed the gurney out of the emergency examining room. "Maybe that's why Dr. Winstead does it, too. Because he's good at it."

Carol hunched her shoulders carelessly. "Maybe. But he'd make bigger bucks at something else."

"If his family's wealthy, he probably doesn't need them."

"Yeah, I suppose. Wealthy families set up trust funds and stuff for their kids, don't they?"

Nan smiled. "You should ask Dr. Winstead."

"I wouldn't dare." But the young woman's eyes sparkled. "It would be great to have all the money you wanted, wouldn't it?"

"I don't suppose anyone ever thinks they have enough." Nan pushed the gurney through the door Carol held open for her, and out into the hall. "Thanks, Carol. I can get it from here."

FEVER PITCH

When Nan had the gurney about a hundred feet down the hall, she heard the door open behind her and Carol call, "Oh, Dr. LeBaron?"

Nan turned back to look questioningly at the young woman.

"Dr. Winstead said to tell you he needs to talk with you later about the malpractice suit."

Nan had learned to live with uncertainty in her chosen profession. It was delightful to be able to pin a diagnosis on a patient quickly and skillfully, but a number of the diseases neurologists worked with were more a process of elimination than a simple matter of reading elevated lab values or seeing distortions on X rays. More than that, a lot of neurologists' patients had diseases for which there was very little treatment. Which made it very important that Nan could be supportive to those patients. She had learned to discuss their diseases with them in a clear and helpful way that said a patient was more than just his or her disease. She was levelheaded and, as the nurse Carol would have said, "good at what she did."

One of the first things she'd learned to do was leave the hospital behind her. Not that the hospital didn't follow her home, with constant calls and pagings, but she had managed to reach a place where she could separate herself from the doctor part of her. Which was why she didn't understand

Peter's insistence that she let medicine take over her life.

It seemed to her as she trundled the gurney down the hall that Peter was looking for an excuse to withdraw from her life, not that medicine was crowding him out. He had, after all, known from the start that she was expected to put in long hours. Hadn't he insisted that he didn't want any woman sitting in his pocket? Well, she certainly wasn't.

The scan room was expecting her patient, since Carol had efficiently called ahead. Nan moved into the control room while a nurse and technician moved her patient onto the bed of the machine. Dr. Woo nodded pleasantly to her as he readied the equipment for a new scan. Comatose patients had to be handled differently than ones who could obey instructions. On the other hand, their unconsciousness rendered it unnecessary to make all the explanations that got repeated over and over in the course of a day. Nan enjoyed watching the video screens show the computerized images of a patient's brain, but she would never have wished to train as a radiologist. Her rewards in medicine came directly from patient contact, something radiology as a specialty couldn't provide.

Slice after slice of brain image appeared on the screen. Eventually Dr. Woo said, "There. Do you see the hypodense region? Interesting that it's so clear now. The hematoma must have been really recent when he was brought in earlier. Better get the neurosurgeons in, Dr. LeBaron. This guy needs help."

"Thanks, Dr. Woo. I'll put in a page."

She glanced once more at the John Doe, silently wished him luck, and left to make her call.

Ever since Angel Crawford had gotten married, Nan had had the flat to herself. The three-unit building was a Victorian with a three-color paint job that emphasized in burgundy and navy the detail around the doors and windows and under the eaves, against a dark gray wood background. The flat itself had high ceilings, hardwood floors, and dark-stained wainscoting in the entry and dining room. Nan's bedroom, the larger of two, was spacious but with windows that looked out only on two light wells.

Because it had been a busy day at the hospital, and because she couldn't quite believe she'd agreed to it, she had entirely forgotten that Roger was moving in. When she arrived at the flat, only two blocks from the hospital, she had been alarmed to see the downstairs door standing open. Only for a moment, of course. There was a car parked in the driveway with its doors open and a pile of clothing on hangers in the backseat. Men's clothes. How could she have forgotten he'd said he would be moving in today? And why had she agreed that he could?

Roger came loping down the stairs and out onto the vestibule where he noticed Nan standing by his car. He seemed to take in her skeptical expression, and his face fell. "You've changed your mind, haven't you?"

"Of course not! I was just wondering if I had the energy to help you get these upstairs." Nan forced a welcoming smile. "It'll be great to hear someone else moving around the flat."

"I probably make more noise than Angel did," he confessed, coming slowly down the stairs to stand a few feet from her. He began tugging at his belt. "It would be all right, if you'd rather I didn't move in, Nan. I don't know what made Jerry come up with the idea."

"I'm *glad* you're moving in," she insisted, stooping down to grab a handful of hangers. "It'll help with the rent, and it'll provide companionship. When I'm here. I spend a fair amount of time with my boyfriend Peter."

Roger lugged a cardboard box full of shoes, belts, and ties out of the car. It looked like he'd just tossed them in at will. "I didn't bring any cooking stuff."

"I have everything we'll need."

Nan followed him up the stairs with an inward sigh. She remembered how she'd once told Angel that he was a nice enough guy, but that his nervous mannerisms would drive her crazy. Would they? Not if she kept in mind that the poor fellow had just lost his wife. He'd married Kerri knowing that she was dying, of course, but he was taking it very hard, Jerry said. Couldn't seem to sleep in his own house right now. Nan would be doing a good deed in letting him share her flat. Well, who wouldn't take a poor, suffering, depressed, fidgety anesthesiologist into her home like a lost puppy? Certainly Nan had found it too difficult to say no.

Trooping up the three flights of stairs, Nan realized she'd begun counting on the exercise just the walk home and climb to the flat gave her, especially on days when she didn't get a run in. It would be handy for Roger, too. He was thin but rather pale. Probably hadn't been outside exercising in the sun enough. As she followed him into his room, Nan thought chances were that he wouldn't want to stay long. Just until the worst of his depression retreated and his insomnia got better. Pretty soon he'd want to be back in his own house, his own bed. He'd lived there for years before his marriage, and he'd be able to live there again soon, she felt sure.

"Doesn't anyone use the backyard?" he asked, staring down into the wasteland of weeds. "Would they mind if I sort of cleaned it up?"

Nan deposited the loaded hangers on the stripped bed that had come with the flat. "I'm sure we'd all be delighted. But it's almost December. Is there anything worth planting at this time of year?"

He shrugged. "I'll find out. It just looks so depressing out there."

"Well, yes." Nan came to stand beside him at the bow windows. "I guess no one's tackled it because it's a lot of work."

"I don't mind. Anything to keep me busy."

She would have liked to ask him if there wasn't something at home, something he'd benefit from eventually. But of course she knew better. "Maybe you could paint this room."

"I hate painting," he admitted. He tugged at his earlobe and sighed. "I appreciate you letting me stay here. I'll try not to be a pest."

"You're not going to be a pest, Roger. I'm glad to have you." And suddenly she was. "I miss my brothers sometimes. And my friend Peter isn't at all like anyone in my family. You'd probably fit in with them, though if you ever meet them you probably won't think that's a compliment."

"Why not?"

"Oh, they're rowdy, and a little bit redneck, and unsophisticated."

"Sounds just like me," he said ruefully.

Nan laughed. "Hardly. But I think you'd like them. They're salt of the earth people."

"I hope I get to meet them sometime."

"You probably will. They're coming for Christmas."

FEVER PITCH

* * *

Christmas was still several weeks away, but Steve Winstead had already bought himself a Christmas present, of sorts. For years he had lived in the five-unit building in Pacific Heights that he'd inherited as his share of his grandmother's estate. It was an elegant building with spectacular views of the bay. It was also next door to his parents' mansion. They might refer to it as their house, but it was a mansion. Steve had grown up in a kind of luxury that tended to spoil one for the simpler things of life.

By the time he reached college age, he was sated with a social life that included cotillions and weekends at Lake Tahoe. His parents had expected him to go to college, of course, and even have a career, something refined like the law or architecture. They had even accepted with good grace his decision to go into premed. But they were not so sanguine about the direction his career had taken since then. Though they would never have said so to any but their closest friends, emergency medicine struck them as rather crass and unrefined. His mother, Bitty Winstead, had recently remarked to him when they were seated on the deck off their summer home that she supposed he frequently got blood on his clothes.

God almighty! Blood on his clothes! Steve revved the engine of his British racing green MG as he waited to pull out of the parking garage at

Fielding Medical Center. He'd done two twelve-hour shifts back to back, finally getting out of the emergency room just after seven. Daylight had long since vanished, but it was reasonably warm and he felt no need to put the top up on his car. He was not unaware of the picture he made in his MG, his fine blond hair blown wild by the wind, his eyes narrowed against the whipping strands.

But it was Steve's impression that people liked seeing someone enjoy the good life. Oh, they might be envious, momentarily, of the money it took to support a luxurious lifestyle, but mainly they got a vicarious pleasure from seeing someone race along in a sports car, or glide across the waves of the bay in a stunning sailboat. If this was a slightly naive view, Steve was so accustomed to his wealth and the world he had grown up in that he was unaware of it.

Fielding Medical Center was only a short drive from the Golden Gate Bridge. For years Steve had driven across the city to Pacific Heights, not a particularly inspiring drive most days. Now, with the key to his new home attached to his key ring, he aimed across the bridge to the north. At night in an open car, the Golden Gate Bridge was a particularly fascinating sight. In stopped traffic, Steve could look up the lighted towers and see stars beyond. He found it particularly energizing to be leaving the city, leaving behind the hospital,

FEVER PITCH

and Pacific Heights, and his family. No one he knew lived in Belvedere.

Highway 101 wound quickly north, and Steve took the turnoff to the Tiburon peninsula. Tiburon, an exclusive community, was still a little newer and more developed than Belvedere, its sister community comprised of one hill around which narrow roads wove their way to the top and back. In nooks and crannies of the hill, extravagant homes boasted astonishing views of the bay and San Francisco. Not all of the homes were large or extravagant, but all of them felt special—hidden away, like some cherished secret. His new house was like that, a surprise you came on at the bend in the road, shingled, wrapped around by ivy and jasmine.

True, it was a fixer-upper, but Steve intended to enjoy himself making it into the perfect place for him. Hell, the flat in Pacific Heights still mainly had his grandparents' furnishings, so old and heavy and worthy. The management company would find decent tenants for it, probably someone of his parents' generation who wanted something smaller than the house they'd lived in for years. Steve's new house—which was all of sixty years old—needed a new roof, and the interior painted, and a kitchen and bath remodeling, and the floors sanded. Everything, really. It had been neglected as an elderly man grew more and more incapacitated, until he finally was forced to leave for a nursing home. To Steve it seemed like the perfect opportunity to get his hands on something that he could make into his own. And be out of the social pull of San Francisco at the same time.

Turning onto Belvedere Avenue, he noticed for the first time how the lights from houses scattered around the hill shone like bulbs on a Christmas tree. A fanciful thought, for one of his skeptical disposition. But he smiled slightly, nonetheless. Certainly the whole endeavor—buying the house, planning its restoration—felt like a celebration of freedom. It was just one more step away from the stifling atmosphere of being the only child of wealthy, prominent parents. Even becoming a doctor and having a life of his own hadn't entirely severed that tie. Not that he wished to disown his parents, but he did wish to disown that sticky trap of belonging to the social register, the ingrown pettiness of a small, privileged group. There were more important things in life, and that particular group didn't even seem to know it.

Steve wound the MG up twisting Madrona Avenue past his house hanging over the road, until he doubled back and came on the garage behind it. The garage was too full of ancient relics from the previous owner to allow a car to be parked in it, so Steve pulled off to the side of the road and turned off his engine. For a long moment it seemed like perfect silence, and then the sound of wind in the trees, the faraway murmur of an-

FEVER PITCH

other car, the scraping of a vine on wood, whispered on the night air. Steve combed back his straight hair with long fingers and took a deep breath. This would be the first night he spent in his new house.

He had cadged a foam pad from one of the nursing floors, and stuffed a sleeping bag in the car that morning, knowing that he was coming over. It didn't matter if there was no furniture. The electricity and plumbing worked. What more could he ask?

Well, probably it would have been smart to bring some food, he thought as he stood in front of the empty refrigerator. This appliance was so old the term "ice box" came forcibly to mind, with its rounded edges and its tiny freezer section overflowing with ice. Steve grunted and decided to unplung the refrigerator so the ice would melt. It did not occur to him, because he'd never defrosted a refrigerator, that the melting ice would collect in water on the bottom shelf, to await his next opening of the door.

From his briefcase he withdrew a yellow legal pad, which he had purposely brought with him to begin a list of the projects he wanted to get started on. Wandering from room to room, he scratched down all the details he became aware of, floors needing sanding, every room needing paint and most needing curtains or blinds as well, ugly light fixtures that needed replacing. The list grew longer as he climbed the stairs to the second story. The carpet on the stairs was a downright hazard, there was no bulb in the overhead light, the shower curtain was in tatters. He hadn't realized how much was needed for a whole house. Beds and tables and chairs and lamps and sofas and towels and bedding and kitchen utensils. On principle he refused to bring anything from the Pacific Heights flat. Everything here would be different and exactly his taste.

When the phone rang he was startled. It seemed so unlikely that anyone knew his number. And he'd forgotten that he'd asked the real estate agent to be here for the phone-service installation. She'd seemed a little annoyed about that, come to think of it, but had refused his offer to pay her. Well, who was supposed to do that sort of thing? He couldn't very well take time off from the emergency room to be here, could he? The call would be from his mother. She was the only one to whom he'd given his new number, and then with the rebellious thought that he wished he didn't need to give it out to anyone, at least not yet.

"Hello."

"Steve? Hi, it's Ruth Ann."

Now, how the hell had she gotten his number? Though he'd dated her off and on over the last year, he'd been relieved when she told him recently that she was seeing someone "seriously." There had been that quality to her voice that told

FEVER PITCH

him she was rebuking him, that she could just as easily have been seing him "seriously." Heaven forbid! "Ruth Ann. How'd you get my number?"

"From your mom. I saw her at the club today, and she said you'd moved. Was I astonished! To Belvedere! I had no idea!"

"Well, I haven't even really moved in yet. The place is empty." Steve knew he wasn't being encouraging, but he didn't want to encourage Ruth Ann. She was part of the set he was trying to draw back from.

"I'm having a party, Steve. And I hope you'll come." Her voice became coyly playful. "It's an important party. We're going to make an announcement."

"Well, that's wonderful," he said heartily, preparing an excuse in his mind. "When's the party?"

"December twelfth. It's the only day most of the family could make it. I hope you can."

"Oh, I'm sorry, Ruth Ann. I work that night." Did he? He had no idea.

"Really? Oh, that's too bad. It's a weekend. Do you work weekends?"

"Sometimes. Three days and one night a week, twelve-hour shifts. We take turns on the weekends, you know, especially in a holiday month like this." He found himself pacing restlessly, ready to end the conversation. "Anyhow, I wish you all the best, Ruth Ann. You certainly deserve it."

"Thanks, Steve." Her voice had dropped to a

soft register that sounded almost sad to him. "He's a nice guy, Jeff is. I know you'd like him. But you'll meet him some other time."

"Sure I will. Well, thanks for calling, Ruth Ann. Take care."

He stood for a long moment staring down at the instrument after he'd hung up. It occurred to him, though dimly, that he had not treated Ruth Ann well. Not tonight, on the phone. That had been all right, if perhaps he'd rushed her a bit. But over the course of the last year. He'd used her, in a way. Not exactly purposely, and certainly with her willing acquiescence, but at no time had he intended a lasting relationship between them, and the whole time he knew that's what Ruth Ann was hoping for.

That was the trouble with two people having different expectations. Steve had told himself that he'd been perfectly straightforward with Ruth Ann, told her right up front that he wasn't interested in marriage. And she'd said that was fine with her, they'd just have fun together. But he had known that wasn't what she wanted. And he'd continued to see her. Was that using her? At the time he'd refused to believe that it was, but tonight he saw it differently.

Tonight it made him annoyed with himself. And with her. Why couldn't she just say what she really wanted? Of course, if she had he would have been gone. Her only hope was to ingratiate herself

FEVER PITCH

into his life and into his emotions. That's how it worked, wasn't it? Steve had never been struck by lightning, falling in love at first sight. He didn't believe such a thing existed. So obviously love grew with acquaintance and proximity and intimacy, didn't it? So was she right to hang in there? And was he wrong for letting her? He might have changed his mind, too.

He wished she hadn't called. But he was good at putting things out of his mind. Steve decided to drive back down the hill and pick up a bite to eat in Tiburon, maybe have a beer, think about what he was going to do with the house. This was a clean slate for him. He was starting over, and this time he was going to do it right.

Chapter Two

Steve stopped outside the open door of the office where he could see Nan LeBaron seated at one of two desks. Unfortunately, there was someone seated at the other one as well, and he didn't wish their conversation to be public. He stood in the doorway, knocked on the door frame, and said, "Dr. LeBaron, I wonder if I could speak with you a minute."

"Sure. I tried to return your call yesterday." Nan waved him to a seat, but he shook his head.

"Could you walk with me to the lecture hall? I have to give a talk there in a few minutes."

Though she seemed reluctant, the neurology fellow put down her pen and rose. "I only have ten minutes until an appointment," she said.

"Won't take long." When she fell into step beside him, he started for the doors at the end of the hall. "It's about the depositions. I think we should talk about the case before we each have to give our depositions."

"Actually, that's exactly what you're not supposed to do, according to a book I was reading. You want us to coordinate our stories?" she asked, her hazel eyes sparkling.

"I don't know how you can take this so casually, Dr. LeBaron. Our reputations are at stake." He pushed the door open into the stairwell and allowed her to precede him. "And I don't want us to coordinate our stories. I just want to see if we both remember the case the same way. It was some time ago."

"And we've both gone over the records interminably."

"Not interminably. Carefully. Everything is very well documented."

"Yes," she agreed, descending the stairs side by side with him. "The only problem is that we disagreed, and the patient died."

"You think that was my fault."

"Look, Dr. Winstead. I know the mortality figures for stroke as well as anyone: 45 percent at one month. Not great odds. And the breakdown for strokes, 85 percent caused by clots and 15 percent by bleeds, made it more likely that you were right, since you thought it was a clot. I saw signs that it was a bleed."

"But there was the left-hand and body weakness and right-facial weakness of a classic crossed syndrome. We'd have known a hell of a lot more if the other emergency hadn't coopted the MRI."

"I know." Nan held the door for him this time as they came out on the first floor of the east wing. "I realize the CAT scan showed no bleeding, but you know as well as I do that sometimes they're too small to show up, or that it might have taken longer for a bleed to show."

"And if it was a clot, the heparin might have saved him."

"An autopsy would have shown if there was a further bleed caused by the heparin you gave."

"But they didn't want one, then. It might have saved us all a lot of trouble."

They had reached the door of the lecture hall, and Steve glanced at his watch. Still a few minutes. "There's legitimate debate about how to treat a stroke. You've probably treated plenty of patients with heparin."

"Of course I have. I wouldn't have in this case."

Steven remembered her urgent insistence that he reconsider his decision. But she'd only been a third-year resident then—knowledgeable, yes, but relatively inexperienced yet. His experience had supported his conviction that it was a clot, and perhaps it had been, already broken down by time. He was trained to respond quickly, aggressively to save lives. There was a heavy toll in that. Human beings were bound to make mistakes, even well-trained and skillful human beings, because medicine was not an exact science, but partly an art. You couldn't always know what was going on in a human body. And in emergency work you had to make constant split-second decisions. If they were wrong, someone could die. Over time those catastrophes mounted.

His companion was watching him, perhaps evaluating the nature of his silence. "Are you worried that I'm going to try to make you look bad in my deposition?"

Steve shook his head in wonder. "I like your directness, Dr. LeBaron. Yes, I suppose that's exactly what I'm worried about."

"You didn't breech the standard of care any more than I would have. It's your emergency room, you had a perfect right to make the final decision."

"They can make any disagreement between doctors look bad."

She shrugged. "So what? We'll have lawyers who know how to defend against that kind of distortion."

"They can argue that we might have waited."

"Waiting could have meant death as well."

A medical student squeezed past Steve through the door into the lecture hall. "I've got to get in there," Steve said, glancing again at his watch. "Just don't let them pressure you into saying things you don't mean, okay?"

Nan bowed her head and said meekly, "Yes, Doctor."

Steve could see the glint in her eyes, but couldn't tell whether it was amusement or anger. Who was this woman? Maybe he needed to know her better to protect himself. "Thanks for talking with me. Maybe we can compare notes after our depositions."

"Maybe."

As she walked away from him, he fervently wished that they gave their depositions at the same time, where he could cover for any mistakes she made, fill any holes she left in their defense. Though Steve was challenged by unknown disease in a patient, he felt very uncomfortable with a person as unknown quantity, especially when his reputation might be at stake. Dr. LeBaron, who obviously didn't take this whole matter very seriously, could be a real threat to him. He watched her tall form recede down the hallway, her blond French braid looking as casually constrained as she was herself, and he felt a twinge of dismay.

In the cafeteria Nan carried her tray to the open deck area where only a few braved the mild December day. Nan herself welcomed a breath of fresh air after the antiseptic smell of the clinic she'd just finished. To her delight, her former roommate, Angel Crawford, soon joined her at the gritty table.

FEVER PITCH

"You sure know how to pick your days to sit outside," Angel complained.

"It just feels like fall. Don't you like fall?"

"I love fall." Angel grinned at her and set her own tray with its large salad and whole wheat roll down beside Nan's. "I've got news for you."

Nan raised curious brows. "What? Is Cliff behaving himself?"

"You might say that." Angel tucked herself onto the metal chair and sighed. "I'm pregnant, Nan."

Tears pricked at Nan's eyes. "Oh, Angel, how wonderful! Wouldn't you know you'd be able to get pregnant at the drop of a hat."

"That's not *quite* how it happened, but I do feel very lucky."

Nan reached over to give her friend's hand a warm grip. "I'll bet Cliff is thrilled."

"He is. He grumbles about my having to work so hard to finish the family-practice residency, but, hell, this year's so much easier than the last two that it feels like it's going to be manageable."

"And no doubt Cliff will make it easier by waiting on you hand and foot when you're at home," Nan teased.

"He's getting pretty good at meshing his hours with mine, so we eat out a lot." Angel speared a cherry tomato and popped it in her mouth. After a while she said thoughtfully, "We're going to Wisconsin for a few days over Christmas. I hope to hell he likes it."

"Yeah. It could be a problem if he doesn't."

But Cliff had promised that they would go back there to live, because it was what Angel wanted to do, and they both knew he'd keep his promise. Angel sighed and looked out over the view of the Golden Gate Bridge. "Probably we'll both miss it here."

Afraid that her friend was weakening, Nan said, "Now, don't forget why you want to go back, Angel. Wisconsin is where you can practice medicine the way you've always dreamed, being the modern version of the old family doc. It's a great dream. Cliff will do fine in his university setting. In fact, he should love being a big fish in a smaller pond."

"I hope so." Angel returned her gaze to her friend's face. "Did Roger move in?"

"Last night. He has a lot of nervous energy, but he's a nice guy. He said he slept just fine, so maybe this is what he needs for a while. He's talking about taming the backyard."

"He'll need a machete and a flame thrower," Angel said.

Nan shrugged. "If it'll help him. Angel, do you know an E.R. doc named Steve Winstead?"

"Sure. He was my attending when I did my rotation in the E.R. last year. Super competent, abundant energy, abrupt, standoffish in a social way. I hear he's rich."

"Apparently everyone's heard he's rich. We've

both been named in a malpractice suit over a patient who died a year ago."

"Hell, I'd hoped that had been settled. I'm sorry, Nan. That's such a drag."

"I don't mind so much. Rachel has promised to give me some tips. But this guy seems to mind a lot. Well, maybe not that. He seems to be worried that I'll screw things up for him."

"As I recall, it wasn't a question of either of you doing anything wrong. Just a judgment call."

"On which we disagreed."

"That happens." Angel regarded her curiously. "He's not putting pressure on you, is he?"

"We've just had a little talk, but I'm not sure I like his attitude. He was polite enough. There was just this undercurrent that he couldn't trust me. Rather annoying."

"Don't let it bother you. That's just the way he is, Nan. He makes everyone feel like they're a little rough around the edges at times. But he was generous with his positive feedback to the residents, too, so they respected him." Angel grinned. "And he's cute."

"You old married women aren't supposed to notice things like that."

"I wasn't married when he was my attending. Neither was he, for that matter. But I never heard of his dating anyone around the hospital."

"There are plenty of other people to date in San Francisco."

"So there are. Tell me about your Christmas plans."

Nan's Christmas plans, as she'd informed Roger, included the invasion of her parents and her two brothers. Periodically, during the three and a half years Nan had been in San Francisco, her family had come, en masse, to visit her. They never objected to her long hours on duty or her inability to spend massive amounts of time with them. What they did do, rather unnervingly, was storm the hospital to see "where she worked." While any family might have done this, most would have been relatively discreet in their foray, asking for a chance to visit her shared office, to peek at the layout of her clinic, to have a meal in the medical center cafeteria. Not the LeBarons.

The LeBarons were from Oklahoma, and they wanted everyone to know. They took pride in their state, and in their town. Before Nan was born, her father had worked in the oil industry, honest hard labor and small-time managerial positions. Through a fluke, her parents had inherited a small piece of land complete with mineral rights, which her father insisted on prospecting for the liquid gold. And he'd found it, much to everyone's surprise. Several oil wells now supported the entire family in a style to which the elder LeBarons had grown accustomed, far outstripping their neighbors in wealth.

FEVER PITCH

The money was a two-edged sword for the Lebronskis. Long before Nan was old enough to know her own name, it had been changed to LeBaron, a name her father had taken a fancy to because it spoke to him of foreign elegance. Going from a relatively simple household to one of consumption had carried its obligations. The LeBarons treated the neighborhood to extravagant parties. They hired nephews and nieces to work for their small company. They had wealth that said they were among the richest families in Oklahoma. And yet they had no concept of real elegance. They were what Nan had heard referred to as the nouveau riche, and a prime example of the breed.

And they were wonderful people. A lesser child, entering the sophisticated world of medicine and San Francisco, would have been ashamed of them. Nan held them in real esteem, having a realistic appreciation of both their intrinsic value and the way her new world viewed them. Peter, for instance, had been instantly put off when Nan's father had asked him how much he'd paid for his house. Mr. LeBaron was curious about such things and never hesitated to ask, feeling that one had nothing to hide in answering such a simple, uncomplicated question. He'd been puzzled by Peter's unwillingness to answer. And hurt by Peter's even greater reluctance to allow the LeBarons to visit his architectural firm. Obviously Peter was not looking forward to another visit from the LeBarons. Perhaps, Nan thought, that might explain his sudden pulling back from her life.

During the first week of Roger's stay in her flat, she didn't see Peter at all, though she talked to him on the phone twice. Finally he showed up to take her to a movie one evening, but brought her back immediately afterward. Roger was just arriving home as they drove up in front of the building. Nan climbed out of Peter's Acura Legend and waited for Peter to get out so she could introduce the two men.

Roger shook the younger man's hand. "Nice to meet you. It was good of Nan to let me live here. I'll try to stay out of the way."

"Oh, I'm not coming up," Peter assured him, much to Nan's chagrin. "I have to get some work done before I hit the sack." He gave Nan a peck on the cheek, waved a casual good-bye, and drove off.

Nan very much wanted to blame Roger for this defection, but she suspected he'd only proved a good excuse. With a tsk of annoyance, she began to climb the three flights of stairs. Roger trailed after her, coming at such a slow pace that Nan turned to observe his reluctance when she had reached the front door. She was surprised to see his troubled expression.

"What's the matter, Roger? Aren't you feeling well?" She slid her key in the lock and pushed open the door. The entry was inky black, since neither of them had been home earlier to leave a light on. Nan groped for the switch on the wall, and the light snapped on, catching Roger in a blatant attempt to marshal his expression. "Something *is* the matter. Please tell me. Maybe I can help."

"No, no. It's nothing. I'm fine. It doesn't have anything to do with me."

A curious thing for him to say, Nan thought as she tossed her purse on the hall stand. "Who does it have to do with?"

"That's not what I meant. Really, it was just a stupid thought I had. I'm sure I'm wrong."

Nan remained standing in the entry as Roger edged toward the hall, tugging agitatedly at his left ear. "What are you wrong about?"

"Nothing. Well, I mean, I'm off to my room. A lot of stuff to put away still, you know? See you in the morning."

"Sleep well." But the more Nan thought about it, the more she became convinced that there was something Roger wasn't telling her. There was that edge of guilt to his look, his desperate attempt to disappear. Definitely he was not being frank with her. And Nan very much suspected that it had something to do with Peter. Why else the prodigious frown as Peter had pulled away? Nan had thought at the time that Roger didn't approve of Acura Legends.

His door was already closed, and she tapped lightly on it. "Roger? You better tell me. I have a feeling I need to know."

With hesitant steps he returned to the door and inched it open. "I could be wrong," he said. "I'd hate to be wrong and cause you a lot of worry."

"Oh, hell, just tell me. I like things out in the open."

He swung the door the rest of the way open and waved her to the only chair in the room, a wicker-basket-type with a bright cushion on it that he'd brought from his house. Beside it on a table was one of several pictures of Kerri that he'd also brought. He took a seat on the end of his bed. His expression was pained. "Look, I hate to be the one to tell you this. It seems terribly unfair after what you've done for me."

"It's about Peter."

"Yeah. I've seen him before, but I didn't know who he was, you know?"

Nan could feel her stomach muscles tighten. "When had you seen him?"

"It must have been a week ago, and I happened to see him twice in the space of a few days. That's why I remembered. That and the way he breathes, you know? Patients like that are hard to intubate. I was just thinking at the time that I hoped he never showed up in my O.R."

"Where did you see him?"

Roger scratched the bridge of his nose. "The

first time at the Galleria in Stonestown, standing in front of Victoria's Secret."

"And he wasn't alone."

"No."

"He was with a woman who didn't look like his mother."

Roger smiled briefly. "Right. She could have been his sister, if he has one, of course. But he took her in to buy something."

"And the second time you saw him?"

"He was with the same woman, in line at the Kabuki. They were . . . kissing."

"Oh, hell." Nan leaned back in the chair and rubbed her temples. "I knew he'd been drawing back, but I'm always such a sucker for trusting someone. Why don't people just tell you? It's so much more decent, and less painful in the long run."

"I'm sorry, Nan. Really, I am. But I'm dead certain it was him. You know how someone just catches your attention."

"Yeah, I know. No, I appreciate your telling me. Much better that I know. I was fond of him." She rose tiredly from the chair, which squeaked in protest. For a moment she stood lost in thought, and then she blinked her eyes and said, "But I wasn't in love with him. Maybe that's why he did it. I think Peter wanted to be loved, to be adored. Well, maybe this woman does. Good night, Roger."

"Good night, Nan."

Purposefully she strode up the hall, closed her bedroom door behind her, and picked up the phone. It was a difficult, painful, ten-minute discussion, and when it was over she hung the phone up gently. Funny how a few minutes can change your life, she thought, dry-eyed but tense. She had begun to think of Peter in the long term. Foolish of her, of course. Her attachment to him had been real, but not as strong as she would have expected for their having seen each other for almost a year. Still, he was familiar, he was fun, he was a good lover, and he didn't know a damn thing about medicine. All very fine qualities in a man.

In two months she'd be thirty.

Her family was coming for Christmas.

And Nan was in the midst of a malpractice suit.

Since the Emergency Department at Fielding Medical Center was always chaotic, Steve had decided not to have his deposition taken there. Instead he drove to downtown San Francisco, and parked under the Bank of America building. The attorney hired by his malpractice insurance company had offices high up in the building, and the high-speed elevator ascended so rapidly he thought of scuba divers and getting the bends. The offices themselves, he deduced, were an interior decorator's modern interpretation of the sunbaked, earthen-colored simple forms of early Rome. There were mini-columns and glass vistas into offices that looked out over the city and the bay. There were conference rooms with endlessly long marble tables and high-backed, uncompromising chairs. The whole pretentious setting made Steve want to laugh.

The partner who was handling his part of the suit was Fillmore Rush, an unlikely name that sounded more like it belonged to an actor. Rush was a tall, solidly built man of middle years, graying elegantly at the temples and always dressed impeccably in suits that hinted of foreign tailoring. Steve imagined that he was a very expensive attorney, and probably very good at what he did.

Rush had assured him on their first meeting in the medical center director's office that physicians typically felt betrayed, threatened, and vulnerable when they were sued for malpractice. No lie, Steve had wanted to respond. But he'd kept his thoughts to himself. He remembered the family of the deceased very well indeed, and he thought he had explained everything to them quite clearly at the time of the death. They had seemed to understand. But they'd gone out to hire an attorney to sue him, and Dr. LeBaron, and everyone else in sight. Which, the attorney assured him, was the usual way a medical malpractice case was handled.

Steve didn't care how they were usally handled. He would have felt a lot better if he'd never found out. It was no help that half a dozen of his colleagues had discussed their own malpractice suits with him in an effort to ease his frustration. He could not rid himself of the idea that most malpractice cases were simply an exercise in making fees for lawyers. And his attitude, though not uncommon among physicians, was of no help to him in dealing not only with the opposition lawyer, but his own.

Fillmore Rush escorted him into the conference room with the impossibly long marble table and introduced him to the opposition attorney, Robert Whiting, and the court stenographer, Pamela Torres. Rush had explained to Steve that this was the discovery portion of the lawsuit, and that the deposition was the main vehicle employed. He would be questioned under oath by the opposing party, which his lawyer assured him was a good thing. Oh, sure, he thought as he set his briefcase on the table and took a chair. But he had learned over a long time to keep his expression impassive and his mind in high gear when faced with unfamiliar situations.

What they would discover, Fillmore Rush had explained, was just what facts the other side knew. What he hadn't said, but Steve obviously understood, was that Rush would also learn how good an impression Steve was likely to make in court.

Steve knew he could be persuasive, and he knew he could control his emotions under the intensity of the courtroom cross-examination. But he hated to be caught off guard, and that was exactly what happened a half hour into the deposition.

"Did you tell the family that an autopsy would be useful?" Robert Whiting asked, in his calm yet pointed fashion.

"I did. It's something I always do."

Steve noticed that his attorney almost imperceptibly shook his head. Right. The first rule of testifying, apparently, was that you never volunteered more information than you were asked for, even if it sounded like you were saving your own butt. He made eye contact with Fillmore to show that he'd understood.

"Even though the family was visibly upset, you suggested an autopsy?" the opposing counsel asked.

"Yes."

Fillmore smiled beneficently at him.

"Tell me, Dr. Winstead, why did you think an autopsy would be useful?"

"It's always helpful to know the exact nature of a disease that kills someone. Also, we're a teaching hospital and autopsies are teaching tools for medical students, residents, and clinicians."

"So you had no personal interest in the results?"

"I'm not sure I understand what you're asking."

"Didn't you want to find out if you had made a mistake?" Whiting asked.

Steve could think of several answers to that particular question. The one that sprang first to mind was that it bore a striking resemblance to the age-old: when did you stop beating your wife? But Fillmore Rush had explained quite patiently the preceding day on the phone that in giving evidence the rule was to clarify the question if necessary, not to stall but to get on with answering the question. "No, my purpose in suggesting an autopsy was not to find out if I'd made a mistake."

"Would an autopsy have identified whether the stroke was caused by a bleed or a clot?"

"Probably. If the clot was older, it might have already broken down and been harder to identify."

"But the family refused to agree to an autopsy, did they?" the opposing attorney asked.

"Yes. They were adamant."

"And there was no doubt in your mind that death was caused by a cerebrovascular accident?"

"None."

"But you were not the physician who signed the death certificate, were you?"

"No. I believe Dr. LeBaron signed the death certificate."

"Why would that have been?"

"We both consulted on the case and were familiar with its details. I had other emergencies to attend to, and Dr. LeBaron agreed to handle the paperwork." Steve felt certain that had been the progression, since it was the ordinary way things happened in the emergency room.

"But it was you who spoke with the family first?"

First? What did he mean by first? Steve frowned slightly. "I spoke with the family, yes."

"Why was that, if Dr. LeBaron handled the paperwork and was familiar with the details of the 'case'?"

Steve knew that people outside the medical field detested the way physicians referred to cases and illnesses without seeming to assign humanity to them. Very deliberately he said, "I had met Mr. Murphy's wife when he was brought in. She answered a number of questions about the circumstances of his illness before going to wait outside the Emergency Department."

"Did you and Dr. LeBaron disagree about how to handle Mr. Murphy's case?" Whiting asked.

Don't hurry your answer, Fillmore Rush had told him. So Steve let a moment pass as he thought how best to respond. A simple yes was obviously not enough in this instance. "We disagreed about the cause of Mr. Murphy's stroke. The CAT scan showed no bleeding, and we were unable to check that finding on the MRI because the equipment wasn't available."

That should cover it, he thought. But the opposing attorney came back quickly with, "What would an MRI have shown?"

"That would be speculation," Fillmore Rush interceded. "Dr. Winstead can't know what a scan would have shown."

And for a while they quibbled about how to phrase the question so that Steve could answer it. He followed their discussion with only half his mind. There was something here that hadn't been clarified, something he needed to know. If he'd been the first one to speak with the family, who had been the second? Is that what Whiting had meant? When the two attorneys had decided on a proper course of examination, Steve filled in all the technical detail requested, but his curiosity was aroused. At the completion of the deposition, he waited impatiently for the other attorney and the court reporter to leave so that he could speak alone with Fillmore Rush.

The senior partner took him into an office with a panoramic view over the north and east of San Francisco. Clouds scudded across the sky making bands of shadow race over the buildings below. It would be nice, Steve thought, to work in such a setting instead of a windowless, oppressively sterile white suite of rooms. But he wouldn't have been an attorney, like his father, for all the money on earth.

"You handled that exceptionally well," Fillmore complimented him. "You'll make a good witness,

FEVER PITCH

as long as you maintain that air of frankness you had just now. It's very hard for the other side to batter down that kind of impression."

Steve thanked him but asked, "What did he mean, asking if I was the first to speak with the family? Did someone else speak with them?"

The older man pursed his lips. "I don't have the transcript of Dr. LeBaron's deposition yet. Is it possible she spoke with them?"

"I can't see why. I had already done it."

"Hmm." Fillmore made a note on his legal pad, where he'd jotted a number of things during the deposition. "I'll be sure to check it. Do you want me to give you a call when I find out."

"I'll speak with her myself."

"That might not be wise."

Restlessly Steve rose to his feet and picked up his briefcase. "Oh, I'm sure it won't be a problem, Fillmore. Dr. LeBaron is a very easygoing sort of person. She won't mind my curiosity."

His attorney looked skeptical, but rose along with him and offered his hand. "Still, I'll give you a call when I've read her transcript."

"Good idea."

Steve checked his watch as he left the ersatz sunbaked Rome offices. Almost noon. Dr. LeBaron might be free. He picked up his car phone and had her paged.

Chapter Three

Nan had explained to Dr. Winstead that she wasn't intending to eat a real lunch and would not be able to join him. When he pressed her for when he could meet with her, she told him that her entire afternoon was filled and that she probably wouldn't get out of the hospital before seven, which was when he would be coming on duty. "What *are* you doing on your lunch hour?" he'd asked, just as though doctors didn't often work straight through. And what business it was of his she couldn't imagine. Nonetheless she found herself waiting, at quarter past twelve, outside the main hospital building for him to meet her to do a thirty-minute run.

The path running along the cliff above the Golden Gate provided an exceptionally good track when she had the time. Actually, she wasn't used to running with anyone except one of the other women, and she didn't relish the idea of trying to keep up with some jock who probably ran five miles a day in good weather. But when Winstead arrived he was dressed in scrubs and running shoes and didn't look like this was his usual form of exercise. He was hardly champing at the bit.

"Doesn't anybody just walk anymore?" he demanded, frowning at her. "Aren't you going to get cold in that?"

"In that" referred to a sweatshirt and shorts, and since the day had become overcast and cool, she felt a little awkward standing still. "So what do you usually do for exercise, Dr. Winstead?" Nan asked, taking off at a comfortable pace.

"I play squash, indoors, like any sane person in San Francisco," he said. His foot slid on loose pebbles, and he added, "You could break a leg this way."

"I'll bring a rescue squad if you do."

Even though he wasn't as accustomed to running as she, he'd obviously done it often enough to find her pace less than strenuous. He was hardly even breathing fast after they'd been running for five minutes in silence. Nan had almost begun to blot him from her mind when he said, "You've already given your deposition."

"Yes, I did it yesterday."

"How did it go?"

"Fine. He wasn't very rough on me, the lawyer

Whiting. I guess you don't have the same defense lawyer, huh?"

"I guess not. Mine's name is Rush."

Nan shrugged and slowed her pace to descend a steep part of the trail. One of the joys of this run was the scenery, and she kept her eyes on the water and the Marin hills and the bridge rather than on her companion. She fell easily back into her rhythm after her descent and drew a deep breath. There was a touch of salt in the air here, and a faint whiff of eucalyptus. She had almost managed once again to forget Winstead was with her when he asked, "Did you talk to the Murphys at the time Mr. Murphy died?"

For a while she ran without speaking. This was going to be the tricky part. It had seemed quite possible that he'd never actually find out about that. The suit would be dropped, or settled, and even their day in court might not have brought it out, necessarily. Her breath was coming a little harder as the path started upward again. "Yes, I talked with them."

"But why? I talked with them right after he died."

"After I signed the death certificate and was about to go back to the floor one of the nurses came and told me Mrs. Murphy was becoming hysterical." She glanced over at him. "You hadn't seen any sign of that?"

His face was impassive. "I remember that she

cried. Her sister was there with her, and a nephew, I think. They were calming her down."

"Mmmm." Nan lengthened her stride as they reached level ground again. It was almost time to turn around and head back.

"What's that supposed to mean—mmmm?" he asked.

Sweat ran down the sides of her face, and she wiped it away with the sleeve of her sweatshirt. "It means I understand how you saw the situation."

"And how is that?"

"You didn't think Mrs. Murphy needed any more assistance than she was getting. You thought you'd taken care of the situation."

"That's right. I had."

Nan paused briefly to tighten the laces of her shoes. He ran in place beside her, into the movement now and not wanting to stop. Her troubled gaze settled on his face for a moment, but there was nothing to be read there. "This is where I turn around," she explained as she headed back in the opposite direction.

"Do you know why most malpractice suits are brought?" she asked him as they moved together past windblown juniper bushes.

Winstead snorted. "Because lawyers stir up trouble when there's a disagreement as to treatment. Genuine disagreement, with no standard of care agreed upon."

"No," Nan said, trying unsuccessfully to make

him meet her gaze, "they're brought because of a lack of communication most of the time. They're brought because a doctor didn't make a family understand what was happening, or upset them with his or her hardness at the time of a death or catastrophic illness, or neglected to spend time with them when they needed reassurance or emotional support."

He continued to run at the same pace, but he shrugged irritably. "Look, Dr. LeBaron. I talked to the Murphys. I explained what had happened. I said I was sorry about their loss. What more could I do? I'm not a psychiatrist. I had other emergencies to attend to. They understood that."

"No, Doctor, they didn't." She chewed on her lip, trying to decide whether to be perfectly frank with him. That wasn't really her responsibility, and she wasn't sure he was ready to hear what she had to say. But he looked genuinely puzzled. Probably he had no idea how remote he seemed when he wore that impassive expression of his. A blond warrior, hardened by battle, unable to bend because it made him uncomfortable. Nan slowed to a walk, then stopped and leaned back against the flaking bark of a eucalyptus tree. "Do you want me to lay it out for you, or do you want to go on believing there's nothing wrong with the way you treat bereaved families?"

He had stopped in front of her, his hair disheveled and his eyes hooded. She could see that he wanted no help from her. And yet there was something in him, some nagging idea that made his jaw twitch and his hands bunch. "Tell me."

"You have a reputation for being a brilliant diagnostician, and for handling patients reasonably well, interpersonally. Most of them like you. Some of them, when you're impatient, which you are fairly regularly, find you annoying."

"They find me obnoxious," he admitted, with a slight smile. "But I don't get impatient all that often, really. Just with people who waste my time with broken toenails and sniffles. That's not what an emergency room is for."

"Your staff knows better than to give you the worst of those offenders, if they can juggle things around. Besides, they'd rather save you for the hard stuff."

"Thank God. That's why I do emergency medicine."

Nan nodded. "When Mr. Murphy came in, you did what you could for him. There's no saying that my recommendation would have kept him alive, either. You felt it was your responsibility to see his wife, since you'd spoken with her earlier. Otherwise you would have let someone else do it."

"How do you know that?"

"It was explained to me," she said carefully, "when someone came to me and asked that I speak with Mrs. Murphy."

His brows drew farther down over his eyes.

"You're saying that the staff in the emergency department is aware that I try to avoid talking with bereaved families?"

"Sure. You can't hide that kind of thing, Dr. Winstead."

"Steve."

Nan blinked at him. What an extraordinary time to suggest she call him by his first name. "Right. Steve."

"I thought I'd hidden it pretty well. I always talk to them when I have to."

"They know that and they appreciate it. They also try to protect you when they can."

"Damn it! I don't want them protecting me. It's part of my job. A very unpleasant part, but still part of what I should do automatically. I've done it for years."

"But not well," Nan suggested, her voice even. "Apparently this isn't the first family that's been upset."

"Jesus! Why didn't they tell me? I'd have tried to do something about it."

"Well, now you can."

"Too late, though, isn't it?" He raked strong, energetic fingers through his fine hair. "Are you sure this is all the malpractice suit is about?"

Nan let out a long sigh. "More or less. Just before we were notified that the family had filed suit, Mrs. Murphy called me. It couldn't have been easy for her to track me down, you know?

And she said that she'd asked the attorney not to include me in the suit, but he'd insisted. And to make her feel better about it, he explained that when someone is left out, the others named subtly seem to indicate that just that person was the responsible party, since he or she isn't on trial."

Nan grinned. "Sounds like human nature to me."

"But they might have believed you could have saved him. That's much more likely."

"Except that I didn't tell them we'd had any disagreement. And I'm sure you didn't. So they couldn't have known."

Steve stared up into the branches of the eucalyptus tree for a long moment. "I suppose it wouldn't help for me to talk with them now."

"I'm sure your attorney would strongly recommend against it."

After another long pause, he asked, "What did you tell them that day, the day Mr. Murphy died?"

"Probably the same thing you did," she admitted, "but they felt that I was accessible. They felt that I cared. You were like a stone wall, Mrs. Murphy said. You seemed cold and heartless to her. I'm sure that's not how you meant to come off. But we Americans have gotten into a habit of believing that someone is to blame for everything. And when you're upset, and you feel you've been offended by some standoff, cold-fish doctor, you tend to want to believe he's to blame."

"In most cases that wouldn't get them far," he

said, comprehension dawning in his troubled blue eyes. "But in this case, with the MRI unavailable, and a debate in the field about how to handle stroke victims, some of the right pieces fell into place. A friend who's a doctor said, Well, maybe they should have done such and such, and pretty soon Mrs. Murphy contacts a lawyer, or a brother-in-law is one . . ."

Nan was having a hard time absorbing what was going on here. Right in front of her eyes, a doctor was learning something about human nature and the part he'd played in bringing a malpractice suit down on them. He sounded curious, concerned, and not the least defensive. How was that possible? He was not going to be able to make the suit go away; he might very well suffer a real loss because of its impact. He returned his gaze to her and asked, "How did you learn to talk to them right?"

There was the catch. He thought it was some trick she'd learned during her training and that he could learn it, too. Nan shifted away from the tree and began walking back toward the hospital. "I learned to say the same words you did, Steve. You know how to do that. What's missing is—oh, hell, it sounds so psychobabble to say it, but you have to be open and vulnerable and sensitive to their pain."

He shook his head. "You have to maintain a distance, Dr. LeBaron. Every good doctor knows that. You can't let your emotions get in the way of your judgment."

"But your judgment is over by then. Your patient is dead. What's left is the family's pain and confusion and anger. If you keep a distance from all those things, you're just going to alienate them."

For several minutes he walked beside her, saying nothing. His eyes were on the path, but she doubted that he saw it. He was probably silently arguing with her points, and finally he said, "But there are so many deaths when you work in an emergency room. So much pain. You can't take all that on. *I* can't take all that on."

Nan felt the strongest desire to catch his hand and hold it. Odd of her. "You don't have to take it all on, Steve. You just have to let people know you *feel* something, that your expression of sorrow is real. That when someone dies, it's not just a professional failure or something. You see, that's how these families read you. Most of them believe you've worked hard to save their father or mother or child, but they don't see any humanity in you. They see an impassive face, hear a cool, controlled voice, and they think, 'Well, that son of a bitch! He doesn't give a damn. This is just another body to him.'"

They had reached the side entrance to Fielding. Nan thought he would say something, but he was lost in thought. "I have to get in and change," she said, turning away from him.

He seemed to come out of his trance with a start. "Well, thanks for telling me, Dr. LeBaron. I wish someone had done it sooner."

"My pleasure," she said, giving the words an ironic twist. "Please call me Nan, Steve."

"I'm sorry about the malpractice suit, Nan."

"Yeah. Well, maybe I'm wrong about what caused it."

He stared straight into her eyes. "I doubt it."

As Steve drove back across the Golden Gate Bridge, he wondered whether it was easier for him to believe that he had made a mistake in his handling of the stroke or that he was regarded by others as a "cold fish." Very unappetizing choices. Of course, he was bound to make a certain number of mistakes under the pressure of emergency situations. That was one of the things that eventually drove some people out of emergency medicine. Too many life-and-death situations demanding determination of cause on the subtlest of clues and instant action in situations where the human body was already strained to the limits of its resources.

There were bound to be deaths. And the deaths were seldom caused by the medical people present. Death was an inevitable part of life, after all. Sudden, disastrous illness struck, and sometimes a physician could keep death at bay. Often he couldn't. The accident victims, too, were heart-rending. Young men and women who an hour earlier had seemed to have long lives in front of their healthy bodies. Then a speeding car or an urban encounter with a gun-wielding felon, and that healthy body was no more. How did you see that day in and day out and not build a wall to protect yourself?

From sunlight into the dimness of the tunnel on the Waldo Grade, the MG sped on with Steve paying minimal attention to his driving. That was another thing he'd trained himself to do—concentrate on serious matters when he was handling routine tasks. He'd learned that his mind would switch automatically if some demand were placed on the routine skill. If another car cut him off, his attention would instantly return to his driving. In a smiliar way he'd learned to be somewhere else when he was placed in situations fraught with emotion. Not because he didn't feel any emotion, but because he felt a great deal.

Years ago, he couldn't have been more than seven or eight, when his grandmother had died, his parents had brought him to the funeral home to see her laid out in her coffin. Steve had been very fond of his grandmother. She had spent a great deal of time with him, had had her cook bake his favorite treats, had read to him before he went to bed in her house on the many nights his parents had been out socializing. And, of course, he had known when they took him to the funeral home that Grandmama was dead. But he had not expected what he saw, the waxen face, the eternal stillness. Death was a new and frightening concept to him then, and worst of all he had lost the person who seemed to care the most about him. And he had cried.

Simple as that. He'd cried. What else were you supposed to do when someone you loved died? But he had cried for real, a child's sobs of devastation, and in the hushed and solemn atmosphere of the funeral home, it had seemed unbecoming to his parents. He'd been sent home, with his grandmother's chauffeur, and left in the house with only the cook, who had comforted him but had not understood the gravity of his loss, or his shame. It was a very deeply learned lesson.

Not that it was ever spoken of. His parents had never mentioned the incident, either to castigate or comfort him. There was just an unspoken understanding that it wasn't "done," this sloppy emotionality. Their attitude seemed to be that it was self-indulgent and antisocial. Didn't he have before him the example of his parents, who never raised their voices, never shed a tear, and only laughed in modulated tones? Steve patterned himself on their model, and flattered himself that he had gained superb control over his emotions.

Now here was Nan LeBaron telling him that not only she but all the other people in the emergency department were aware of this superb control, and they found it a weakness and an offense. Hellfire! There was no winning. And didn't the medical establishment constantly harp on the theme of keeping a distance, not becoming emotionally involved? They couldn't have it both ways. But apparently they were asking exactly that.

Well, he could meet their requirements. He'd always managed to do it in the past, and he'd do it this time, too. It was just a damn shame that they couldn't be more consistent. And that this particular area was already so painfully difficult for him. He *hated* to bring that kind of news to someone. Death was so incredibly final. And yes, it often felt like a failure to him. Sometimes, for the chronically suffering, it was a blessed release. At those times it felt almost like a failure to save someone. Fortunately, most cases, most people with an emergency medical condition, were more straightforward than that.

Steve parked his car in his newly emptied garage. Gradually he was beginning to bring order to the chaos of his new living arrangement. Every task took two or three times as long as he estimated for it, and always he had to abandon some project in the middle to take off for his shift at the medical center. He had decided not to tackle the kitchen until he had a better idea of what he was going to want there.

In the meantime he'd rented a sander and spent

three days sanding and then staining the hardwood floors in the living room, dining room, and bedrooms as well as the upstairs and downstairs halls. None of these spaces were particularly large, but in order to do things right, he had had to spend generous amounts of time working in the house.

But the physical labor and the sensation of accomplishment were buoying him along. Steve had carried in two gallons of urethane from the car with him and set them down in the kitchen alongside his bed. Since it was the only room other than the bathrooms that wasn't going to be sticky with urethane, he had decided to camp there for the duration. Even getting to the bathroom could prove a challenge if he didn't plan things right.

When he had put on old jeans and a torn T-shirt, carried the urethane and his paintbrush upstairs, he threw open every window on the floor for fresh air. He had exactly four hours to work before he needed to leave for the hospital. He snapped on the rubber gloves he'd brought home with him and pried open the gallon can. Only then did he read the label of the can, which informed him that he would need at least two coats of the urethane, probably three, and with luck it would take only a day's drying time in between.

Hell, it would be forever before he got to furnish the place and actually live in it! In four hours, though, he'd surely be able to finish the entire upstairs. Steve dipped the brush in the urethane and got down on his knees. When he was halfway across the room from the window sill where it rested, the phone began to ring. He considered letting it go. The machine downstairs would take a message, since he'd forgotten to turn it off when he came in. Or even to check it, he thought with a frown.

So he abandoned the paintbrush and raced down the stairs to grab the phone before the machine answered on the fourth ring. "Winstead."

"Your mother said I might get you if I called this afternoon," his father said. "How's the new house?"

"A mess at this point. I'm urethaning the floors."

"Why don't you have it done for you? It seems such a waste of time."

"No, actually I'm enjoying it, so far. It may get old," he admitted, because, later, his father would tease him about getting help if he did.

"I was wondering when I could come and see the house," Steven Winstead, Sr., said.

"Well, Dad, it's going to take at least a week to finish this project, what with a couple of coats and all the time it takes to dry. And then, I don't have any furniture."

"No furniture? I don't understand. What about all the stuff from your flat?"

"I'm leaving it there."

"But, Steve, it was your grandparents'. You know how tenants can trash a place. It could be ruined."

"That's not likely to happen, and it's insured."

"A rather cavalier attitude."

I learned it from you, Steve thought. But he only said, "It'll be fine, Dad."

"So when can I come?"

"I'll have you and Mom over for dinner as soon as the place is presentable. But that might not be for a while."

"That's something I wanted to talk to you about," his father remarked diffidently. "Your mother's . . . concerned that you haven't been in touch much since you moved out there."

He made it sound as though Steve had moved to some godforsaken spot inaccessible to a normal San Franciscan. "I've been real busy, Dad, with work, and the house, and the malpractice suit. I gave my deposition this morning."

"You should have taken me with you. Rush is no fool, but he won't be as attuned to your interests as I would be."

"He was fine. It went pretty well. I don't think they have much of a case."

"It wouldn't have gotten this far it they didn't have something," his father warned. "Don't take this too lightly, Steve. It could damage your career."

"I know. I'm not taking it lightly." Steve remembered that he'd thought it was Dr. LeBaron who was taking the case too lightly. Turned out she had a much better grasp of the situation than he had. Which irritated him, and made him feel something of a fool himself. On the other hand, they were going to have to pay attention to the lawsuit, no matter what had brought it on originally. But he wasn't going to feel comfortable working with Nan LeBaron after their discussion this afternoon. Hell, why did things have to get so complicated?

". . . Are you?" his father asked.

Steve realized he hadn't been paying attention and said, "Sorry. I didn't catch that."

"That's just what you used to say when you were a boy and you sat around daydreaming," his father muttered. "I asked if you were working too hard?"

Too hard for what? A socialite turned dilettante physician? "I'm working as hard as usual, which is pretty hard. But that's the nice thing about emergency medicine. You don't take it home with you."

"Hmmm. Well, then maybe you could call your mother a little more often."

That was rich, considering how Steven Winstead, Sr., treated his wife. "I'll have the two of you over to see the house when there's a dining room table, okay? That may be a while."

"I hope you're planning to spend Christmas with us."

"I'll certainly see you sometime during the day, but I do have other plans." To be alone, precisely. Not to have the stifling burden of family obligation one more year. He'd tried working Christmases for many years, but his family hadn't let him escape that easily. Before a shift or after a shift, they had insisted. He lived right next door, didn't he? How could he not spend time with them?

Well, this year he didn't live right next door to them. And he would do what he pleased, with a very small concession to their concept of family unity. Steve was thirty-three years old, and much as he loved the Bay Area, he was going to move away if this latest ploy didn't work in getting him some breathing space from his family and San Francisco society.

When he had hung up the phone from his father's call, he slowly climbed the stairs to the second floor and realized that, once again, the work was coming along more slowly than he'd anticipated. He'd be lucky if he finished two of the bedrooms before he had to leave. Maybe he really should get someone in to do some of this work.

Not that he minded that it would be awhile before he could have his parents to visit. But he liked the idea of coming home to something more than an empty house that needed everything done. His usual impatience was creeping up on him. He'd intended to conquer it, this time. Seeing the house in need of everything, he'd thought he could slowly dispose of task after task, each one given his thorough attention and insistence on excellence. Like the floor sanding. The machine didn't get right into the corners and he had, since it was his first endeavor, sanded each of the corners by hand, a lengthy and ultimately annoying process. And then the staining. At the paint store, they'd seemed to think that a can of this or that would do, but Steve had found it necessary to do a trial on oak strips to find what combination of stain colors most closely met his visual image of the finished floors.

When he finally reached the doorway of the second bedroom, with only minutes to spare before he had to leave, he thought how good they looked. And how much he really didn't want to have to do all that other work. Hell, someone could be working on them while he was at the hospital. The floors could be drying while he was out shopping for furniture. He understood that took a long time, too, that furniture had to be ordered and there was a six- or eight-week delay before it was delivered. Six or eight weeks! Who the hell could wait that long? Steve decided to call the real estate agent and get a few names of painting contractors. Then he took his brush out to the sink in the garage and cleaned it out with paint thinner. Yes, this was definitely getting old.

Nan's first patient at the afternoon clinic was a woman who had had multiple sclerosis for five years. Though she had been on the newest medication, Vanessa had recently suffered a further attack that had increased her disability. She was discouraged, angry, and ready to lash out at anyone who seemed to underestimate her suffering. Nan had seen the warning signs when she first came into the examining room.

"Why doesn't the medication work for me?" Vanessa demanded even before Nan could speak to her.

"It only works for a certain proportion of the people with MS," Nan explained, as she had before. "It seems to work better for people newly diagnosed, or in earlier stages of the disease."

"Well, can't you give me something that will work for me?"

"Unfortunately, this is the first big breakthrough we've had. Down the line I'm sure there will be refinements or new drugs that might work, but there's nothing available now."

"There must be," Vanessa insisted. She stabbed the cane she had recently required almost full-time at the black-and-white tiles on the floor. "There has to be something that will help me. This is ruining my life!"

"Let me check you out," Nan said. Sometimes just a doctor's touch was helpful in calming a patient. Reluctantly Vanessa let her conduct a full physical examination, which inevitably showed that the decreased weakness was still there. The demyelination caused problems with sight, sensation, and movement of limbs. Nan found the usual vision problems, the lack of coordination, the numbness. Later, permanent motor neuron damage sometimes caused painful muscle spasms, but that hadn't happened yet with Vanessa. Still, her progressive nerve damage could put Vanessa in a wheelchair in the not too distant future.

But it began to impinge on Nan's awareness that there was something else different about this visit. Vanessa's husband wasn't there. Usually he was. Casually she asked, "Did Jeff have to work today?"

Vanessa looked down at her hands. "He's been away."

Uh-oh. That didn't sound good. Nan had once heard a long-time neurologist tell a colleague that husbands never stayed with their wives when they got multiple sclerosis, but wives usually stayed with their husbands when the situation was reversed. "Are you managing okay while he's not there?"

"It's very difficult," Vanessa said in a strangled voice. "He used to help me."

"Will he be gone much longer?" Nan asked gently.

Vanessa's eyes became moist. "I don't know. He says it's too difficult for him, my disease. He says he can't bear to see me getting sicker. What does he think I feel?"

"A lot of people don't feel strong enough to cope with a spouse's illness, Vanessa. Maybe it would help for him, or even both of you, to see a counselor."

Vanessa drew a shaky breath. "He won't go. I've asked. I've even insisted. But you can't make someone do what they don't want to do."

"I know. I'm sorry." Nan laid a comforting hand on her patient's shoulder. "In that case maybe you should go alone, just for some support. MS is difficult enough without other emotional burdens. Would you like me to refer you?"

"I suppose." She sniffed back a sob. "It's just going to get worse, isn't it?"

Nan knew she was referring to the MS, not her marital situation, but chances were they were both going to get worse. "Over time of course there's degeneration, but no one can predict how fast or slow the progress will be. We've been more successful in recent years keeping things from degenerating so fast. I wish I could offer you more hope than that, but it's a disease where we just have to wait and see."

"Yeah, see yourself fall apart." Vanessa glared

at her companion. "Maybe if I'd gotten this five years later, I'd have had all the benefits of the new drug. It isn't fair."

"No, it isn't fair." Nan tore the referral she'd been writing off her pad and handed it to her patient. "Get yourself some help. You deserve it, Vanessa."

"Lot of good that will do me." The young woman grabbed her cane and stomped to the door before Nan could move to open it for her. "I'm learning to manage for myself. It looks like I may have to."

"I'm really sorry," Nan said to her retreating back.

Nan had decided years ago that there was no reason patients visited with an incurable disease should exhibit any more grace under pressure than the average person. Sure, it was more comfortable for doctors if their suffering patients were pleasant, accepting individuals who put up with untold misery, but it was really asking more than one should of them. They had every right to be bitter, especially when their physical misery was added to by emotional devastation, as could well be the case with Vanessa. If Jeffrey left his wife, there was nothing Vanessa or Nan could do about it. Nan thought she'd be howling, too, if fate had dealt her such a hand.

Chapter Four

Déjà vu, Steve thought as he looked down at the sixty-year-old male on the examining table and up at Dr. Nan LeBaron beside him. "Thank God the MRI's available tonight," he murmured, giving her a half smile.

"Yes, but my guess is we agree on this one," she said almost absently as she concentrated on writing in the chart. "And Dr. Krause will be taking over for me in a few minutes. He's been briefed on the phone, and I'll wait until he gets here, but I have an appointment I can't miss."

Though for the life of him he didn't know why, he asked, "Professional?"

She regarded him with surprise. "Actually no. My parents are coming in, and my brothers, and I'm supposed to pick them up at the airport. They'd make it to my place if I wasn't there, but I'm determined to manage it this year. It's become a challenge."

"In for the holidays?" he asked sympathetically.

"Yes." They walked beside the gurney onto which the patient had been transferred as it was pushed toward the corridor. "It was my turn to host Christmas. We take these matters seriously in my family."

"Yeah, it's hard."

Nan frowned. "Oh, I love it. Don't you?"

"I could just as easily do without."

"Not me. I've even got Roger stringing popcorn and cranberries to hang on the tree. And I made gingerbread cookies so the flat smells great. My biggest problem now is figuring how to fit five giants into my car. A friend gave me the keys to her minivan, but it turns out it's a stick shift."

Steve paused in the doorway. "If you don't have to go for half an hour, I could drive it for you."

"I beg your pardon?"

"Well, I'll be out of here in twenty minutes or so. Kevin's already here. I just have to fill him in." Steve staunchly upheld his offer, though she was looking at him as though he'd lost his mind. "You tried to help me the other day. I'd like to repay the favor."

With her hazel eyes narrowed and her head cocked slightly, Nan said, "There's nothing to repay, Steve. I'm just glad you thought I was trying to help you."

"Weren't you?"

"Yes, actually I was. But there are a lot of people who wouldn't have seen it that way."

"Well, I did. And I'd be happy to help you now. I'm just going home to a house with sticky urethaned floors and no furniture."

The gurney was far down the hall now, and Nan turned to follow it. "Okay. I'll meet you at the entrance to the C garage in thirty minutes. And thanks."

Steve watched her retreat, her long-legged stride meshing well with the tidy, efficient image the French braid suggested. Always he had felt most comfortable when he could repay the debts he owed. This was a small matter, perhaps, but an important one to him. He glanced at his watch and returned to the desk to finish briefing his replacement.

She was already there when he arrived a little over twenty minutes later. The lab coat had hidden her burgundy suit with its ruffled white blouse that softened her doctor image. Though it was cool, she wore nothing over it and she seemed a little chilly standing there in the dark entry. She held out a set of car keys to him.

"Rachel says it's on the second floor. It's blue and older and has a personalized license plate that says MOMS VAN. She apologized for that. Apparently her kids gave her the license one Mother's Day when they were young."

"It just goes to show that one has to think ahead," he said as he took the stairs two at a time. "Who's Rachel?"

"Rachel Weis. She's a medical ethicist here. Used to be in risk management."

Steve shrugged. "I don't think I know her."

They found the minivan with ease, and Steve unlocked the passenger door before going around to get in on the driver's side. "They shouldn't give drivers' licenses to people who don't know how to drive stick shifts."

"I love the way men make proclamations like that. As if I'd ever need to drive a stick shift under ordinary circumstances. And, hell, in San Francisco it's hard to learn on one."

"All the more reason. What would happen if someone had to drive a stick shift who'd never driven anything but an automatic?"

"Obviously they'd get some doctor to drive them where they needed to go," Nan retorted. "It happens all the time. Whenever I have to take a stick shift to the airport, I ask a doctor to drive me. There's hardly any better use for a doctor that I can think of."

Steve grinned. "All right. So not everyone needs to know how to drive a stick shift. I presume we're headed to the San Francisco airport and not Oakland."

"Right. United."

"Where are they coming in from?"

"Tulsa."

"Did you grow up there?"

Nan turned her head to look at him. "I did. I have a bit of a chip on my shoulder about it, Steve, so spare me the Okie jokes."

"I don't know any Okie jokes," he said, glancing briefly at her before pulling out onto Geary. "I'm sure very nice people come from Oklahoma."

She sat silent for a few minutes, apparently lost in thought. "It was a clot this time," she said, referring to their patient. "Looks like there's a good chance of his making it."

"Good." Steve was not comfortable with silence as they drove down the long stretch of Geary. He had, after all, been raised to handle small talk with ease. As far as he was concerned, that was all the people he had grown up with knew how to talk. And the only thing doctors seemed to end up talking about was medicine. He was still debating what topic to raise when Nan spoke.

"How come you don't have any furniture in your place?"

"I just bought a house in Belvedere. I left the old furniture in my flat, so I need to fill this one up from scratch. It's kind of unnerving, you know?"

"I'd think it would be. Good furniture is expensive, and it takes forever to order it. And then you have to make things go together. How about an interior decorator?"

Steve screwed up his face in distaste. "How is someone supposed to know what I like? And besides, have you seen some of these places that decorators take credit for? They're bizarre exaggerations of normal furnishings. Or they have some *theme* to them—the Southwest, or Victoriana, or ultramodern. Everyone wants their house to look like a Mediterranean villa, or a French Provincial chateau. I just want comfortable furniture that looks nice in this house. It's a little shingled cottage, really. Needs everything. I just sanded and stained all the floors, but I ran out of steam doing the urethaning. Last week I called help in, but, hell, these guys only show up when they feel like it. The house may never even be *ready* for furniture."

Nan laughed. "That would save you a lot of expense. Where do you sleep?"

"In the kitchen."

"On a bed?"

"Sort of. I bought a cot and set it up there." He scratched his head. "Maybe I should have painted the walls first."

"Are you going to do them yourself? When do you have the time?"

"I don't, really. Everything takes so damn long. I was going to make it really *mine*, you know?" Why had he said that? What did Nan LeBaron care about his house? Steve hurried on to say, "I've lived in the same flat for a dozen years, and it's never felt like anything but my grandparents'. They'd lived there for decades before that. I needed something of my own."

"Hmmm. I think interior designers are supposed to consult with you, like architects, and find out what you like."

"But I only know what I like when I see it somewhere," Steve protested. "I can just hear someone asking me if I want cabbage roses or corduroy on the couch pillows. Ugh!"

She shook her head. "But it takes a long time to pull a whole house together. Angel and I didn't do anything much in the flat because we were too busy, and a couple of pieces of furniture came with the place."

"Angel Crawford? Is she your roommate?"

"She was. She got married recently to Cliff Lenzini."

"Right. I remember hearing that. I also remember trying to talk her into switching to emergency medicine. She was really good."

"She'll be a terrific family-practice doc, too."

"Do you live alone now?" He shouldn't have been asking her all these questions. They probably sounded as if he were prying.

"I have a temporary roommate," Nan said, and went on to explain Roger's presence in her life. "But he's going to stay at Jerry's while my family is here, because Jerry has moved into Rachel's house."

"Naturally," Steve said dryly, since he assumed he didn't know any of these people. But when Nan had explained each of their Fielding connections, he said, "Jesus! You're an incestuous bunch, aren't you?"

"I suppose so." Nan reached down for her briefcase, which obviously served her as an old-fashioned doctor's black bag as well. Steve caught glimpses of files and instruments—no doubt there were papers on the malpractice case and department business, as well as the standard rubber reflex hammer, tuning fork, stethoscope and ophthalmoscope, blood-pressure cuff, and skin-prick wheel. What Nan apparently was looking for, however, was a tissue. She finally withdrew one, blew her nose vigorously and smiled. "Fielding is a big place, bigger than a lot of small towns. And medical people have a tendency to hang out together."

"I've never understood that," he said thoughtfully. "I mean, is it because their interest in medicine is so consuming, or because their being in medicine puts them in a social strata where other people don't belong?"

"It doesn't have to be one or the other of those," she protested. "I think it's more that nonmedical people can't ever quite comprehend the uniqueness of being on the inside of medicine. Like the life-and-death issues, the special knowledge, the position of power. And doctors only really feel comfortable with other people who grasp all those nuances. They feel a little fake with other people, as though they aren't really being completely honest."

"I don't see that. It's other people who don't understand what it means, not that physicians try to hide anything."

"Well, it's too big a job to explain. And then, Steve, so many people are intimidated by doctors. Not just people when they're sick, but people you're introduced to outside the medical world. Sometimes I just say I'm in the health-care field."

"Now that's cheating." He increased the van's speed to merge with the freeway traffic.

"Maybe. But it gives people a chance to get to know me before they identify me as a doctor. Because when they learn I'm a doctor, they react differently."

He had, of course, witnessed just that kind of situation. On the other hand, among his parents' social circle sometimes his being a doctor was regarded with a bit of high-handed disdain, as though one really shouldn't get one's hands dirty when one could surely have found some simpler avenue for looking busy. They were lawyers, architects, senior management in large corporations, directors of charitable foundations, but not, for the most part, physicians. Another reason why he'd chosen his route, no doubt.

Steve had become so enmeshed in his thoughts

that he'd almost forgotten where they were in their discussion. He found that Nan was regarding him expectantly, so he asked, "How does your family feel about your being a doctor?"

"They don't understand why I wanted to become one, but they're proud that I've done it. Not that they particularly comprehend what a neurologist does. When I try to tell them, they easily get distracted." She quoted her mother with amusement. " 'Oh, yes, dear, I think Cousin Jane had that kind of condition. Didn't she, Fred? You know, where her hands were always shaking. Couldn't hold a cup of coffee for the life of her. When we were younger we used to bet on how many minutes it would be before she spilled something. We were just awful!' And then they go off on an excursion into family eccentricities and forget all about Parkinson's."

Steve thought it sounded a great deal better than the way his family avoided any mention or discussion of medicine, as if it were something slightly unsavory. "What do your brothers do?"

"They work with my dad."

"That's not very helpful," he teased. "What does your dad do?"

"He owns a small oil company."

Steve blinked at her. "Owns an oil company? As in oil wells and derricks and those things that look like giant metal grasshoppers grinding away?"

"Right."

"Do people know this about you?"

"No, why should they? Angel knows, of course. She thinks it's funny. It's not like I came from Old San Francisco money," she said pointedly.

"Money is money."

"No, Steve. You're not naive enough to believe that."

He wished he were. With a drawn-out sigh, he shrugged his shoulders and said, "Maybe not, but it buys the same things."

"Even that isn't quite true. My family wouldn't be interested in buying the same things yours would."

"Like what?"

"Oh, I imagine yours buys season tickets to the opera and antique furniture and artistic treasures."

He laughed. "Yes. What does yours buy?"

She squinted at the roof of the van and began to detail the most incredible list: "Opal rings from the Shoppers Network, sporting equipment to fill a whole private gym, a fully equipped private screening room and a stash of laser discs that's as large as the neurology department's medical library, the occasional dining set, kinetic art of the lava lamp variety, a small private zoo of llamas, parrots, koalas, kangaroos and such, enough trucks to transport most of Oklahoma's population, various vacation trips to no point farther than Mexico, Hawaii, or Canada, and certainly not east of the Mississippi . . ."

"Stop!" he begged, laughing. His curious glance captured her gaze. "Does this bother you? What they do with their money?"

"Not particularly. But it bothers other people."

Her voice seemed to suggest that he would be one of those people it bothered. Steve realized she'd made a judgment about him, but since it was probably not entirely inaccurate, he decided to challenge her own statement instead. "But you wouldn't have told me if it didn't bother you, Nan. You seemed to be poking fun at the nouveau riche aspect of it all. Like, you wouldn't buy those things, and you know they're not the kinds of things my family would buy."

"They are, nonetheless, things that give pleasure to my family."

"I don't think that's the point." But he decided to abandon that line for the time being. "What do you buy, Nan?"

"I bought medical school."

"That can't be your whole share."

"Yeah, but it's none of your business, is it?"

Steve felt stung by the suddenness of her retort. "I beg your pardon. I didn't mean to pry. I thought . . ." He was surprised to feel her hand come to rest on his on the steering wheel.

"I didn't mean that. I get very confused around some of these things, Steve. It certainly has nothing to do with you." Nan let out a hiss of pent-up breath. "I've invested most of my money in Oklahoma real estate and mutual funds. Nothing exciting or ridiculous. I live very simply, mostly because I'm too busy to find the time to entertain myself."

A stubborn silence fell over the occupants of the van. Steve was not satisfied with her apology. Her hand had quickly retreated from his after a brief squeeze, which, he suspected, was meant to rob her words of any sting. But she had made him feel gauche, just when he'd thought they were being rather extravagantly open, for two people who hardly knew one another. Two people who had more than he would have suspected in common. Two people with decidedly ambivalent feelings about their families, if he was not mistaken.

The traffic increased as they drew near the airport. Steve expertly swung the van over to the right-hand lanes that fed up and over the freeway. As they approached the terminal he asked, "It was United, right?"

"Yes. But you'll park, won't you? It's still a few minutes before their flight is due."

"Of course."

For the first time he realized that he was actually going to be meeting her family at the gate. A rather awkward situation, really, with the two of them now not even in charity with each other. He wished he'd thought about it before he'd offered to drive the minivan. That's what being a good Samaritan would do for you: get you in trouble. He parked the van and came around to open her door, but she was already out and standing there facing him, her lower lip caught between her teeth.

"Look, Steve, I know I've upset you. I can't quite explain why I did that." She stared absently into the dark parking garage. "Actually, I do know, in a way, but it's very hard to explain. And I'm very much afraid you're going to find out, anyway, when you meet my family. But I don't think you want me to explain."

True, he didn't. This whole last hour was beginnning to seem especially odd to him. He'd had no business offering to drive her in the first place. And then to find that he rather enjoyed her company, felt a kinship with her, was disconcerting. Her unconscionable flare of anger at him would let him discount this whole episode. And he was more than willing to do that.

When he said nothing, she turned and moved toward the closest doorway. "Not that one," he said, indicating one in the opposite direction. "United is this way." He kept a hand on her elbow, guiding her along, though she obviously didn't need his assistance. The rough texture of her suit jacket felt familiar to his hand, as though he'd done this before. He could smell a light, spicy fragrance from her hair. "All right. Tell me," he said.

Nan looked undecided for a moment. "They're great people, my family," she finally said. "I really love them. But they embarrass other people, sometimes, and that tends to make me . . . oh, I don't know, uncomfortable. It's so hard to explain, Steve. I just broke up with this guy, Peter. The first time my dad met him, Dad asked Peter how much he made." She glanced up to see if he understood.

Steve could feel his face closing down. But his mind was working overtime. "So when I asked an intrusive question about your income, you told me to mind my own business. Sort of like offering me a way to deal with your father."

"Was it that simple?" Nan looked uncertain. "I don't think so, but maybe. It was like showing you that the question could be very kindly meant, even if you weren't going to answer it. Steve, I'm very much afraid that my family might misunderstand why you're here with me. I'll tell them, but they read all sorts of things into small stuff. I never should have let you drive me here. I'm really sorry."

"So am I," he muttered. But he gave her elbow a squeeze. "I'm a master at stonewalling, Nan. Being forewarned should give me a distinct advantage in handling your family. Trust me, it will be all right. Tell me about Peter."

Taken off guard, she blinked at him. "Well, Peter is an architect, and we've been going together rather casually for the last year."

"Only now you aren't."

"That's right. I did tell my folks on the phone the other night, so they'll probably think they need to cheer me up. They're good at that."

Apparently she wasn't going to tell him why they broke up, and why should she? That was her very private personal life, after all. "What do they do to cheer you up?"

"Once they took me to a karaoke bar and insisted that I perform with them. That was great!" She grinned at his horrified face. "Well, you have to flow with them or it's no good, of course. We've been to circuses together, and once they arranged for me to drive one of those sulky carts on a horse-racing track. The boys—I shouldn't call them that, but they're both younger than me—have really imaginative ideas. Most of them involve some degree of embarrassment, if you're stodgy or uptight. Which I am, a little, but not majorly. And I do understand that a lot of other people are even more so. That's why I know my family embarrasses other people. I'm not sure that they actually embarrass me, or whether I simply sympathize with the people they do upset—like Peter. Probably like you, Steve. So I'm just forewarning you."

Steve would have protested that her family's

antics could not possibly embarrass him because he wouldn't put up with them. But he could see that for Nan's sake one would have to put up with them. Her relationship to her family was different than his, after all. More complex, possibly. Well, probably not. In a strange way he started to look forward to meeting the LeBarons, just so he could prove that he was perfectly capable of coping with whatever they could dish out. Hell, he was a fifth-generation San Franciscan!

"I can handle it, Nan. Don't give it another thought."

She smiled and said nothing as they stopped in front of a screen showing the incoming flights with their gate numbers. "Gate 76" they said together and turned toward the sloping corridor down to the metal detector. Passengers and visitors alike went through it. Steve automatically placed the car keys in the waiting tray, but he managed to set off the alarm anyhow. With a tsk of annoyance, he reached into his pants pocket to deposit his own keys in the tray and came through as Nan scooped up her briefcase.

He was struck by how attractive she looked with her high arching brows over such sparkling hazel eyes. Her lips were delicately full with an adorable little open spot in the middle where they almost seemed not to meet. She had a determined chin and a well-defined nose, but her cheeks were fuller, like her lips, and of that desirable peaches-

FEVER PITCH

and-cream complexion that the British so prized. A rather striking combination of elegance and wholesomeness, Steve thought. He scarcely had to slow his stride for her to keep up with him as they followed the long corridor down past a photo display of San Francisco Victorian houses.

"I like the colors on that one," Nan said, indicating one of the more subtle three-color combinations. "But my dad," she said with a grin, "would prefer this one."

Steve could see the appeal of the more flamboyant color choice—a rich burgundy with a gray verging on silver. "It's not bad," he admitted. "Just skirting the tacky. That's why I've decided to paint all the inside walls of my house white. You can't make a mistake that way."

"Coward! You'd take risks in the emergency room for a better result. Why not in your house?"

"I know medicine. I don't know paint colors." He glanced at a clock near the gate that showed it was still ten minutes before the LeBaron flight was due to arrive. "Let's walk a few more minutes, okay?"

"Sure."

As they wandered on down the terminal corridor, Steve continued talking about his house, though why he thought Nan would be interested, he hadn't the faintest notion. "There's a room I'm going to make my study that I thought about painting something outrageous—a deep red, maybe. I saw a room like that once, and it looked great. But there would have to be a lot of light in it, or it would feel really heavy, don't you think?"

"Probably. But they have all kinds of recessed lighting now that will do anything you want it to. Mom got into that, too." Nan laughed. "You should see her kitchen."

"Describe it to me."

Nan did, with its central island flooded in light, its kitchen sink bathed in light, its blue tile countertops reflecting so many lights that the whole place twinkled like a Christmas tree. The two of them fell into laughing as she continued to detail the sources of light and the surprises Mrs. LeBaron had in store for any visitor caught in the myriad spotlights.

"Uh, Steve?" Nan said when her recital was finished.

"Yes, Nan?"

"I just wondered why you were holding my hand," she said meekly.

He looked down at their joined hands and felt a shock of emotion rush through him. Why indeed? But he decided it would look gauche to drop her hand at this point, and he retained it. "Well, I suppose because we're walking along among all these people, and if we're holding hands, they aren't going to try to pass between us."

She shook her head with amusement, but made

no attempt to withdraw her hand. "That's a mildly imaginative answer. I'd give you a four on a scale of ten."

"All right, I can do better." He thought for a moment and said, "There's an old medical ritual where the art of healing is passed on by means of an older physician holding a younger physician's hand. It's something like the laying on of hands, but different."

"Better," Nan admitted. "Maybe a six or six and a half."

"I should have a third try. Everyone gets three tries, like three wishes."

"Have at it."

But the only thoughts that came into Steve's mind were surprisingly romantic ones. Her hand felt warm and comfortable in his, and he had a sudden and strong desire to hold her against him and kiss her. He felt powerfully attracted to her, just then, and to her situation. His own decision to help her out tonight seemed suddenly an act of fate. He cleared his throat. "I'll need a little time on that, and your family's flight must be almost at the gate."

She regarded him curiously but said only, "Okay. Look, here come the first passengers, and my family always flies first-class."

Nan stepped forward, automatically withdrawing her hand from his, breaking the spell he seemed to be under. Three wishes, indeed! Steve should have stuck with the one where he hadn't ever done this, driving her to the airport to meet her family.

As Nan moved forward, Steve stayed well behind, observing her as she waited. Almost immediately a little round woman and three giants came up the passageway and burst through the door into Nan's arms. All four of them at once, from the looks of it. They were hugging and kissing and several exuberant voices were exclaiming about how good Nan looked and how long it had been since they'd seen her. They were, without doubt, the noisiest arrivals in the area. Other people stopped to look at them, their expressions varying from amused tolerance to frowns of annoyance. Well, Nan had warned him.

Turning to him finally, Nan said to her parents, "This is Steve Winstead from the hospital. He agreed to drive me out because the car I borrowed was a stick shift." She caught her mother's eye and added, "He did it as a favor, and I don't want to impose on his good nature too far, so let's get your luggage and be off."

Mrs. LeBaron's name was Trudy, which she insisted on being called. "And may I call you Steve?" she asked, her voice chipper and her little eyes flashing with obvious suspicion of the real nature of her daughter's relationship with this man.

"Of course." Steve made a point of shaking hands with Mr. LeBaron (Fred), and both brothers, John and Jim, who looked like twins but who assured him without his asking that they were not. All three of the men easily cleared six and a half feet. Steve, at slightly over six feet, felt almost annoyed with them for all being so tall. Only Trudy was short, and she couldn't possibly have been more than five four. So obviously all the height genes had come from Mr. LeBaron, who was at present announcing to the world that "It's damn good to be here, Nanny. Roughest flight I've been on in years."

Nanny. Steve exchanged a bland look with Fielding's foremost neurology fellow and offered to carry Trudy's carry-on bag.

"None of that. None of that," Fred LeBaron boomed. "Trudy only lets me carry her bag. Not even the boys unless I'm not around. Doesn't trust anyone else."

Which was patently untrue. Steve suspected Trudy LeBaron trusted everyone. She had already taken hold of his arm and had begun a lengthy explanation of how they had arrived at its being Nan's turn to have Christmas even though they had been out two years ago. This involved John and Jim sharing the honors, and the elder LeBarons giving in to necessity—they were not going to see Nan for more than two days if she came to them in Oklahoma. "This being a doctor really isn't easy on families," she said, looking hopefully up at him. "You're not a doctor, are you?"

"I'm afraid I am."

Trudy sighed and gave a shake to her head of deeply waved golden hair. "It's what she wanted, you know, but we had no idea. She's too busy to call half the time, and she's impossible to reach." Trudy extended her other arm and drew Nan in beside her. "Not that we blame you, dear. It does seem that you work too hard, but if you enjoy it . . ." Her voice trailed off in the mystery of why someone would want to work that hard.

Steve grinned at Nan but said only, "Doctors are like that, Mrs. LeBaron . . . Trudy."

"Will you look at that?" demanded Fred LeBaron in a voice that could undoubtedly be heard above a field full of oil derricks in loud motion. "Isn't that the damnedest thing? Those are exactly the colors we painted the new office."

He was pointing to the Victorian Steve and Nan had discussed on their route past it to the gate. Nan laughed. "I knew you'd like those colors, Dad. Steve liked them, too."

"Is that right, son? Well, you'd love the new office building. Architect designed, no expense spared. It's the talk of Tulsa."

Son? Where did this man get off calling him "son"? Steve was about to take exception, if nonverbally, to Mr. LeBaron's designation, when he caught Nan's quizzical expression. Well, she'd warned him. There was nothing to take offense at, after all. It was probably something people in

Oklahoma said all the time. But then Mr. LeBaron asked, "So how much do you earn a year, son?"

Indignation snapped at his heels. *No one* had the right to ask such a question, no matter whose father he was. Nan's voice echoed in his mind, telling him her investments were none of his business. "Not as much as you I'm sure, sir, but enough," he replied ruefully. He caught Nan's surprised look and shrugged slightly. He'd told her he could handle it, and he would. Or his name wasn't Steven P. Winstead, III.

Chapter Five

After the way Peter had behaved around her parents, Nan had not expected such tolerance from Steve Winstead, a notedly impatient and obviously blue-blooded man. Peter had been appalled by the gauche questions Fred LeBaron had asked, and the smotheringly cozy attitude Trudy LeBaron exhibited toward him. Though Steve was maintaining a certain reserve, he wasn't treating anyone as if he was shocked by their behavior.

Nan had tried to warn Peter, but he hadn't paid much attention to her at the time. After his first exposure to her family, he had taken her aside and criticized them in such derogatory terms that she had felt more embarrassed for him than for her family. "I know they're difficult to accept," she had said, "but they're my family and I love them. They're good people."

"They're abominably nouveau riche," he'd protested. "Your father is loud and rude, your mother looks like an aging madam, your brothers practically pick their noses, they're so country hick."

"Not another word! Maybe we aren't quite meant for each other," she'd said caustically.

Unfortunately, their romance at the time was fairly new and though Peter stayed away during her family's visit, he returned afterward, apparently pushing the alarming LeBarons way to the back of his mind. Maybe his realization that he was about to meet them again had spurred his recent defection.

Nan watched her family gather around the baggage carousel now, the three giants and the short, round woman with golden hair. Her heart swelled with love for them—this boisterous, intrusive bunch. Even as she watched, her brother John helped a frail elderly man lift his suitcase off the moving black rubber of the carousel, and Jim reached down to retrieve a doll a small girl had dropped. They were very good people, and if their behavior didn't meet with San Francisco's sophisticated expectations, it didn't make them any less worthy.

She steeled herself to glance across at Steve, but he was talking with her mother and paying no attention to her. Strange man. When he'd taken her hand as they walked, he had done it as though it were the most natural thing in the world to do. He was talking at the time, looking at her, and his hand had simply slipped around hers. His expression hadn't changed. He hadn't, in fact, seemed to notice what he was doing at all.

Maybe he did it all the time, walking with some woman. Nan had been taken off guard, even though she remembered wanting to squeeze his hand the day she'd told him some home truths about the reason for the malpractice suit. Well, she thought now, it was nice having someone hold your hand. Kind of friendly. It didn't mean a thing. Especially not with this man.

The amount of luggage her family had brought was truly astonishing. "Well, dear," her mother explained, "it's Christmas, after all. We've brought all the presents, and even some decorations, since you didn't have much last time."

"But you bought me strings of lights and ornaments then!" Nan protested, laughing. She remembered the boxes of Christmas items that she had stored in her closet. They took up so much room, she'd never bothered to expand her wardrobe.

Trudy confided to Steve, "Scrawniest tree you ever saw. We're going to go out and chop one down this time. There are Christmas tree farms around, you know. Why don't you come with us?"

"Mother," Nan said warningly.

"Well, he's going to need a tree, dear. Everyone needs a tree."

"Unfortunately, my house is being renovated.

I'm going to have to skip it this year." Steve smiled benignly on Nan. "I'll just enjoy the one at the hospital."

"Oh, no!" Trudy protested. "You'll enjoy ours with us. A hospital Christmas tree! They probably don't even have blinking lights."

"No, I don't think they do," Steve said sadly.

"He's teasing you, Mom." Nan reached for another suitcase her mother unnecessarily indicated was hers. They had the largest set of matching luggage—in black and purple—that she'd ever seen. Steve grabbed hold of it before she or either of her brothers could. Her father, she noticed, was deep in conversation with a stranger wearing a dog collar—literally, asking her, in his usual curious and decidedly high-volume way, why she wore it.

"I think that's all of them," her mother said, distractedly counting the suitcases, duffel bags, and garment bags that covered a few square yards of floor space. "Ten, eleven, twelve. Yes, they're all here."

Nan groaned, but each of the men slung one bag strap over his shoulder and gripped two in his hands and followed Steve as he made his way through the throng over to the escalator down to the parking garage. Nan linked arms with her mother, and kept a firm grip on her briefcase, which she wished she'd left in the minivan. Even Rachel's minivan was going to be stretched to the limits. How had Nan ever considered bringing a car to meet this menagerie?

Her mother was filling her in on aunts and uncles, cousins and their children, friends and neighbors. It seemed a shame to pull these family-oriented people away from their own home during the holiday. But they'd insisted. "You're more important to us than all the cousins in Oklahoma," her mother had insisted. "And we love San Francisco."

Steve had the back of the van open, and bags were being piled in under his somewhat casual supervision. "This garage could use more light," her father said, squinting into the cavernous spaces around him. "I'll bet people get mugged here."

"I imagine they do," Nan said. "Mom, why don't you sit up front with Steve? I'll ride in the back with Dad, and John and Jim can sit in the middle."

"No, no. You're to sit up front with Steve where you belong." Trudy grasped the sides of the van and levered herself up through the side door. "My! That's a tall step. Mind your head, Fred."

With a maximum of fuss, the others arranged themselves around the minivan as though it were a hotel room they'd just taken over. Nan shook her head with fond exasperation and climbed in beside Steve. "Home, James."

"Actually," he said, "I don't know where you live, Nan."

"Did you hear that, Mom?" Nan asked. And without waiting for a reply, since due to the commotion her family was making Trudy probably hadn't, she added, "Near the hospital. I'll guide you when we get closer."

The ride back seemed much briefer than the ride out. Her family asked a stream of questions, told a variety of stories and jokes, and discussed what each most wanted to do now that they'd gotten here. Steve spoke when he was included in the conversation, and seemed intent on his driving when he wasn't. Nan stayed turned halfway around in her seat to see everyone and answer their endless queries.

"I'll be off on Saturday so we can get the tree then," she said. "But let's remember to measure how high the ceilings are before we leave."

"Would Steve like to come with us?" Trudy called.

"No, I'm afraid I'm working Saturday," he said.

When they were discussing the performance of the Nutcracker to which Nan had gotten tickets, her father said, "Maybe Steve would like to go with us."

Since Nan had bought the tickets months before, she did have an extra one that had been meant for Peter, but she didn't say so. Steve said, "That's kind of you, sir, but I don't think I could."

Pretty obvious he wasn't interested in palling around with the LeBarons, since he didn't even know when this event was taking place. But Nan could only admire his calm in the face of her family's relentless goodwill. He never gave the impression of humoring them, the only mode in which Peter had seemed able to operate. Fred LaBaron had asked Nan ruefully if Peter had some kind of burr up his butt. Physically it seemed unlikely, but metaphorically her father was right on.

When they arrived at the three-story Victorian Steve helped unload the minivan, but Nan insisted that he had done more than his duty and wouldn't hear of him climbing the three flights of stairs to her flat. She gave her mother the key and hopped back in the van with Steve. "My car's in the hospital parking garage. Yours must be, too. If you'll drop me and the van there, your mission is accomplished."

"Doesn't Rachel need her van?"

"No, she drove home with Jerry. She'll get it tomorrow."

"Right. She and Jerry are living at her house, and Roger is temporarily living at Jerry's while your family is here," he recited from their earlier discussion.

"It's not all that strange. After all, you're going home to a house without any furniture."

"True."

They drove in easy silence the few blocks to the

hospital. He fed his plastic pass into the machine by the gate, and the arm swung up. "Where's your car?"

"On the second floor. Yours?"

"Same."

When she indicated her car, he pulled the van into the space beside it and shut off the engine. "I'm sure you wish to hell you'd never offered," she said, "but I really appreciate it. Now I owe you, so don't hesitate to ask a favor." She pushed open the door and climbed down into the cold, silent garage. "It's kind of eerie here at night, isn't it?"

He locked his door and walked around to drop the keys into her hand. "Yeah, but it's safe enough, apparently, with us being the only ones who can get in. Nan?"

"Mmm?" She was using her own keys to unlock the burgundy convertible LeBaron, her own private joke on her name. There was no way it could have held all the LeBarons at once with their luggage. When he didn't speak, she turned to find him regarding her intently. "Is something the matter?"

"I wonder if we could talk a little more about the malpractice case sometime. You'll be busy while your family is here, but afterward. Before the court date."

"Of course." While he held her door open, she

slid onto the seat and smiled up at him. "We'll get through that okay. I'm not worried about it."

"I can tell," he said dryly. His hand came to rest briefly on her shoulder. "Enjoy your visit with your family."

"Thanks."

Nan was curious about what he drove, but he didn't move to one of the few cars remaining on the floor. So she shrugged, started the LeBaron and, with a wave, drove off down the ramp and out of the Fielding staff garage. He had unsettled her, standing there looking curiously expectant before he'd finally and firmly closed her car door. Almost like a date waiting to be kissed, Nan thought, frowning. As she drove the short distance home, she couldn't help but wonder what Steve Winstead really wanted from her.

Between her family's visit and her work Nan was run pleasantly ragged for the next week. No one was as good as John and Jim at finding the most interesting, enjoyable things to do, no matter where they were. And coming home each evening to her mother's wondrous home cooking was a very special treat. Nan remembered that she and Angel seldom kept more than yogurt in the refrigerator when they lived together, and though Roger had been experimenting with cooking, the kitchen had remained fairly barren. Fortunately no protestations about Mrs. LeBaron being on vacation had the slightest effect on her desire to cook for her daughter. "We can eat out any time," she said more than once.

Nan came home one evening to find her family huddled over the medical center newspaper that she'd brought home the previous day. They were obviously arguing good-naturedly about something to do with it, because Fred LeBaron stabbed the paper with a blunt finger and said, "It says right here that his parents couldn't afford to come with him. That means they're still in Italy. So what are we going to do about it?"

Oh, boy, we're on another crusade, Nan thought with an amused shake of her head. "What's up?" she asked, tossing her briefcase on the floor beside her mother's chair.

"A little boy's been sent here from Italy for neurosurgery, and his parents couldn't come with him." John looked up from the paper. "Dad thinks we should fly them over."

"Well, hell, it's Christmas," her father explained. "How would you like to be a five-year-old alone at Christmas?"

The picture that illustrated the article showed half a dozen staff members surrounding a small child with a bandaged head. Holiday activity was already in full swing at Fielding, and Nan knew a lot of attention was paid to the children, but it was not the same as family. "If we're going to do it, we have to do it right." She took the paper and quickly scanned the article. "Okay, tomorrow Mom can talk with the Patient Relations people, and Dad can call the family housing group to see what's available. John should talk with a travel agent, and Jim can speak with Francine about an interpreter."

"So what are you going to do?" Jim demanded, grinning at her.

"I'll pay him a visit and find out what I can about his medical condition, okay?" She looked at her mother. "I'm starved. Are we eating out?"

"Heavens, no. There's a meatloaf in the oven and potatoes ready for mashing. You can show me what to do with the artichokes."

And with no more discussion, the LeBarons embarked on one of their famous, or infamous, rescue projects that served to utilize their talents, their energy, their financial resources, and their unbounded generosity. Within two days the whole project had been arranged, not quietly, because that wasn't a LeBaron attribute, but with no wish for self-aggrandizement, either. The medical center learned of the project, but they did not learn who the donor was. Which was exactly as Nan would have wished it.

But Steve knew who was reponsible. He couldn't exactly have said how he knew, because no one presented him with the complete story, but enough of the pieces fell into his lap that he was able to fit the puzzle together. One of the major pieces occurred when he found himself, as a last-minute substitute, in the role of Santa Claus for the children's Christmas party. He had been on the very point of departure, several hours late, when the director of volunteers came rushing up to him. "Don't go," she begged. "We need you."

"I'm exhausted," he'd said, tugging ineffectually at the piece of tape that had stuck to the bottom of his running shoe. He shouldn't have stopped to do that.

"Steve," she said, fixing him with her no-nonsense look, "our Santa Claus has come down with the flu, and there's no one else around. The party starts in thirty minutes. It's very important. We can't disappoint all those children."

Steve had known Sandra Lopez for half a dozen years. She had sent him all her best volunteers to work in the Emergency Department, and she had kept the hospital in general afloat with volunteer helping hands that were too often not sufficiently appreciated. He *was* tired, but not too tired to help out in an emergency. Santa Claus, though? Who the hell would believe in him as Santa Claus? They should have found the guy who was bringing the Italian parents over to be with their son.

"I presume you have a costume," he said, and allowed himself to be led off to the volunteer office, where he was duly provided with a red suit, black boots, a magnificent mustache and beard combination, a stocking cap with a white pompom, and a pair of half glasses.

Sandra eyed him appraisingly when he opened the door of her office and stepped out. "Not bad. You're a little *younger* than our usual Santa, but the kids aren't likely to notice. Want me to put a little lipstick on your nose?"

"So the kids will think Santa's a lush?" he grumbled. "No, thanks. You're not sending me up there alone, are you?"

"No, you have an elf," she assured him seriously. "Terri is one of our candy stripers, and she did it last year, so she knows the routine. Thanks, Steve. And good luck."

He felt ridiculous, and a fraud. The girl, Terri, who could not have been more than ten, candy striper or not, regarded him skeptically. "You ever do this before?" she asked.

"Never." And never again, he silently added.

There was a book cart emptied of its books and magazines and filled with Christmas stockings stuffed with tiny toys and handmade, cuddly teddy bears. Terri handed him one girl bear and one boy. "It's easy," she said. "Just say 'Ho Ho Ho' and hand them one of these."

It was not easy. It was heartbreaking. In every room there was a sick child, sometimes a dying child. In the playroom there was a forest of IV poles pushed by kids too young to be so ill. There were parents who told him their son had been waiting for him. There were parents who told him their daughter had lost her sight the previous day. There were children with grotesquely shaped heads and twisted bodies. There were children wrapped around with bandages from major surgery. He felt the worst kind of fraud handing these innocents a stocking and wishing them a merry Christmas. How could they possibly have a merry Christmas?

In one room he came upon Nan LeBaron, sitting with a child who obviously spoke no English. *"Buon natale!"* he said, handing out the boy bear peeking from his stocking. In Italian he asked the child what he wanted for Christmas, and if he knew who Santa Claus was. Nan peered rather closely at him, her brows rising in surprise.

"As I live and breathe," she muttered, grinning. "If it isn't the jolly old elf himself."

He had known, seeing her there, that it was her family who was trying to help this boy. Though there might have been other explanations for her being in the boy's room, Steve did not believe for a minute that they were the real reason. "It's wonderful, what your family's doing," he blurted.

Nan frowned at him. "How could you possibly know that? My mother hasn't called to invite you to dinner, has she?"

"No. Was she planning to?"

"I hope not. And, Steve, not a word of this, please."

"Of course not." He returned his attention to the child, rumpling his dark curls. "Best of luck, kid," he said in English, repeating it in Italian. And with a hearty "Ho Ho Ho" he followed meekly as Terri marched back out of the room pushing the laden book cart before her.

The afternoon drained him. He returned to the volunteer office to rid himself of the stifling Santa Claus outfit, feeling the sweat dribble down his face and neck. Sandra Lopez was still up at the children's party playing Bingo, and the volunteer office was deserted—except for Nan LeBaron. Before he could ask her why she was there, she said, "I think I was rude upstairs. I didn't mean to be."

He tugged off the ridiculous hat and lifted the beard over his head. Nan handed him a tissue, and then another, to wipe away the perspiration. "I hope they dry-clean this outfit between uses," he said.

"They probably do. You can't be the only one to bake in it."

"Jesus! How can anyone bear to be a pediatrician?"

"Most kids are healthy. And most sick kids get better. Was it hard?"

He watched his fingers as he unbuttoned the red jacket and unbuckled the belt. His throat had tightened, remembering the heartrending patients, and he needed a moment to bring himself under control. "All those kids believing in Santa Claus, and all those parents hoping for miracles. It was . . . painful."

Nan nodded and helped him out of the heavy jacket. He stood there in his undershirt, staring at the colored yarn strung with beads around his neck. "One of the kids gave me that," he said. "She made it for Santa Claus because he always gave things away and never got anything." Steve lifted fiercely glistening eyes to Nan's. "And this kid was bald as a billiard ball from chemotherapy."

Then she did something that completely took him by surprise. She put her arms around him and hugged him, tight. Just for a moment, but when she stepped back she was smiling wryly. "You never cease to amaze me. Look, I didn't mean it when I said I hoped Mom hadn't invited you for dinner. If you wanted to come, we'd all love to have you. Tonight she's fixing roast beef with our favorite gravy and oven-browned potatoes. You're probably busy, but I wanted you to know you're welcome."

"I'm not busy." Things seemed to be coming unbidden from his mouth this afternoon. But he found that he had a real desire to be enveloped in her crazy family again, just for the evening. And maybe he could kiss her good night, even though they hadn't ever been on a date. He could pretend that it was a friendly, thank-you sort of kiss. Her lips just seemed to beckon to him. The last few days he'd found himself thinking about them, seeing them in his mind's eye. They were just lips, for God's sake. But he wanted to kiss them rather desperately. "What time should I come?"

"Six-thirty, if you want to unwind first. Seven, if you just want to eat."

"I'll be there at six-thirty."

Because of a last-minute emergency, Nan wasn't. When she arrived, at just a few minutes before seven, she found Steve sitting back in her favorite chair, listening to Jim tell a tall tale about a trip to the Andes. To her astonishment, the woman she'd recommended as a translator, Francine Polardi, was also there. Nan raised questioning brows at her mother, but Trudy merely smiled broadly and winked. Oh, my God, Nan thought. They've latched onto another innocent soul and swept her off with them. Francine waved cheerfully but continued to pay considerable attention to Jim's story. Steve rose to give her his chair.

Not wanting to make a fuss, Nan said, "Thanks. Sorry I was held up." She dropped into the chair and, there being no more seats in the room, Steve sat on the floor nearby. Nan's father was surreptitiously wrapping a Christmas present at the coffee table in front of the sofa, and everyone else sat spellbound until Jim, a natural storyteller, finished his story with a dramatic flourish. Francine laughed and said, "I'll tell it to Tomasino in Italian. He'll love it."

"Maybe I could come with you when you tell him." Jim sounded diffident, but Nan knew him well and caught the undercurrent of real eagerness. Ordinarily an extremely laid-back fellow, this intensity alerted Nan to something unusual going on. And she doubted that it was Jim's affection for a child he hadn't met.

Francine nodded. "Okay. How about if we meet on the pedi floor on my lunch hour tomorrow?"

Trudy LeBaron had disappeared into the kitchen, and John with her. After a few minutes of general conversation, John returned to say, "Soup's on. Sorry, Nanny, you don't get an old-fashioned tonight."

Though Nan hadn't maintained her family's love of a cocktail before dinner, she sighed extravagantly. "Everyone's so *mean* to me."

Both brothers instantly pounced on the childhood complaint with their usual insistence that Nan had always had things better than they. "See what you missed by being an only child?" she said to Steve, reaching down to give him a hand up.

"I had no idea."

He held her hand a moment longer than necessary, and once again she pondered what was going on. Nan felt as if she'd missed something along the way, something she should have picked up, like a symptom of neurological damage that had escaped her notice on routine examination. He didn't even quite look like himself. He looked relaxed and almost good-natured.

Not that he was such a terror, she reminded herself. Though he had a reputation for impatience and a short temper when he was at the end of a double shift, he was also known to be remarkably accurate in his diagnoses and especially good with frightened patients. His steadiness and matter-of-factness were attributes that patients often liked, and staff depended on.

"Why are you staring at me?" he asked.

"Was I? Sorry. I was just thinking." Nan realized he'd never been to her flat before, and she led him from the living room into the dining room while the others gathered up their glasses and chairs to take with them. "It's sort of mix and match in here," she apologized. "Angel and I usually ate in the kitchen but Roger likes the dining room, even with all the different chairs. There were four when I moved in, and I've picked up more for when my family visits, only they don't match."

"They look comfortable. Maybe I'll get some like that for my house." He motioned toward the door. "Could we help your mom?"

"No, it's John's turn. We've been working on the same schedule since we were kids."

"Who does the dishes?"

"If John has helped before dinner, then Jim and I do."

Steve looked significantly toward where Jim was escorting Francine into the room. "Maybe you and I should do them tonight."

"I know I've missed something here," she grumbled as she took the seat he held for her. "I'm convinced this is not your typical behavior, and it can't just be that you're grateful to me for telling you your graveside manner stinks. Sure, you can help me do the dishes, but only if you'll let me in on what's going on."

"Nothing's going on," he said, a look of perfect innocence on his handsome face.

And though she would have preferred to pursue the matter, it was not something destined to happen when her family congregated in their usual high spirits. There were plans for Christmas to finalize, and, since both Steve and Francine knew about Tomasino's parents, arrangements to discuss. John and Jim competed in telling stories that made everyone laugh, and every once in a while someone would ask Nan how her day had been. But somehow no one could stay on the subject of medicine for long, and Fred LeBaron would be mentioning how he'd changed the spark plugs on the LeBaron or Trudy would be soliciting advice on the menu for New Year's Eve.

"We'll do the dishes," Steve said when everyone was rising after the meal.

This caused a certain amount of confusion—a guest being burdened with such a task—but in the end Jim gratefully handed over the onerous chore. Nan shook her head to her mother's offer of help and dutifully showed Steve where the kitchen was. "Have you ever done dishes before?" she asked.

"Well, not exactly."

"How close have you come?"

"I've stacked dishes in the dishwasher and soaked pans for a cleaning person to take care of."

"I don't have a dishwasher."

"Really?" He looked around him in fascination. "I'm surprised your parents haven't given you one."

"They would have if I'd let them. But the woman who owns the building is ancient and doesn't believe in modern conveniences and wouldn't hear of anyone installing one."

"Then you should have moved."

He looked so earnest that Nan laughed. "Probably. Look. Since you offered, I'm going to teach you how to do them, okay? You never know when it's going to come in handy."

"Is there some skill to it?" he asked doubtfully.

"Sure. You have to know what to wash first, and what kind of cleaning implements to use. You want an apron?"

"Me? Of course not."

"Oh, these macho men," she sighed. "It's like

putting on scrubs, Steve. It protects you from the worst of the ravages you're about to encounter."

"Do your brothers wear them?"

"If they have decent clothes on."

"Hmmm. All right, but nothing with frills on it."

Nan found a large striped navy apron that Roger wore hanging on the back of the kitchen door. Since Steve looked like he didn't even know how to put one on, she slid it over his head and told him to turn around. While she tied a bow in back she said, "I'm going to let you wash, because that's the hard part. We start with the cleanest dishes, the glasses, and a sink full of soapy water."

She rather liked his looks in the apron, standing here by her sink. His blond hair gleamed under the paper globe, and his face was reflected in the dark window. He wore a look of concentration, much as he might have sewing up a laceration. In his awkward hands the wineglasses looked particularly fragile. "Don't they get broken all the time banging against this hard surface?"

"Sometimes. Jim is the one who breaks them, mostly. He gets caught up in a story and starts to wave his hands and smashes them against the side. Now watch how I do it," she said, when he started to rinse the soapy glass after swishing it in the water. "Run your fingers along the rim and then down the sides and the base, to get it really clean."

"Is that necessary?"

"In my house it is. If you're going to do something, you might as well do it right."

"Where have I heard that before?" he muttered. But he did as he was told.

When he turned the water on to rinse the glass, Nan reached past him and swung the faucet over to the other sink. "If you let the water run into the soapy side, it will dilute the suds."

"Gee, this is really complicated," he teased, turning his head just as her face neared his shoulder. And without seeming to give it any thought, he kissed her, lightly, on the lips, and drew back. "I had no idea what I'd missed all these years."

Nan blinked at him. She expected to experience a flash of anger at the liberty he'd taken, and it didn't come. Her lips seemed to reverberate with his touch for several moments. "Well," she said after a while. But could think of nothing more to add. Picking up a dish towel, she began to wipe the glass he'd placed in the drainer. This was all very strange.

They worked in silence for some time, until the glasses were done and Nan instructed him to soak the flatware in the sink while he washed the plates. "And maybe we should be soaking the roasting pan, too," she said, feeling as if she weren't quite with it. "I'll scrape the grease into a tin, and you can squirt dishwashing liquid in it for me."

Nan felt the pulse beating in her throat as she

FEVER PITCH

worked near him. She was never unaware of exactly where he stood or when he glanced casually over at her. He seemed taller than she'd remembered, his hair a more burnished gold, his eyes a deeper blue, his chin even more rugged than she recalled. There actually seemed to be two things going on. One of them was definitely Steve's agenda, but the other ... Something was going on inside her that she couldn't account for, which she was unfamiliar with. Well, she would figure that one out later. For now she said, "Steve? What's going on here?"

Chapter Six

Steve knew he wasn't going to be able to ignore her questions much longer. He continued to swab a sponge over the roast beef and roast potato leavings on a stoneware plate. "Look, Nan, I wish I could tell you. I just seem to be very attracted to you this evening. I'm sorry if I offended you. I didn't mean any harm."

"You can't just go around kissing people because you're attracted to them," she said sternly.

"I don't, mostly."

"And you held my hand the other day."

"Well, that was just friendly. You didn't mind that, did you?"

"I didn't mind, but I was surprised and confused."

"No more surprised and confused than I am." He wiped his hands on the front of his apron and reached for her hands. She hesitantly allowed him to take them. "I don't understand what's going on. I feel like it's not just me, Nan. I think something is going on with you, too."

"Steve, I just got out of a relationship. I'm not looking for something like that."

"I'm not, either! Honestly."

"Then you shouldn't be kissing me and holding my hands." But she didn't withdraw hers from his grip.

"I know I shouldn't. And you shouldn't let me."

Nan sighed. Her eyes stayed glued to his face. "This isn't good, Steve. We don't know each other, we're involved in a malpractice case together, we come from two different worlds. There are any number of women you could get involved with. I'm definitely one of the ones you shouldn't. And I don't need anyone in my life right now. I don't want anyone in my life right now. So let's just let this go, okay?"

He agreed with everything she said. And more. He could think of half a dozen other reasons why they shouldn't start anything. But her face was so close and her lips so tempting that he slowly lowered his head and sought them eagerly with his own. His kiss was slow and tender and provocative and hungry by turns. Not a short kiss by any means. And Nan followed him, allowed him to take her where he led, her eyes closed, her body swaying slightly, almost unsteadily. His heart was pounding when she finally drew back.

"All right," she said. "That was lovely, but that's the end of it, okay?"

"Okay." He turned toward the sink again and plunged his hands into the greasy water.

"Maybe you should empty that out and start over," she said.

"I'm sure you're right."

Nan watched as he followed her instructions, and after a while she began to talk, not about anything in particular but just the sort of things one talks about with one's friends—what her family had been doing, their plans for the holidays, one or two of her own cases. And after a while Steve felt more relaxed and he talked, too. He told her a little more about his family, and his new house, and a horrendous night in the emergency room. When Trudy LeBaron came into the kitchen to check on how they were doing, she found the two of them arguing the merits of the newest treatments for migraine headaches. She smiled benignly on them, remarked that Steve looked very handsome in his apron, and left them alone.

The tension had started to rise again in Steve's body, but he was determined to ignore it. Together he and Nan finished the dishes, for which he received her modest praise and her wickedly rueful grin.

"Another first for Dr. Steven Winstead," she

teased. "No accomplishment or task is too lowly for the good doctor."

He wanted to grab her then, to pull her into his arms and swing her around in the narrow, confined space of the kitchen, to seek her lips again with his, to press her body against the length of his torso. But he did none of these things. With great restraint he merely tsked and told her to mind her manners. He felt as though, in a way, she was daring him, but that might have been only his wish. Because if she was daring him, he would be perfectly willing to accept the challenge.

It was actually a relief to him when they joined her family and he was distracted by the friendly bickering among them and their plans and schemes for the holidays. But he could still feel the pull from Nan, even when she was halfway across the room, and after a while he excused himself, saying that he had an early morning. The three men jumped to their feet and shook his hand, while Trudy offered him her cheek to kiss. He nodded good-bye to the woman whose name he'd forgotten and followed Nan to the door.

"Thanks for inviting me."

"Our pleasure."

She had opened the front door and stood waiting for him to leave, but he held out his hand to her, not with any idea to shake hers, but to draw her out onto the landing. Nan stared at his hand for a long moment and then slowly, almost reluctantly laid hers in it. He drew her out and pushed the door almost closed—and took her in his arms. "Oh, hell," she murmured against his chest. Then she lifted her face for his kiss, and made no effort to appear shy or nonparticipatory. She was with him every moment of the prolonged and breathless exchange. Her mouth was silken and warmly moist, excruciatingly inviting and not entirely satisfying. He wanted to let his hands wander, but even in his intoxicated state realized that that would not be a wise move. Instead he snuggled her against him and sighed deeply into her ash-blond hair. "I should go," he said.

"Yes. Please do." Her voice sounded husky with desire.

Steve left.

Nan had never been so confused about a relationship with a man. Steve was right, of course, that she could call a halt to whatever it was that was going on, whenever she wished. But Nan had no clear idea of what was going on, or whether it would continue. After all, what were the chances that without making any effort to do so, she and Steve would run into each other where they could carry on this nonsensical thing they had going on? If they did have something going on.

And yet each day after he had come to dinner, there was an encounter. The first day he appeared at her shared office clutching a deposition, saying, "I really need to talk with you about this malpractice suit, Dr. LeBaron."

Nan's office mate had said, "Take my desk, Doctor. I need to get down to the clinic."

As soon as she had left, Steve closed the door behind her and stood staring unnervingly at Nan. "What's the problem?" she asked.

"I haven't been able to get you off my mind," he admitted.

Nan remained firmly seated at her desk. "Maybe you're not trying."

"Are you?"

"Of course. I don't mean that I haven't thought of you. And those kisses. I have. But I know better than to build anything around them. You do, too, Steve."

"I'm not building anything around them." He stood there like a blond diver poised on a diving board, awaiting the perfect moment to make his heroic plunge. His head was held alertly cocked toward her and the whole lanky length of him seemed attuned to the slightest lowering of her guard. Unfortunately, he didn't have to wait long. Nan could not seem to be in the same room with him and maintain her resolve. What harm could it do to kiss him, when that's what she wanted to do? She knew he wasn't asking for more than that.

"We're nuts," she said, rising to walk toward

him, where she placed her fingers on his chest and tilted her head up.

"Undoubtedly," he murmured against her forehead.

And then their arms were around each other and their lips joined. Nan felt the currents of excitement flash through her. This was not familiar territory, not this intensity, this unquestioned need. She pressed her body against his and wrapped her arms around his waist. After a while their kiss broke off by mutual consent and they merely stood there together, their torsos touching, Nan's head resting against his shoulder, his hand stroking the back of her neck. Even as desire rose in her, she felt incredibly tender toward him.

Steve sighed, kissed her forehead, and said, "I'd better get back."

"Don't forget the deposition papers. Did you have anything you wanted to ask me about them?"

"Not that I remember." His lips twisted ruefully. "I'm not sure I remember my own name right now."

"I'm sure a Winstead never forgets his name."

"Does a LeBaron?"

"Sure. It used to be Lebronski when I was born."

His eyes narrowed. "Seriously?"

"Seriously. So you see you have every reason to keep your distance."

"We'll discuss it when we have more time, Nan.

I've already taken more of a lunch break than I usually do."

And with a peck on her forehead, he disappeared through the office door, and Nan, weak-kneed, sat down at her desk to try once again to understand how this could be happening.

He came to her office, or she went to the emergency room, or they arranged to meet on the jogging trail. Never anywhere that they could stop and take time. It was as if they were determined not to let anything develop, as if this would burn itself out like a comet if they would just be cautious for a while.

The day before Christmas, Nan left a message asking him to meet her after work. She chose a waiting room that would be deserted, near the south entrance. In white tissue paper with a red bow she lugged the gift she had brought for him and hid it behind a chair. She was due to go out to dinner with her family and couldn't afford to wait long for him, so she was about to leave a note when she heard running steps in the deserted corridor.

"Sorry," he said, brushing back his hair and coming forward to clasp her hands. "Merry Christmas, Nan. I felt sure you wouldn't have time to see me today."

"I have to go almost immediately, but I wanted to give you something." She reached behind the chair and pulled out her present. "My family's crazy about Christmas, and I am, too. I couldn't resist giving you something because that's what Christmas is like for me. But I didn't expect anything from you, and I didn't want you to feel awkward, so I'm going to explain that this isn't something I went out and got for you. Obviously," she said, with a grin. "Open it."

Steve gave her a curiously mischievous smile in return and tore off the tissue paper. Inside was an aqua-colored, wooden howling coyote with a red bandana around its neck. "I love it!" he said, reaching down to turn it around. "So if you didn't go out and buy it for me, where did you get it? And more to the point, what is its significance?"

"Well, my mom sent it to me a couple of years ago after they took a trip to Santa Fe, and my place has never seemed appropriate for it, so I've kept it in my closet all this time. But I thought it would be perfect for you in your empty white house. Something colorful to keep you company. And because," she added thoughtfully, "he's kind of a 'lone wolf,' howling at the moon."

"That's how you see me?"

Nan reached up to place a hand on his chest. "I think you're a very exciting man, Steve. I don't really know a lot about you, because that's the way we've chosen for it to be. But, yes, I think you treasure being alone at the same time you howl with loneliness. That's not a criticism. I can perfectly understand why someone would choose to be a person unto themselves. Families can be invasive. They don't give you the kind of privacy you sometimes need. And some people need that privacy more than others. But it's a lonely place to be, sometimes." Nan stood on tiptoe to kiss him. "That's all I meant, Steve."

He held her gently, placing kisses on her nose and lips. "You're a dear. Thank you. I'll set my coyote in the corner of my bedroom to keep me company."

Nan wondered if indeed he needed company. Perhaps, given the oddity of their relationship, he actually had a woman in his life already. Ordinarily she would have trusted that he didn't, but her recent experience with Peter was making her wary. If Nan wasn't the most trusting person on earth, it was only because her mother was more so. Even medicine hadn't drummed the trustingness out of her. But with Steve it was different.

"Are you working tomorrow?" she asked.

"Yes. I don't need the day off like other people do, and I can see my parents in the evening, briefly." He reached into the back pocket of his scrubs and drew out a small, flat jeweler's box. At Nan's look of alarm, he cleared his throat and said, "It's just a trinket, Nan. Something I thought you might enjoy."

Reluctantly Nan snapped open the catch on the box. Inside lay a delicate, twined golden chain with a small, perfect diamond dangling from a tiny gold arrow. "It's stunning. I'd hardly call this a trinket, Steve."

"But it is, in a way. Jewelry is easier to choose than something like a coyote." He grinned at her. "You just go to a store and say, 'I want something for this elegant, warmhearted woman,' and they show you about a hundred pieces, and you point to one."

Nan had gotten her breath back by now, and her manners. "Thank you. It's truly lovely." He had told her, hadn't he, that it had no significance? The golden arrow was just a design appreciated at a jeweler's shop. "If I'd known we were going to exchange real gifts . . ."

"I wouldn't have given it to you if you hadn't given me something," he admitted. "Not because I wouldn't have wanted to, but because it might have embarrassed you."

Nan took the fragile chain from its box and held it in the palm of her hand. "Would you put it on for me?"

"Sure. I wanted to see it on you." His fingers, skilled in delicate maneuvers, easily attached the clasp at the back of her neck. Then he adjusted the arrow and diamond just above her heart, in the V-shaped opening left by her green silk blouse. "It looks perfect."

There was no mirror in the waiting room, but the darkness outside made the window into a reflecting glass. Nan stood before it and fingered the sparkling stone. "It's too much, Steve."

"Oh, what's too much? I wanted to give it to you, and it would please me if you'd accept it. Will you?"

She was torn. Not because of its value as much as because of its significance, or lack thereof. Only because she knew it would hurt him if she didn't, she said, "I will. Thank you. And merry Christmas."

They clung together, briefly. Their lips and tongues met and merged, and Nan felt the excitement rise as usual. But he drew back, saying, "You probably have to go," and she wondered if his comet was indeed burning out and the necklace was merely a parting reminder.

"Yes, my family's waiting."

"I'll walk you home, if you like."

"I brought the car. I'm going to pick up Roger. He's going out to dinner with us."

"Roger?" he said blankly. "Oh, your roommate."

"The holidays are a little hard for him. Mom insisted that he spend tonight and tomorrow with the family."

"Of course. So I won't see you tomorrow."

Nan looked surprised. "Well, no. It's family all day tomorrow. Opening presents in the morning, having a big family dinner in the afternoon, and in the evening we go caroling." She blushed. "It's an old family tradition. We do it wherever we are—Tulsa, San Francisco, one year in Banff. It probably sounds hokey to you."

"Most people do it before Christmas."

"That's why we do it on Christmas Day, to be different," she said. "Actually it's because we like the exercise of walking around, and continuing the holiday spirit a little longer. For better or worse, my family is quite unique."

Steve tilted her face up toward him. "I'll miss you tomorrow. Give my best to your family."

"Thanks. See you soon."

Steve watched her go with a feeling of sudden loss. She hadn't even thought to invite him to join her family that evening at dinner, or the next to go caroling. He'd be done with his shift by then. Maybe she thought he didn't like her family. Or maybe she thought going caroling was beneath him. Neither assumption was exactly true. And she couldn't know what his answer would be if she didn't ask. Of course he'd told her he was going to see his family in the evening, but before she knew that she could have asked him. And there was no reason she couldn't have asked him for this evening, except that she didn't want him there.

Disgruntled, and not sure exactly why, since Steve didn't want to go caroling with the LeBarons, he picked up the coyote and headed back to the emergency room where he'd left his jacket.

FEVER PITCH

He was the butt of several jokes about the coyote, which only made him smile whimsically and refuse any information on its origins. Samples of the keen wit of the emergency personnel were: "Now that's the kind of pet a doctor needs," and "I think someone is trying to tell you something about your voice, Steve." He wished them all a happy holiday, they commiserated with his having to work the next day, and he departed, coyote under his arm.

In the MG he positioned the coyote on the seat beside him, strapped in with a seat belt, and drove off to a solitary evening in his unfinished house.

Nan forgot to remove the necklace before she walked into her flat with Roger. Roger, of course, hadn't known or cared if the necklace was new, though he did remark that it was a unique piece and he wished he had seen something like that to give to Kerri while she was alive. At home, however, the first thing her mother said after greeting Roger was, "My word, Nan dear! Where did you get the beautiful necklace?"

She hadn't prepared an answer, and could have kicked herself for forgetting to return it to its jewelry case. "It's a Christmas present from a secret admirer," she ad-libbed. "And don't ask who, because it's a secret."

Her brother John raised his brows until they practically reached his tousled forelock. "This is the first I've heard of a secret admirer. Why haven't we met him?"

Nan wanted to say, You have, but instead she turned to Roger to ask if he'd like a drink before they went out. Her family were not going to forget about the necklace, but she really could not tell them anything more. What was she supposed to say? Oh, it's from that fellow, Steve Winstead, whom I've never gone out with in my life. He just thought he'd give me a valuable piece of jewelry because it was Christmastime. Even to Nan it sounded ridiculous. Why had she accepted it? Stupid, stupid. Was this some subconscious wish to have to answer for her recent behavior?

Keeping secrets from her family was not something Nan was accustomed to doing, and yet she was aware of the invasiveness of their curiosity, as she had hinted to Steve. Well, this time she would not be cajoled into revealing her secret. Some things were, indeed, not meant to be shared, even with one's beloved family.

By some method she did not recognize at the time, everyone except Nan and her father took the rental car her brothers had insisted on. She drove, and her father sat beside her with a worried look on his face. "You know, honey," he said after a while, "I'm a little worried about this necklace thing. Seems to me it can only mean one of two things. Either this fellow you're seeing is a shady sort of character, or you're ashamed to have him meet us. Either way it's a bit worrisome."

"Well, Dad, I think you have to have a little faith in my judgment and discretion. I'm a grown woman, and I know what I'm doing." Oh, sure, she thought. In a pig's eye.

Her father, not ready to drop the topic so easily, pursed his lips and scratched his head. "Now that last guy you were seeing, he was downright rude. Made no bones about how gauche he thought we were, did he?"

"Peter is a snob, with no apparent reason."

"But you went with him for quite some time, didn't you?" her father pressed.

"Yes, as a matter of fact I did."

"That doesn't show terrific judgment."

"Well, no one's perfect. Peter had a few good traits that offset his snobbishness. With him I think it was more a matter of aesthetics."

"We're not aesthetic enough for some San Francisco architect?"

Nan was stopped at a red light. Her glance over at her father was considering. "You and Mom and John and Jim all treasure your Okie roots. You take a certain pleasure in making them apparent to people who consider themselves more sophisticated than you. And if you're going to do that, Dad, you have to expect some people to look down on you."

"I don't see that for a minute. We're decent

people. No one in the world has a right to look down on us."

"I didn't say they did. I said some people would do it because they think they're more sophisticated. You can pretend that such a thing doesn't exist, but you know it does. And you court that kind of disapproval."

He drew himself up to his full height, which made his head touch the ceiling of her LeBaron. "I never," he said. "I'm sure I don't know what you mean."

Nan sighed. "Tonight, when we're at the restaurant, you can look around you and see how sophisticated people behave. They don't call waitresses 'sister,' and they don't act like they've never seen a wine list before."

"You're ashamed of us!"

"No, Dad. I love you all dearly, and I'm willing to accept the way you choose to behave. But I don't kid myself that you haven't noticed that other people behave differently out in public."

Fred LeBaron was silent for a long moment. "So you're not ashamed of us, but you're embarrassed for us to meet your beau."

"I don't have a beau, and if I did, you'd meet him."

"I call the waitresses sister at home, and they don't mind."

"How do you know they don't mind? Probably some of them do and some of them don't. In San

Francisco, and anywhere else with any pretensions to sophistication, not only don't they like it, they think you're a bumpkin. Which I'm sure doesn't make the least difference to you and the rest of the family. I try, personally, to follow the philosophy of 'When in Rome, do as the Romans do.' It doesn't give me any particular satisfaction to have other people think I don't know how to act better."

"Who says it's acting better?" he asked, all belligerence. "I don't believe in acting different for different people and different places."

But Nan knew he was bluffing. Her father was not an unobservant man, nor a particularly insensitive one. "You wouldn't behave the same way in church that you do on a hunting trip, Dad. Different situations call for different behaviors. I've learned that as a doctor and as a woman."

"Well, as a woman it seems to me you're avoiding the real issue, which is that you've accepted an expensive piece of jewelry from someone you shouldn't have."

Nan laughed. "You sound like some Victorian father, Dad. Trust me. I'll get it all worked out."

Her father grumbled something about hoping that she would. He did not call their waitress sister that night.

Several times on Christmas Day Nan thought of trying to slip away to the hospital, but it never proved feasible. Roger came over early and was obviously trying so hard to be upbeat that she felt she should be there to support him. Not that her family wouldn't have done it, but he was her roommate and friend, and she felt she should be there. But she missed Steve and that exhilarating, slightly daredevil feeling she experienced when they kissed. To say nothing of the smoldering need which, never satisfied, continued to build with each encounter.

The present opening lasted for two hours, with one gift opened at a time and everyone exclaiming over its appropriateness, its lack of inspiration, or its humorousness. The LeBarons had a point system, from one to ten, for grading the inspiration level and uniqueness of gifts given. Each of them strove to get the highest scores they could, though they didn't keep tally during the morning. She wondered what score Steve would have given her for the aqua coyote. And she wasn't sure, either, what score she would give the necklace. Expensive, yes, but that was not the criteria the LeBarons used. Jewelry seldom called forth a rating above five.

While she and Trudy were working in the kitchen—on Christmas her father and brothers saved their energies for the dishes—her mother probed further about the necklace. Her approach was slightly different from her husband's.

"Sweetheart, Christmas is for family, and it

pains me that your young man wouldn't want to spend Christmas with us. Did you ask him?"

"Mom, he has family of his own."

Trudy looked shocked. "You mean he's married? Oh, Nan, you wouldn't be involved with a married man!"

"Really, Mom," Nan said, exasperated, though she wondered, momentarily, if it was possible this attraction to Steve would be there even if he were married. Surely not. "I meant he has parents he sees on Christmas."

"And they couldn't spare him to you for just a few hours? That's very sad."

"That's not what I meant."

"He must be very fond of you if he gave you such a lovely necklace."

"You know how we rate jewelry, Mom. It hardly makes a dent in our scale."

"Yes, but he doesn't know that, probably. Lots of people think jewelry is the ultimate gift."

"It doesn't require a lot of searching or imagination," Nan said.

"It's the thought that counts," Trudy said.

"Well, we believe in giving it a whole lot more thought than that."

"Nan! That sounds very unappreciative."

Nan sighed. "I don't know how to feel about it, Mom. I don't think it means anything except that he wanted to remember me on Christmas, and money doesn't mean a lot to him." She hadn't mentioned that Steve was rich, had she? "I wouldn't have accepted it at all except that he would have been hurt. Now, really, that's all I have to say on the subject." And a great deal more than she'd meant to say.

Trudy scraped vigorously at a large potato in her hand. "Your father told me a little about what you said on the subject of behavior. He thinks the reason you haven't brought him to see us is because you're ashamed of us. He thinks maybe that Peter fellow broke up with you because of us, and you're afraid to introduce us to your new friend." There was a question in her voice, but she didn't meet Nan's eyes.

With a catch in her throat, Nan put her arm around her mother's shoulders. "You know that's nonsense. I love you all dearly."

"Family can be trying, though," Trudy admitted sadly. "I remember Mother Lebronski and her dreadful dogs. Let them do anything they pleased, she did. Pee on the rugs, and chew on shoes. It was a fetish with her."

Nan laughed. "I remember. I vowed never to have a dog for years after that, until I realized they weren't all misbehaved. You know you're not like that, Mom."

"But I suppose there are other things. Like my hair. People stare at my hair sometimes."

"Do they? How tacky of them."

Trudy looked up from the peeled potato she was

placing in a pot of water. "There weren't any other women at the restaurant with hair like mine."

"So you want to be unique. That's your prerogative."

"Or maybe it's my fetish. Maybe it's what embarrasses you about me." Her eyes regarded Nan keenly, waiting for some indication of the truth.

On Christmas this should not be happening. Christmas was not a day for hard truths, or even gentle explanations. Roasting turkey scented the air, and pies sat lined up on the windowsill as if they were all in Oklahoma for the holiday. The Italian boy's parents had been invited to dinner, and there was an attempt at zabaglione in the refrigerator. What possible difference could it make how Trudy wore her hair?

With his typically judgmental attitude, Peter had said she looked like a madam. If Trudy had behaved in some sexually provocative manner, there might have been some content behind the charge, but it was just his prejudice. Granted, most women of fifty-nine did not have golden hair. On the other hand, most of them did dye their hair, and why not choose a color one appreciated?

"Well, Mom, your hair color is a personal choice. True, it's not what most women around here choose, but that's not your problem."

"You're not answering my question, are you? Is there something wrong with wearing your hair this color when you're my age? Other women in Tulsa do it."

"I know they do. You can't change your hair color when you go traveling."

"I suppose I could but I'd rather not."

"Of course not."

Trudy had begun peeling another potato, her lips pursed thoughtfully. "When I was a teenager, we thought girls who bleached their hair were loose. Is that somehow the impression people here get when they see my hair?"

"Loose? Not exactly. I'd say it's more on the order of a brazen hussy." Nan winked at her mother. "Exactly what you are, you see."

"I'm not sure I like being thought of as a brazen hussy," Trudy confessed, but with a grin. "I'll have to think about that."

"Not for more than a minute. If you like your hair that color, you should wear it that way."

"The boys have never teased me about it. Except to call me Goldilocks. Do you suppose that's meant as a hint?"

"I doubt it. Hey, isn't it time to baste the turkey again?"

Chapter Seven

Usually Christmas Day was slow in the emergency room. Steve had planned to use the extra time to catch up on some paperwork. This Christmas defied the rule, however, and he found himself resuscitating a heart attack victim, removing a bullet from a gunshot wound, and pronouncing the death of a street person found by the police, as well as the usual variety of lesser ills and problems. Despite the fact that he was busy, Nan kept running through his thoughts.

He had put the coyote in the newly ready bedroom, where it was the only item other than his cot. Steve had turned down several invitations for Christmas Eve get-togethers, but when he arrived home, alone, he almost regretted that he had. He had gone to bed early and awakened early, the howling coyote the first thing he saw. It had brought a smile to his face, and then a pinched feeling in his chest. Maybe Nan would change her mind and come by the hospital after all. She must have patients to check up on. Her family would surely understand.

But by the end of his shift, he hadn't seen her. Which made him feel almost annoyed with her. Maybe he'd scared her off with the necklace. He had been shown less expensive necklaces, but the one with the arrow had somehow seemed the right one to give her. Stupid of him. He should have given her a coffee table book about hummingbirds, something impersonal but attractive.

At a little after eight, Steve arrived at his parents' house with his Christmas gifts for them. His mother, Elizabeth (Bitty) Winstead, was a woman of fifty-five, short, and always well-groomed and well-dressed. She was reserved, more so now than he remembered as a child. Though her hair was a silver-gray, she had never seemed to grow into the image of her own mother, a warm, loving woman whom Steve had treasured. She presented her cheek for him to kiss, exclaiming, "Merry Christmas, darling! We were keeping our fingers crossed that no medical emergency would keep you from getting here."

His father, Steven P. Winstead, Jr., was a tall man, ten years his wife's senior. He stood much as Steve did, with lanky ease, and offered his hand to his son. "Glad you could make it. We had dinner with the Robinsons because we knew you couldn't get here until late." He was still dressed in the sport jacket and tie he'd worn out, and looked vaguely amused by Steve's blue jeans and plaid flannel shirt. "There's coffee in the living room. Or maybe you'd like a drink?"

"Coffee will be fine, thanks."

Steve followed them into the elegant living room with its twelve-foot ceilings and its view over the bay toward Marin County. Though he'd grown up in this house, the living room had then been used only for special occasions. He suspected that without his chaotic youthful presence, his parents used it routinely now, when they were at home. Their Christmas tree, however, was a miniature thing, set on a table in the huge window that overlooked the view. Steve knew, from past years, that it was purchased from Bitty Winstead's favorite florist, predecorated and in a pot that could later be planted, though he wondered if it ever was.

There were several wrapped gifts lying on the table near the tree. Steve withdrew the four presents he had brought from a Nordstrom holiday bag and placed them with the others. Like his parents, he hadn't wrapped them himself. Well, how could he, living in a house with nothing? But he had learned when he was much younger that his awkwardly wrapped packages were regarded with amused tolerance by his parents. His mother had once casually mentioned during the early part of the Christmas shopping period that department stores would wrap packages for a minimal price, and Steve had not missed the cue. He had not wrapped a gift in the better part of twenty years.

Jewelry was always acceptable to his mother, even if it wasn't to Nan, and he had bought her a pair of dramatically dangling earrings. "Why, Steve, they're beautiful!" she cried, instantly removing them from their box and replacing the pair she had been wearing. "How do they look?"

"Wonderful," he and his father said together.

"You have a real eye for jewelry." His father sounded almost envious. He placed a finger carefully behind the hanging earring to better observe it. "This is very fine craftsmanship."

"Isn't it?" Steve handed his father a small package. "Merry Christmas, Dad."

The elder Winstead opened the handsomely wrapped package to discover within a lushly soft leather belt in the color Steve knew he liked best. He ran appreciative fingers over it and smiled. "You certainly know our taste, son. This is great."

Well, someone appreciated his gifts, Steve thought. How was he supposed to know what to get Nan when he hardly knew her? His mind threw up an entirely different question then: what would his parents' reaction have been if he'd brought Nan with him? Surprise, certainly. He'd never brought a woman home, though they had often enough brought women home for him to meet. Steve sometimes wondered if they thought he was gay, or that he couldn't attract the "right" kind of woman, since they worked so hard at introducing him to friends' daughters, people who would fit into their circle.

Though Nan herself wouldn't have posed a problem for them, perhaps, her family would have appalled them. His parents had no tolerance at all for people who weren't as cultured or sophisticated as they were. In an odd way they were more narrow-minded than the worst back-country bigot. Not that they were likely to meet the LeBarons, or understand the simple good-heartedness that motivated them. Steve was brought out of this reverie by being handed a package to open, his parents watching with eager smiles.

They usually gave him clothes, and today he unwrapped a bulky Norwegian sweater. "Wow! This is terrific. Did you get it on your trip?"

"Yes," his mother said. "Not in Oslo, though. We saw it in a village and met the woman who actually knit it. We thought of you immediately, didn't we, Steve?"

"Sure did," his father agreed. "We could just see you wearing it après-ski. Your mom insisted that I get one, too. Not exactly like it, of course. Different colors, different design, but done by the same woman."

Steve struggled into the navy-and-white sweater and found that it fit perfectly, as he might have known. He skied occasionally, but no more than twice a year. Still, it was a lovely sweater and he thanked his parents sincerely. Maybe he would take Nan skiing. He shook the thought from his head and handed his mother her second present.

When they had finished opening their packages, he remained in the living room while his parents went to get dessert. Steve's mother returned with fresh coffee and pumpkin pie—but his father had disappeared. "Your father had an errand to run," his mother explained, not looking at him. "He said to wish you a merry Christmas in case he didn't get back before you left."

This was one of the major reasons Steve hated to visit his parents. And his father knew that if he said good-bye to Steve in person, Steve would not be so acquiescent as Bitty Winstead about his disappearing. Because when the elder Steve Winstead disappeared on such an occasion, it was known, if never acknowledged, by both Steve and his mother that the older man was off to see his mistress. Steve had told his father on more than one occasion that this was not acceptable behavior to him, but he could hardly say such a thing in front of his mother. In his family such things were not spoken of out loud in the presence of one another.

Steve hated his father's philandering. He hated his mother's acceptance of it. The whole situation reeked of an ugly disloyalty that made him writhe with discomfort. Tonight he decided he wouldn't let the matter rest. He accepted a piece of pie and said, "Why do you let him do it, Mom?"

"What's that, dear?"

"Let him go off to see some other woman?"

Bitty looked as though he and not his father had been guilty of the indiscretion. "It's not something we discuss."

"But I need to discuss it, Mom. I need to understand why you permit it."

"What do you think my options are, Steve?"

Steve shrugged. "Tell him you won't put up with it."

"That won't work unless you have an 'or else.' And I don't have one."

"Of course you do. You can divorce him."

Bitty laughed bitterly. "Oh, sure. Have you looked around at the divorced women my age? They're a mess. Oh, lots of them have money, but they don't have any position to speak of. They don't get invited to parties, or find escorts to the opera, or have the respect of their contemporaries. Things haven't improved in the last thirty years for women, Steve. They're still the double losers in a divorce. They seldom get their real share of the property, and they end up with no social position compared with what they had."

"But your self-respect," Steve protested, leaning forward. "How can you live with someone who's having an affair? All of your friends must know. Dad is hardly discreet about it."

"I suppose that's the worst part. It's awful knowing that people talk about it behind my back. I hate being the subject of gossip. But there's very little I can do about that, and there are plenty of other women in my position." She took a sip of her coffee and looked him in the eye. "This isn't something that's just happened. Your father has always regarded himself as a man who could do as he pleased. Practically from the start of our marriage he's had affairs, some short, one or two very longtime. Your grandmother used to urge me to do something about it. I don't think she meant divorce. She meant that I should discuss it with him, make him understand how unfair it was to me. And I tried."

"But he didn't see that."

"As I said, your father believes he's a law unto himself. He came from a family that adored and petted him, and taught him he could have whatever he wished. He told me he would prefer not being divorced, but he would if I couldn't come to some acceptance of his needs. He acted as though it was my problem. And, as far as I can tell, it always has been. It's never been a problem for him, certainly. And I'm too old to make that drastic a change, especially when I've grown accustomed to the situation. So you see, dear, there's nothing for you to alarm yourself about. How's your pie?"

But Steve was not satisfied with this dismissal

of the setup. "You're not doing yourself a service by simply accepting it."

"Steve, do your patients always do the right thing, even when they've been told what they should do?"

"No."

"Well, it's not only in matters of health where that happens. Some people don't have the strength to do the best thing for them."

"I'm sure you do, Mom."

She smiled slightly. "You're wrong. I don't. What I'm doing is protecting my position. That's more important to me than being free of this burden. You probably can't understand that, but your father does, I assure you."

Steve had no doubt that he did, and that he used it to his advantage. "What if he decides someday to divorce you and marry one of these women?"

"He won't. That's been our understanding all along. And he knows that few of his attractions last long. He is, in his way, fond of me. Especially because I don't bother him about this anymore. Someone new wouldn't be able to do that."

It sounded a very shaky resolution to Steve, but he sighed and dropped the subject. What more could he say? At least he'd talked with her about it, after all these years. That was something. Steve took a bite of his pie and turned their discussion to something less personal.

* * *

The day after Christmas, Nan escaped to the medical center almost with alacrity. Her family was staying another week, but she would see less of them again as she resumed a more normal schedule. Her morning was filled with clinic patients, people who professed, as often as not, to have had a wonderful holiday. Nan was asked many times about her own Christmas and replied, "Lovely, thank you. My family is in town visiting." As most doctors, she didn't share a great deal of her personal life with her patients, but she hated to withhold all information, either. That felt like they had a superficial relationship, which perhaps they did, but there was no reason to make it more superficial than necessary.

Near lunchtime Nan slipped down to the Emergency Department, only to find that Steve wasn't working that day. "He worked Christmas, Dr. LeBaron," a nurse explained.

Feeling disappointed, but also perhaps a little relieved, Nan returned to her office. She had not worn the necklace. No use giving anyone else a chance to ask her who had bestowed it on her. The woman who shared her office looked up as Nan entered.

"Dr. Winstead was here looking for you. I guess about the malpractice suit. I'm afraid I didn't know where you'd gone."

"It doesn't matter," Nan assured her. "He can give me a call."

Nan ate a yogurt at her desk for lunch, working hard to distract herself by dictating admission notes and letters to the local doctors of patients she'd seen for evaluation. Steve didn't call or show up, and having left it as long as she dared, Nan hurried down to her afternoon clinic. She was handed a patient chart by the nurse, who indicated the woman was in the first examining room. Nan had no more than glanced at the name when she heard a hiss from the end of the corridor. There, in full doctor regalia, stood Steve Winstead.

She couldn't help but laugh. "Why didn't you just page me?" she asked.

"Because then I'd have had you on the phone and not beside me." He gripped her hand, pulling her into an empty examining room. Which wouldn't, of course, be empty long. "Nice Christmas?" he asked, but didn't give her time to respond before capturing her mouth with his.

It felt like a long cold drink after a hot, dry spell. She tightened her arms around his neck and allowed herself, briefly, to escape into this madness. The faint scent of his aftershave excited her, the taste of his lips fed her desire. She was about to break away from him when the door opened and they sprang apart. "Damn," she said. "We're going to get ourselves into trouble if we don't cut this out, Steve."

"That door closed so fast there's very little chance the nurse or patient saw who it was." He reached over and opened the door a slit, and turned to grin at her. "All clear. I'll call you."

Which should have been the end of the simple episode, but it was not. When Nan next saw the nurse, she was given a knowing smile and handed another chart, but Nan merely gave her a rueful wink in return. So it was a shock to her when she opened the examining-room door on her multiple sclerosis patient Vanessa Crane to have that young woman start screaming at her.

"You're trying to steal him from me!" Vanessa shrieked. "I saw you kissing him. How could you do that?"

Stunned, and not for the moment comprehending what Vanessa was talking about, Nan leaned back against the examining-room door as though for support. "Wait a minute, Vanessa," she said firmly, since her patient seemed to be working herself up to hysteria. "I don't know what you think you saw, but you're quite mistaken."

Vanessa paid no attention to her, just kept screaming at the top of her lungs. The nurse came rushing into the room, shoving Nan along with the door in her attempt to come to the rescue in this emergency. Nan would have laughed at the whole scenario if it hadn't been such a distressing one for her patient. Nothing she said to reason with Vanessa had the slightest effect. The young woman kept screaming, "You're stealing him! You're stealing him!"

Finally Nan turned to the nurse and asked, "Did her husband come with her?"

The nurse's brows rose. "I think he may have. Want me to find him?"

"Please," Nan said dryly.

It was becoming more and more difficult to think clearly in the face of this screaming woman. Nan was astonished that Vanessa's throat didn't give out. Or that her own repetitiousness didn't finally shut her up. But no. Vanessa seemed determined to create the maximum amount of chaos and confusion in the clinic. Nan knew her screams could be heard in the waiting room, and in every examining room in the area. To add to Nan's exposure, Vanessa managed to include her name as often as she thought of it.

"You're supposed to be helping me, Dr. LeBaron," she shouted. "And you're cheating with my husband. I'll sue you. I'll bring you up in front of an ethics committee. I'll get your license taken away, Dr. LeBaron."

The nurse arrived with an embarrassed, bewildered young man whom Nan had met on several previous occasions. He was tall and blond, and there his resemblance to Steve Winstead ended. "Jeff, she seems to have gotten it into her mind that she saw me kissing you. I wonder if you could clear this up for us."

But this attempt to bring sanity merely exacerbated the situation. Vanessa would no more listen to him than she did to her neurologist. "Don't touch me, you lying son of a bitch!" she screamed when he tried to place a hand on her shoulder. "I saw you with her. You can't fool me. I knew there was something going on. And Dr. LeBaron tried to send me to a shrink." Her voice, raspy from the screaming, still contained a powerful sneer. And she continued with another tirade. By this time there were several people gathered in the corridor, and Nan decided the best way to put an end to the situation was to leave it.

She raised her voice to say, "I'm going to see my next patient, Vanessa. If you want to be seen today, you'll have to calm down and ask for another doctor. Otherwise, I suggest that you leave."

"You would, Dr. LeBaron!" screamed the young woman. "Go, you slut. Just leave me alone! I don't want to ever see you again. And take him with you."

Jeff, who was obviously horrified by the scene, decided that this was his opportunity to escape. He followed Nan out into the corridor, where, even with the door closed behind them, they could hear Vanessa screaming. Her voice was, at long last, beginning to give out.

"What's going on in there?" demanded a red-faced Dr. Mark Schneider. "What's she yelling about?"

Dr. Schneider was the head of the neurology department. Nan knew better than to dismiss the scene with a shrug. Schneider hated this sort of thing. He'd made department-wide changes after a patient left in tears a year previously. She put a hand on Jeff's arm and said, "This is Vanessa Crane's husband. She seems to think that I've stolen him away from her, which is not true, of course. I've never seen Jeff except when he's accompanied her."

"Is that true, young man?" Schneider asked.

It was close to the final straw for Nan. What the hell did he think he was doing, not taking her word for it? Jeff nodded, but his face was a blotchy red, which seemed to denote some sort of high emotion—guilt, perhaps, in Dr. Schneider's eyes.

"Well, young man, I suggest you explain the situation to your wife."

"We've tried," Jeff croaked. "She won't listen. She's totally lost it. She's been getting weirder and weirder." He turned to Nan. "I didn't know you'd suggested a psychiatrist. Maybe she needs one."

Dr. Schneider wasn't interested in Jeff's views of the situation. "Just go in and calm her down," he urged.

"No way." Jeff turned his back on the whole group of people milling around the corridor. "I'm getting out of here. I don't need to stay with a crazy woman. She's really blown it now." And he was gone without a backward glance.

Schneider waved irritated fingers at the others standing around taking in the situation. "Everyone get back to work," he insisted. And to Nan he said, "Come to my office when you're finished with clinic."

Holy hell! Nan thought, and squirmed at the looks the nurses and other doctors gave her. Well, she wasn't her father's daughter for nothing. She reached into the chart pile to take up the next patient's records and walked calmly to another examining room, where with relief she closed the door behind her—to find a middle-aged woman sitting wide-eyed.

"Just a case of hysteria," Nan said as she pulled forward a rolling stool. "Tell me what I can do for you today, Mrs. Potts."

Dr. Schneider's office was spacious, neat, and adorned with a variety of modern art that must have confused his patients. Nothing in the sculptures or paintings met at right angles or seemed to bear a realistic resemblance to a normal human being, or to the natural world around them. If she'd been one of this man's patients, Nan thought, she would have wondered if these representations were somehow a sick joke about neurology patients who mistook their wives for hats or whose difficulties with speaking included being unable to call forth the right noun to describe an object.

Though Dr. Schneider had not actually offered Nan a chair, she took one after his secretary closed the door behind herself. The department chairman was scowling at a metal tube surrounded by rings of bolts and miniature anvils, obviously either deep in thought or purposely ignoring Nan.

"You asked me to come by after clinic, Mark," she prompted him.

Without looking at her, he said, "That was, without doubt, the most disruptive, embarrassing, and disgusting incident that has ever occurred in my department."

"Was it?"

"Of course it was!" He had raised his voice, and his eyes swiveled to glare at her. His right eyelid twitched. "How could you have let something like that happen?"

"I'm not sure I follow you, Mark. How could I have prevented its happening?"

His eyes swung heavenward. "Well, Nan, since it's never occurred before, I presume every other doctor has managed to prevent it."

"That doesn't follow. Maybe no other patient has Vanessa's personality. Since I'm not responsible for her personality, and I didn't lure her husband, I don't see how you can hold me responsible for what happened."

"Who else would I hold responsible?" He allowed his chair to inch back to a position in which he would be facing her directly, from behind his desk. "I assume the young woman had *some* reason to believe you were trying to seduce her husband."

"Do you? I very clearly remember telling you that I'd never seen Jeff outside of his visits with Vanessa. Don't you believe me?"

Nan found it significant that he ignored her question. Instead he said, "My understanding is that the young woman accused you of kissing her husband. I can't think of any reason she would accuse you of such a thing unless she saw you kissing him."

Reluctantly, Nan said, "She probably did see me kissing someone, but it wasn't her husband."

"Who was it?" he snapped back.

"That's none of your business."

"Of course it's my business! She could only have seen you kissing someone, presumably, if it was at the clinic."

"That's not necessarily true, of course, but in fact she did walk into an examining room where I was with a friend of mine."

"What the hell were you doing in an examining room with a friend?"

"Nothing extraordinary," she said, with a tight

smile. "Nothing that would embarrass anyone, or give rise to speculation."

"Nan, I want to know who this person was, and I want to know it now."

"Well, I'm not going to tell you, Mark. If you're worried that it was someone harassing me, don't be. It was, as I said, a friend of mine who popped in to see me. There was nothing sinister about it."

"The idea of someone harassing you never occurred to me."

No, it wouldn't, Nan knew. She had introduced it as a distraction, and obviously it wasn't going to work, because Dr. Schneider continued, "Behaving in this fashion is grossly unprofessional. It will of course go in your record, and I doubt very much if Fielding would be interested in taking onto staff a doctor who behaved in such a manner." He regarded her with narrowed eyes, the right eyelid still twitching. "On the other hand, if I were to find out that the other party was equally responsible for the unfortunate incident, I might be inclined to regard it with a more benevolent eye."

"I'm perfectly capable of accepting responsibility for my own actions, though you do seem to have blown them remarkably out of proportion." Nan shifted slightly in her chair, indicating her readiness to leave. "If there's nothing more, Mark."

"Why the devil don't you just tell me who it was?"

"Because I don't wish to."

"I'll have to assume it was someone you shouldn't have been with, like a member of the department."

"Don't be ridiculous. I nipped into an empty examining room with a friend for two minutes. That's all there is to it. If you want to make a federal case out of it, I'm sure I can't stop you."

Nan rose and stood for a moment looking down at him, since he stayed stubbornly in his seat. "It was indiscreet of me to see my friend at the clinic, and I apologize for that. I hope, however, that you'll take into account your own discomfort with scenes when you reflect on this at your leisure. My notes from Vanessa's last visit, which I'm sure you've read by now, indicated that her husband seemed to be about to leave her."

She shook her head sadly. "You were the first person who ever told me how often men leave their women partners who get multiple sclerosis. Vanessa was upset then, and I recommended counseling. It was very unfortunate that she should have opened the wrong exam-room door this morning, but hardly the stuff of high drama it became when she misidentified my companion. If you find it necessary to hold me responsible for more than a very small indiscretion, well, that's your prerogative. Did you have anything more you wanted to say?"

"First the malpractice suit, and now this," he muttered in an offended, overburdened manner. "What next?" He waved her out with a dismissive gesture.

Nan left holding her head high in her usual dignified manner, but she felt strangely close to tears.

The phone was ringing when she arrived home. Her brother answered it, and looked up to catch her attention. "For you, sis," he said, holding it out to her.

It had been a trying afternoon. People didn't know whether or not to talk to her about the incident in the clinic. If they did, she treated it matter-of-factly, not mentioning the cause, but explaining the patient's mistake. No one seemed to have any reason to doubt her version, and no one had delved any further, which was a good thing since Nan had no intention of involving Steve in her explanation to anyone at the medical center.

Or at home, for that matter. She wasn't going to mention the disturbance at the clinic at all here. Why upset her family, especially when she wasn't willing to come clean about the whole incident? Nan took the phone from John, automatically slipping the earring out of her right ear. "Dr.

LeBaron," she said with her usual professional calm.

"I've been hearing some distressing things about what went on in the clinic after I left," Steve said. "What actually happened?"

"I can't really tell you right now." Her family surrounded her, curious, eager to hear about her day. She was late, as usual, and they were ready to have dinner. "But it's nothing to worry about."

"Really? Not from what I hear. One of the nurses said your department chairman ordered you to his office."

"It wasn't that bad. And you're not involved in it."

"I beg your pardon?"

"I mean, your name didn't come up."

"That's not what I'm concerned about, Nan."

Nan rubbed her forehead, her lip caught between her teeth. "Maybe I could talk with you later. I'm exhausted right now."

There was a short pause. "Your family's there, of course. Listen, we need to talk. I'm still at the hospital. Let me come and pick you up."

"No, that's not possible."

"In an hour. After you've finished dinner."

She did have to speak with him, if only to prevent his doing something she didn't wish him to do. She turned toward the wall and the phone stand, so it would look as if she were about to hang up. Her voice dropped to almost a whisper.

"All right. At the corner grocery." And she dropped the phone into its cradle.

Her family, trying to look as if they hadn't been eavesdropping, immediately began to talk, asking her about her day at work. But Nan barely had the energy to answer them. "Could we eat soon? I'm going to have to go out for a while this evening."

Her mother, looking concerned, hopped to her feet. "Of course, sweetheart. Fred and I can have it on the table in a jiffy."

"I'll help," Nan insisted, following her into the kitchen.

Chapter Eight

Steve was already waiting in his MG when she got to the corner store at the end of her block. It was a damp evening and he had the top up, so it was difficult to make out his expression as she approached. But he jumped out of the car and hurried around to open the passenger door. He made no attempt to touch her, even so much as a hand on her elbow. Nan folded herself into the low seat, and he closed the door.

Neither of them said anything as he climbed behind the wheel and put the car in gear. As he pulled away from the curb, he said, "I would have been happy to pick you up at your flat, Nan."

She looked out at the passing buildings, wondering where to start. "I haven't told them about what happened today. I didn't tell them who gave me the necklace. What's a little more deception among family?"

"Obviously it's not your natural habitat. Why don't you just tell them?"

"Oh, sure. Well, Mom and Dad, I'm in big trouble at work because one of my patients caught me smooching with that guy you met the day you arrived. He's also the one who, though we've never been out on a date, gave me that very expensive necklace I forgot to take off before I got home." Nan shook her head with chagrin. "This has been just plain stupid, Steve. I can't imagine why I've let it go on this long, but it ends tonight."

"Don't say that. Not until we've talked." He swung the car onto the road that wound through the Presidio to the Golden Gate Bridge.

"Where are we going?" Nan asked.

"To my place. Look, we can't talk at yours, and you may not want to take the chance of being seen at a bar or restaurant with me right now. Where else is there?"

One of those odd currents of excitement had run through her when he'd said they were going to his house. "I thought you didn't have any furniture in your house?" Except maybe a bed.

"I don't, much. But there are some of those huge floppy pillows and wood for a fire. You won't be uncomfortable."

That's not what she was afraid of. This was the time to say something if she was going to object, but Nan said nothing. Traffic onto the bridge was light and all the way across Nan sat with her head averted, watching the outlines of familiar land shapes swirl past in the mist, mysterious and intriguing.

As the car started up the incline toward the tunnel, she turned her head back to look at Steve. He was concentrating on his driving as a pickup truck attempted to pull in too close in front of him. With the ease of practice he slowed momentarily, then pressed down on the accelerator and smoothly passed the truck. The windshield wipers slapped regularly against the mist, and the headlights bore two tubes of light ahead of the car.

Steve said, "Tell me what happened after I left."

Succinctly Nan described the scene. She noted his wince at her revelations, and his hand moved from the gear shift to come to rest on hers in her lap. "I'm sorry," he said. "I'll talk with Mark and explain it was my fault."

"No." She said it flatly, finally. "I didn't tell him who I was with because I don't want him to know. You're no more responsible than I am."

"We'd never done that before, my showing up someplace like your clinic. It was stupid of me."

"It was stupid of both of us. We can't really be trusted to see each other, Steve."

He squeezed her hand and removed his to downshift. "I don't think that's the logical solution, Nan. We've been playing a kind of game with each other, and it's been exciting, but there's no reason we shouldn't just try behaving like other people and go out on dates. Is there?"

"Yeah, there is. I only broke up with someone a few weeks ago. I don't want to get into a new relationship right now."

For a while he was silent, apparently considering what she'd said, or how he felt about it. Finally he commented, "There's already something between us, Nan."

"Nothing that can't be ended here." Nan wasn't sure she believed that. It should have been true. And wasn't there something wrong with a relationship that had gotten off on this foot? Why had they been so circumspect and so passionate? Would things have been different if her parents hadn't been there? She sighed and remained silent for the duration of the ride, which lasted for some time.

Steve parked the car in a wooden garage and came around to help her out of the sports car. The lights automatically came on as they descended the few steps to the back door of the shingled house. When Steve inserted an old key and vigorously jiggled it, the lock yielded to his persuasions and the door swung open. Nan found herself in an abandoned-looking kitchen with old linoleum and no shade on the bare bulb over the sink.

"I see the remodel is moving right along," she teased.

"It takes about a thousand times longer than you expect," he admitted. "Most of the painting's done, except in here. I simply can't decide what to do with the kitchen."

"That's probably because you've never used one." Nan slid out of her raincoat and left it on the countertop, assuming there wouldn't be any place to put it. She followed him through to the dining room, which had beautifully urethaned floors, sparkling white walls above wooden paneling, a charming chandelier, and no furniture. "It's a craftsman-style bungalow. You hadn't said. Very nice, Steve."

"After your folks left, I was going to ask if you'd help me choose some things. I have tons of catalogs, and I don't even mind looking through showrooms. It's just that after a while all that furniture starts to look the same to me." He regarded her inquiringly, but Nan pretended he hadn't left a question in that speech. Reluctantly he shrugged and turned through the archway into the large living room.

Here the lights remained off, and he indicated the delightful view across the bay to the San Francisco skyline. Even on this misty night, it was breathtaking. Nan moved to the large window and stood frozen, immobilized by the magic of that scene. She felt Steve come to stand behind her. "It's terrific, isn't it?"

Her head bobbed once or twice, but she found

herself speechless. San Francisco had never looked so tantalizingly beautiful, and Nan had never felt so moved by its power. But it wasn't just the view. She could feel his warmth behind her and knew that at any moment she could be in his arms. And this time, not in a place where anyone could see them, or where they could be interrupted. Longing ached in her throat. She didn't move.

"I'll light a fire. Do you want the lights on?"

"No."

Behind her she could hear him shifting the fire screen and tearing up paper. For a long time she remained mesmerized by the view, and by the unruly needs of her body. This wasn't like her. Nan had always felt in good control of her emotions, and of her appetites.

With the few lovers in her life, she'd enjoyed healthy sexual relationships. Nothing the least bit out of control. Kisses had led to touching, and touching to sexual arousal. This need, this urgency, from simple proximity was not familiar to her. Just being in a room with him, or driving beside him in his car, her body felt strung so tightly that it was likely to snap.

Nan had not really believed this kind of overwhelming sexual attraction could exist between two people who hardly knew each other. She had believed that as you come to love someone, sexual attraction grew. As far as she was concerned, that was the way it should be. Not this *drive* outside of ordinary life.

"I feel like a lemming," she whispered to the window.

"Do you?" he said, just as softly, behind her. His arms came around her waist, with no demands, steadying her. "It's a very human need, Nan. And it doesn't lead to destruction."

"But to the unknown. This isn't like I've felt before. Maybe men feel this all the time. That would explain them a little better, if they did."

He snorted. "They don't. Believe me. Sometimes they like to think they do."

"And you don't feel that way now."

A strangled noise came from his throat. "I didn't say that. I meant that this, what both of us are feeling, isn't all that common. In my experience."

Nan shifted restlessly. "*How* do you feel, Steve? How do *I* feel?"

"Like we have to make love. Like I'll explode if I can't hold you against me, if I can't touch you, if I can't taste every inch of you. I need to connect with you, to discharge all this excitement that's running through me like static electricity. And I think you feel like that, too, Nan."

She groaned and let her body slump back against his. For a while they stood that way in silence, growing accustomed to the idea that they were indeed going to satisfy this burning desire that consumed the two of them. Nan could hear the fire crackling behind them, and she could see the reflected flames dancing in the window in front of her. Turning in his arms, she lifted her face for his kiss.

Every kiss up to this point had led to that kiss, that kiss where she was surrendering to the forces inside her. Her mouth was open to the probing of his tongue, to the demands of his lips, to the moist heat of his need. Nan felt him drawing her into his orbit. The strength of his attraction left her powerless to maintain her distance. And yet she knew that he was caught in her magnetic field, too, lost to any possibility of denying her appeal and the hold she held over him.

Their bodies braced against each other. At every point of touching, Nan could feel the flames leaping, at her breasts, at her groin, in her thighs. Even with her eyes closed, she could feel the flickering of the firelight bathing them in its magical light. Her whole body felt soft and ripe with expectation. Steve's body in contrast felt solid, unyielding, and as hopeful as her own. She dropped her hands from his waist to the hardness of his buttocks, pressing him against her.

"Oh, God," he breathed against her hair. "Would you be too cold without your clothes?"

Nan backed slightly away from him and began to unbutton her blouse, shaking her head ever so slightly to let him know she preferred to do this herself. She removed her blouse, and then her skirt, standing in front of him with her back to the fireplace. He watched her with an almost pained expression. Nan kicked off her shoes, stripped off her pantyhose and hesitated. Not to prolong his anticipation, but to gather the courage to do this, to strip naked in front of a man she knew too little about.

She swallowed nervously and reached behind herself to unfasten her bra. It slid immediately down her arms and she disposed of it on top of her other clothes. Then she stepped out of her underpants, and with a sigh looked up at him as though to say, Here I am. Her body had never felt so lush, so long-legged and firm breasted. So ready for his man's body to merge with her. The longing in her throat had, impossibly, increased.

Steve stood where he was, taking in the length of her with widened eyes. He seemed uncertain whether to touch her or simply admire her. "You're beautiful," he said, his voice cracking. "I can't believe you're here, in front of me, naked and desirable. I want you so badly, Nan. I want to make love to you."

"Yes."

Slowly, as though paying attention only because it was necessary, he removed his shirt, pants, undershirt and jockey shorts. He stood before her just as naked, just as desirable, his body taut with need. Nan could scarcely control the wish to touch him, but she remained for a long moment watching the firelight play over his golden body. And then, by unspoken understanding, they moved toward each other, their skin touching, their bodies already knowing each other.

Her breasts felt the wiry hair of his chest, her groin the fierce need of his penis. They clung together just experiencing the size and shape and contours of each other's body, drinking in knowledge that was new and ancient. Knowing that here was the culmination of the brief, intense moments they'd shared over the last week. Their bodies, if not their minds, had always understood that this was what was called for, what had to happen.

Steve led her to the pillows positioned in front of the fireplace, fluffy as two miniature feather beds. Nan watched as he lowered himself beside her, always touching. And then he began to kiss her, as he'd described earlier, all over her body. Nan could do nothing more than luxuriate in it, for he was so close and so insistent. His mouth played over her face and neck and shoulders. His tongue circled on her breasts, capturing each nipple in turn to draw it into him, to draw her into him. Her moan echoed deep inside her.

But his mouth continued its succulent journey over her body. Down to her waist, down her long legs, even between her toes. And then began to rise again toward the site of her aching desire. Closer it came, that seeking, stroking tongue, those nibbling, hungry lips. Nan could feel the building tension, and looked up at him with dazed eyes.

He smiled at her, his own eyes lustrous with desire—and turned her over. "I don't want to ignore any part of you," he murmured, his mouth beginning once again to move down her body. While his tongue played on her back, his hands followed suit underneath her, sliding from her shoulders to her breasts, from her waist to her legs, and then returning to that wistful spot where she needed him. Nan turned herself back over, cocking her head at him. "I don't know how much longer I can bear this," she said.

"Oh, I don't think you'll have to wait much longer."

His lips were on her lips, his hands on her breasts, and he lowered himself onto her carefully, slowly, and then with increasing vigor thrust into her. The intensity her body had reached was almost too much to bear, and almost a barrier to release. Steve captured a nipple between thumb and forefinger, rubbing it temptingly back and forth, while his body motion shifted to one of rocking against her, back and forth, rubbing himself against the vital spot, again . . . until Nan cried out in shocked release, a haunting cry that sounded almost primitive.

"Oh, my God," she moaned. "Oh, Steve." She felt incoherent with the ecstasy and for a moment experienced only that, while he watched her face, showing pleasure in her joy.

And then Nan moved to please him. She tightened her arms around him and used her body's natural pulsing rhythm to clasp him, to draw him into her, to stroke him again and again. Astonishment and delight mingled on his face, until his climax, a shuddering, overwhelming release overtook and collapsed him. "Jesus Christ, Nan," he whispered.

They stayed locked together for a long, long time, saying little. Nan absorbed the sense of him with her. Now she truly did know the feel of his body, the scent of his hair, the taste of his lips, and the depth of his eyes.

In the shifting shadows of the firelight his face changed many times, and she drank in each new configuration. Light and darkness played over their bodies like some kind of unheard melody, wistful and intoxicating. Nan ran her hands along his arms and down the sides of his body. She nuzzled her head against his shoulder and felt him tighten his arms protectively around her.

"Are you cold?" he asked.

"No." How could she be cold when she was pasted against his glowing body? How very simple it would be to stay there forever. And how impossible.

"But I really have to leave," she added, sighing.

"By the time I get home, my family will already be in bed."

"All to the good, I'd say."

She could feel his smile rather than see it. Yes, certainly it was best. Nan shifted slightly in his hold, and kissed him softly. "This was wonderful, Steve. Thank you."

He ran a finger gently down the line of her nose. "We'll do it again real soon."

"Mmm." This time she drew away from him with a shaky breath. "We both have to work tomorrow."

Reluctantly he released her and watched as she rose. In fact, he didn't move until she had efficiently dressed herself again, looking out toward the view because she was just the slightest bit embarrassed. And then he jumped up and quickly dressed himself. She watched him more circumspectly than he had watched her, but she watched him.

"I feel like maybe you're Cinderella and I have to get you home before midnight," he said, half teasing, half serious.

"My folks will hear me come in, but they wouldn't think of questioning me. Just so long as your car doesn't turn into eight little mice who accompany me home."

After they had crossed the Golden Gate Bridge and were traversing city streets to arrive at her apartment, Nan, who had been rather silent until then, began to talk. Softly at first, but with gathering determination as his protests strengthened her resolve.

"I know it must seem crazy to you, Steve. But I have half a dozen reasons why I don't think it would be a good idea to see you again. Probably the most important one is that on both sides there hasn't seemed to be anything *but* this sexual attraction. I know, I know. It's a very strong attraction, but you can't base a relationship on it. Well, maybe you could, but I can't."

"I didn't say I could. I don't agree that that's all there is between us."

Nan frowned. "If there had been more, we wouldn't have conducted ourselves the way we have. Then there's the problem with my department. Mark Schneider isn't just going to let this slide by, you know. He's a man who's very uncomfortable with disagreeable scenes, and he's going to make sure I pay for today's." When he protested, she put up a restraining hand. "Please, Steve. I don't want him to know who you are. That's very important to me. I want you to promise you won't tell him, or anyone."

Steve brought the car to a stop in the driveway of her building. With a determination of his own, he turned off the lights and the engine, and sat staring at her. "What possible harm could it do to tell him?"

"There's a lot you don't know about me, or him, or the department. Please promise me, Steve."

His eyes narrowed. "Have you had an affair with him, Nan?"

"No, I haven't had an affair with him, though it's not something I believe you have a right to ask. Promise me, Steve."

After a long pause, he said, "All right."

"Thank you."

"Nan, something special happened with us tonight." He reached for her hand, and she didn't resist his effort to lay claim to it. "Didn't you feel that?"

She swallowed painfully, unable to meet his gaze. "Of course I did. It doesn't mean we're meant to have a relationship."

"Well, what does it mean then?" When she didn't answer, he asked, "Are you afraid of that strong a sexual attraction?"

"Aren't you?" she shot back. "Didn't it bother you at all that we snuck around like high school kids to kiss each other at work?"

He grinned. "Not really. It was just part of a game of anticipation. Except that I wasn't sure there was going to be anything more."

"Well, I felt foolish."

His mouth twisted ruefully. "Would you have felt different if you hadn't gotten caught today?"

"I already felt foolish," she protested. "It wasn't

just what happened today. But that certainly brought things into focus for me."

"Then why did you come with me tonight?"

Her chin came up a notch. "Because I chose to let the fire flame itself out rather than smolder for weeks."

He brought her hand to his lips, where he kissed the palm gently. "I don't think that's how it works, Nan."

She could indeed feel her desire rise again, but she forced calm on herself. "That's how I'm going to make it work, Steve."

"But why?"

"I've tried to explain that to you. And there are other reasons." She withdrew her hand from his clasp, folding both hands tightly in her lap. "It's too soon since I broke up with Peter. I can't make that kind of switch. You wouldn't want me to make that kind of switch. And then there are our backgrounds. You've met my family. They're wonderful people, and they're very important to me, but you couldn't possibly feel comfortable with them."

"Why not?"

"Oh, don't be obtuse!" Nan shook her head with a kind of suppressed rage, glaring at him. "They'd embarrass you. They'd embarrass your family."

"Hell, my family embarrasses me."

"I beg your pardon?"

He sighed. "Never mind. We won't go into that. Is there more?"

"There's the malpractice suit. We're going to be pitted against each other if this thing comes to a trial. You know that, Steve. The opposing attorney isn't going to be able to resist. And how's that going to feel if we're involved with each other? We need to stop this thing right here."

"Before it goes too far?" he asked, a mild irony to his voice. "It's gone too far already, Nan. What we need to do is find out how far it was meant to go."

"I don't agree." She held herself stiffly, about to inflict a blow on him, one which would settle the matter. It was for the best, she felt certain. Like the decisions she had to make as a doctor which were wrenching, which required painful honesty, she had to expose the root problem. "Do you remember the day we first ran along the cliff path?"

"Sure."

"I told you my impression about your difficulty with handling death issues."

"And I was grateful to you."

"Yes." She cleared her throat. "That surprised me. I had expected you to deny it, to argue with me. Instead, you looked sad and stricken—and I felt sorry for you."

There was a long silence in the car. Finally he

said, "I see. And you've continued to feel sorry for me, this emotional cripple."

Nan didn't know how to respond, so she said nothing. It might have been partially true, otherwise how was she to explain her behavior? Certainly it wasn't totally true, but if he believed that it was, it would be worlds easier for him to accept her decision. He would, in fact, probably grow to feel contempt for her. How dare she feel sorry for him? Nan could feel tears brimming at her eyes, and she turned her head away. "I have to go in now, Steve."

"Of course." He climbed out of the car, came around to open her door, helped her out of the low-slung car, and watched as she began to climb the first set of stairs.

When she reached the front door, she turned to look back at him, standing there blank-faced, waiting for her to let herself in. "Good night, Steve," she said softly. She didn't hear any reply from him.

In the morning sun streamed into his bedroom. The first thing Steve saw from his cot was the wooden coyote, and there was something gleaming around its neck, caught in the folds of the neckerchief. He frowned at the gold chain, which had not been there yesterday morning when he'd woken and smiled at the howling icon. But then yesterday was a very long time ago. He'd had a restless night, and he tumbled out of bed half asleep, not understanding.

His fingers closed around the chain, lifting it off the coyote's head. In his palm lay the necklace he'd given Nan, with its gold arrow and its flawless diamond. His jaw tightened and his fingers closed over the metal and stone as if he could make it disappear, make that whole ugly scene disappear from his mind. She pitied him.

Last night before they'd left his house, she'd come upstairs to use the bathroom. She had known then, even when she was still in the house with him, where they had made such glorious love minutes previously, that she was going to tell him. And she'd hung the chain around the coyote as a reminder, so that he wouldn't forget when he got home. She couldn't keep a necklace given her by someone she felt sorry for, even if she liked sex with him, even if she was attracted to him.

Steve felt the bitterness burn in his throat. He placed the necklace carefully back around the coyote's neck. Maybe he did indeed need the reminder—for a while.

Chapter Nine

Nan felt as though she hadn't slept at all. But she was not so far past those residency years when that was the rule rather than the exception that she couldn't handle it. Of course she could handle it. She could handle anything she had to handle. What was medical training for if not to blunt your humanity?

Her office mate, Joellen Thomas, was already at her desk when Nan arrived. She looked up with a sympathetic smile. "I hear Mark gave you a little hell yesterday," she said. "I'm sorry to hear it. You know how he is about scenes."

"Well, we had a really special one, just for him." Nan set her briefcase beside her desk and dropped into her chair. "It was one of my MS patients, who thought I was stealing her husband. Nothing wrong with the nerves in her throat."

"Some of them get a little crazy. As Mark says,

the guys almost always bail out." Joellen doodled on a sheet of yellow paper as she continued. "Word is you wouldn't tell Mark who you were with."

"Well, for God's sake, it was none of his business."

"Or mine?"

"Or yours, or anyone's." Nan snapped the rubber band that held a file folder together on her desk. "I did something stupid, and I'm not dragging anyone else into it. For God's sake, it's not as if we were screwing on an examining table. So I kissed some guy! Big deal! It won't happen again."

Joellen's brows rose. "Oh? Did you promise Mark that?"

"I didn't promise Mark anything." Nan's face suddenly showed the strain of the last twenty-four hours. "But he more or less threatened me with getting no further in the department because of this, and the malpractice suit."

"That wasn't your fault!"

Nan sighed. "What difference does it make? It all reflects negatively on him. That's the only thing he cares about."

"He's always been harder on you than the rest of us," Joellen mused, and not for the first time. "I can't believe he doesn't like you, you're such a straight arrow." Her swift grin appeared, and she wagged her finger at Nan. "Except maybe for this.

FEVER PITCH

It should have done you a bit of good to play the naughty girl for once. Instead you get flattened."

"Yeah, well, that's been a pattern in my life, Joellen. It's why I've adopted the straight arrow way of life." Nan looked up to find Angel Crawford standing in the doorway. "They're coming out of the woodwork for this one," she grumbled.

"You should have called me," Angel insisted, coming into the office and giving Nan a hug. "Hell, I had no idea you could cause so much commotion."

"Neither did I."

They discussed the incident for a few minutes, but Nan could see that Angel was not being her usual forthcoming self. Finally she said, "Angel, what's bothering you? Everything's okay with the pregnancy, isn't it?"

"Oh, yes. It's not that." Angel glanced quickly at Joellen before returning her gaze to Nan. "I just . . . wondered if . . . this had anything to do with your roommate."

"My roommate?" Nan, who was thinking of her family occupying her flat with her, took a moment to realize what Angel was suggesting. "Roger? Oh, God, people aren't going to think that, are they? Do they?"

"Not that I've heard," Angel assured her. "It was just, well, you've been living with him, and he's a sweetheart, and you're both very vulnerable right now."

"Me, vulnerable?" Nan snorted. "Because of Peter, you mean? Peter seems like a year ago. I think my parents are right: my judgment seems to be deteriorating. But, Angel, this has nothing to do with Roger. He's living at Jerry's while my family's here."

"I know." Angel looked guilty. "That's actually why I thought it might be him. You know, because you were apart, with your family there and all. And because you wouldn't say who it was."

"How does everyone know I wouldn't say who it was?" Nan's voice had a real edge to it now. "What did Mark do, go out and announce it to the hospital at large?"

Angel shrugged. "Hey, don't ask me. You know what medical centers are. None of us would be caught dead gossiping, but the word is around in no time flat."

Nan forced herself to calm down. "You're right. It doesn't matter."

"Are you going to tell *me* who it was?" Angel asked diffidently. "I wouldn't tell anyone, except Cliff."

"Sorry. It's all past now, Angel. I'd rather keep it that way."

"Okay. Well, we're around if you need any support. Cliff's always felt he owed you one."

A genuine smile dispelled the gloom from Nan's face. "He probably does. But everything will work out in time. Mark's just gotten caught up in his

FEVER PITCH

distress right now." Not that she really believed that. Mark held onto things for a long, long time.

Angel seemed to doubt her reassurance, but she said only, "Call if we can help, okay?"

"Sure."

Angel had only been gone five minutes when Roger appeared in the doorway and beckoned her out. Nan gave a shrug of rueful amusement to Joellen and followed him down the corridor. "You're just going to start speculation that it was you," Nan warned him.

Roger looked surprised. "Me? You mean that you were kissing?"

"Yes. Angel's already come by to make sure the two of us weren't so crazy as to fall into each other's arms in our difficult circumstances. I'm not comparing mine with yours, Roger. She just thought we were both vulnerable."

He looked sheepish. "Well, I came to see if you were sneaking around seeing that Peter fellow, and too embarrassed to do it at home because I knew what had happened."

"Peter," she said disgustedly. "No, it wasn't Peter. By the process of elimination, you all only have a few thousand more men to suggest before you're bound to come up with the right one."

"Aren't you telling, even your friends?" Roger looked a little hurt, and very curious.

"No, I'm not telling anyone. I acted foolishly, and I'm determined to put it all behind me. I can't do that if everyone's whispering some guy's name."

"I guess I can understand that."

"Look, Roger, I'm not telling my parents about this imbroglio, you know? It will pass, and I don't want to spoil their holidays with worrying needlessly. You won't say anything, will you?"

"Of course not. But that's what families are for, Nan, to help you when things get rough."

And hers would certainly be there for her one hundred percent. But there had been too much confusion and strain over the necklace and her secrecy already. She'd said too much, and too little. "I know, Roger, but I can't do it this time. I'll have to muddle through this without them."

"Okay. We're still on for New Year's Eve?"

Nan's head swung around to make sure no one was within hearing. "Roger, people really are going to think it was you if they know you're going out with us that night. Maybe you really shouldn't."

He tugged at the lobe of his right ear, frowning. "What the hell do I care what people think, Nan? Your folks were good enough to invite me, and if it's okay with you, I'll be there."

"It's okay with me," she said, tears stinging at her eyes. "I'm sorry. I seem to have screwed everything up royally."

He gave her shoulder an awkward pat. "Hey, things will get better," he said, and loped off.

* * *

FEVER PITCH

Steve's morning in the emergency department started off with a patient dying. Just as the preceding physician had disappeared out the door, a cardiac monitor shrieked on, warning that the patient in the fourth cubicle had gone into ventricular fibrillation. Steve had run the code and everything had, technically, gone smoothly: the IV drugs pushed, the defibrillator paddles used to shock the patient, the bloods drawn, the oxygen mask.

Nothing had brought the fifty-eight-year-old woman back. She looked like so many other women, not unlike his mother, seemingly healthy and certainly well-groomed. Steve had heard her, just as he came on duty, make a joke to the nurse about how her mother's advice on always wearing clean underwear for just such an occasion had finally come in handy. Now she lay gray-faced and unmoving, lifeless on the gurney. And her family would have to be told. The resident, a young woman whose judgment he trusted, had stepped in, almost too quickly, to say she had met the waiting family and would tell them if he wished.

Ordinarily he would have agreed, also all too readily. Today he recognized a pain within himself that urged him to see this through. But he knew the family would be more comfortable with Dr. Jeffers. "I'll go with you," he said.

Dr. Jeffers, looking a little surprised, nodded. He allowed her to precede him through the emergency department and out past the registration area to the small special waiting room where families were placed when just this kind of thing was a possibility. As Dr. Jeffers pushed open the door, Steve noticed that she seemed to brace herself, to draw herself up to the most of her five-foot-three height. Every eye in the room instantly swung to her. On the faces he could see fear, anguish, and, as soon as they registered her expression, the knowledge that their worst fears were realized.

"I'm so sorry," she said, firmly and in a voice that distinctly reached each of them. "Her heart failed again, and we were unable to get it started. We did everything possible. Sometimes, the heart attack is just so massive that there's no escape."

Steve watched as the man, certainly no more than sixty himself, rose to his feet unsteadily. He said, "I'm sure you did everything you could, Dr. Jeffers."

Tears swam in his eyes, and a younger woman rose to put her arm around his waist. "Oh, Dad. What are we going to do without her?"

The other two occupants of the room, a man with a baby, stood up now, too. The child, affected by the atmosphere in the room, though too young to understand, began to cry. The man rocked the youngster against his shoulder, patting the small back and uttering soothing words.

"This is Dr. Winstead," Dr. Jeffers explained. "He was in charge of Mrs. Linden's care during the critical time. Dr. Winstead, this is Mr. Linden, his daughter Karen Williams and her husband and child."

Steve could feel his instinctive emotional shutdown reaction begin to invade him as he stepped forward. And then he saw the pain in the man's eyes, and experienced an instant kinship with him. The aching sadness he had refused to acknowledge last night, and this morning, gripped his body. Steve knew he had something in common with this man. He extended his hand for the man to shake, saying, "I'm terribly sorry, Mr. Linden. We did everything we could."

He had said the words before, many times. He had meant them every time. But only today did they seem real. The man gripped his hand as if for dear life, and held on a little longer than was customary. Today it didn't alarm Steve, didn't set off that voice inside him that said he would not be able to handle this. He might be awkward, but these people weren't concerned with his polish. They were concerned with his sincerity.

When he turned to her, the young woman was choked with tears and unable to say anything except "Thank you" in a strangled voice. Steve had always shaken hands with both men and women. That was what men did. But he had watched Nan once, unobserved, and seen that she shook hands with the men, and held a woman's hand, pressing it encouragingly, a different kind of connection. He offered Karen Williams his hand now in that way, and she straightened as if given an infusion of courage, which seemed quite remarkable to him.

They stayed for a few minutes, he and Dr. Jeffers, answering the hesitant questions, explaining that in a few minutes the nurse would come to take them to see Mrs. Linden. Then they excused themselves, unhurriedly, assuring the family they would be available to answer any unremembered questions.

When Steve quietly closed the door behind him, he suddenly and vividly remembered the day he had visited his grandmother at the funeral home. He realized for perhaps the first time that there had been nothing wrong with his reaction to seeing the awful figure of his darling grandmother frozen forever in that flower-bedecked coffin.

He had tried to deal with his fear of that crushing sadness by toughing it out in medicine, by staving off death, and by facing it as routinely as any emergency doctor must. But never, ever dealing with it on the simple, personal level that would have made it manageable. It had seemed that every grieving family might trigger his own unacceptable grief. At any moment he might break down, the way they were, with tears and running noses and choked voices. He would become a ridiculous sight, to be scorned by his colleagues and disapproved of by these poor lost families who would feel somehow mocked in their grief.

FEVER PITCH

Dr. Jeffers stopped at the entrance to the E.R. and blew her nose, stuffing the tissue back in her lab-coat pocket. Steve's startled gaze swept up to her eyes. She shrugged in mild embarrassment. "It gets to me. It could be my mom, you know? Karen's about my age. It's such a sad thing, and they're always so brave and grateful, even when we couldn't do much."

"Yes, they are, aren't they?" Steve touched her elbow lightly as he turned to answer a nurse's urgent summons. "Thanks, Dr. Jeffers."

Afterward he was too busy to think anything but medicine for several hours. The stresses of the emergency room could put most any thought out of his mind. What could compare with life and death, after all? But hurrying down the corridor, or drawing on rubber gloves, or picking up a chart, a vision of Nan would flash through his mind. Not statuesquely naked as she had been last night, but in her kitchen, teaching him to do dishes. He would want to tell her he'd learned something today, but she would be gone as quickly as the thought surfaced. And he would turn to his work, and allow himself to be enveloped by it.

As a family the LeBarons had decided to go the Club Fugazi for a performance of *Beach Blanket Babylon* on New Year's Eve. The show, a froth of music and costume and outrageously large hats, was a perennial favorite of theirs, and New Year's Eve had seemed the perfect time to experience it again. Francine Polardi, who had become a regular companion of Jim's, was with them, as well as Roger and a young woman Nan hadn't previously met who was John's date. Since they were all going on to a club Jim had chosen because of the dancing, Nan wore an elegant emerald green silk dress that bared her shoulders and was cut low over the bust. It would have been the perfect dress, she thought as she finished applying lipstick, with which to wear the necklace Steve had given her.

She was finding that she wasn't very good at pushing him out of her mind. And certainly scenes from the night at his house replayed themselves with alarming frequency whenever she wasn't concentrating on something else. The intensity of her passion that night burned through her on each subsequent remembering, not dimming as it should have, as she had anticipated that it would. Well, at least she could keep it all well within her own head, and fevered body.

Roger looked handsome, if slightly uncomfortable, in evening dress. Nan could see that he was determined to keep up his spirits and not drag down anyone's evening. Her family cosseted him, not in an annoying way, but with understanding and a comfortable familiarity that seemed to suit him well. He drove her and her parents to the club, with her brothers coming in her car. As their drinks arrived, Francine leaned toward her to say sympathetically, "I hear Mark's giving you a rough time. I don't know what's gotten into that man the last few years. He used to be a cream puff, you know? Now it's like he's obsessed."

Hopeless to think that her family wouldn't latch onto her boss's name. Nan took a sip of the Black Russian she'd ordered and said negligently, "He's just blowing off a little steam." She could feel her family's eyes on her and knew she was going to have to say something more, to somehow explain without divulging any part of the real story. "Unfortunately Mark and I have never hit it off very well. But we've managed to muddle along, and I'm sure we will again."

"Dr. Schneider?" her father asked, with that alert air of skeptical reverence fathers reserve for their daughters' bosses. "He doesn't appreciate you enough. I've said it before."

Nan gave Francine a warning look. "No one appreciates me enough, Dad."

Roger gallantly leaped into the breach. "Oh, I don't know. I heard Rachel Weis say just the other day that you were one of our up-and-coming neurologists."

Fred LeBaron relaxed back into his seat with a smug grin. "Obviously someone knows what they're talking about. Have I met this woman?"

The conversation that followed drifted far afield from Nan's departmental problems. Out of the corner of her eye, she could see that her mother's face remained concerned, but that she wouldn't press the matter now. With a sigh Nan shifted back in her chair, gave Roger's hand a grateful squeeze under the table, and prepared to enjoy the usual delightful performance.

It was not until they were alone the next day, removing ornaments from the Christmas tree that Trudy LeBaron broached the subject. She set a miniature wooden sleigh in a box she'd brought from home and said, "It seems to me that there's something you haven't told us about your boss."

"There are a lot of things I haven't told you about my boss," Nan grumbled halfheartedly.

"Well, something's happened, I could tell. That dear little Francine wouldn't have brought it up if she hadn't been concerned." Trudy turned to regard Nan with a worried frown. "There seems to be a lot you aren't telling us these days, dear. Don't you think it would be better if you could confide in someone?"

"Oh, Mom, I wish I could." Nan nearly dropped the fragile glass ball she was removing from the tree. She stepped back for a minute to take a deep breath. "I'm trying to get things straightened out. I gave the necklace back. It's just that I've done some stupid things lately that have gotten me in a little trouble with my department." She shrugged. "I can't go into it. I'm sorry. I know you all love me, and that you're there for me. Everything will work out."

"Is is about the malpractice suit? I'm sure your father could give you good advice if it's about that."

"No, it's not the malpractice suit. I suppose that could damage my career, but not if there's any justice in the world." Is there, she wondered? Well, of course there was. It was she who had been at fault in the clinic, not the rest of the world.

Her mother was hesitant. "Are you afraid they won't keep you on at Fielding after your fellowship ends?"

"Yes, I'm afraid of that," Nan admitted. Mark had made no effort to smooth things out between them. Nan had counted on staying at Fielding, until the malpractice suit, until the distressing scene in the clinic. Now even her good reference from her department chairman could be jeopardized. And soon she would need to look for a position for next year.

"If you were to come back to Tulsa, your father could help you find a place in a hospital there," Trudy said, as if she'd been able to read Nan's mind.

Nan laughed. "Yes, I'm afraid of that, too, Mom."

Her mother gave her a playful swat. "What an ungrateful girl you are!" But then she turned serious. "If worse comes to worst, though, it would be a solution."

"I know. But it would be like coming home with my tail between my legs." Nan felt righteous indignation briefly suffuse her. "And for so little reason!"

Trudy lifted the glass ornament from her daughter's unnoticing grip. "Life's like that sometimes."

Nan had to work the day her family was flying back to Tulsa. Before she left for the hospital, she spoke with each of them individually. John assured her he'd had a great time and hoped she'd visit Tulsa soon. Jim said, "I may be back in a couple weeks."

"In San Francisco? To stay with me?"

"No." He flushed slightly. "I think I'd probably stay with Francine, if that was okay with her."

"I see." Nan felt at a loss. "Have you talked with her about this?"

"Just a bit. She wasn't sure it would be a good idea." At her worried frown he added, "I know she's different than I am, Nan. But she's really special. You've learned to behave the way all these people here do. I don't see why I can't."

"Oh, Jim." She shook her head with frustration. "It shouldn't matter. I'm sorry that it does, but it does. Peter was frightful about it. I wouldn't want to see you hurt."

He shrugged, and grinned. "That's my lookout. I'd feel worse if I didn't try. Hey, wish me luck."

"I do."

Her father, his eyes supsiciously bright, hugged her tightly to him when she said good-bye. "Your mom says it's a hard time for you, sweetie. I wish you'd let us help."

"You help me most by being there. I promise I'll let you know if I need anything."

"I hope so," he said sternly. "I have great contacts in Tulsa. Just say the word."

"Thanks, Dad."

Her mother, run to earth in the kitchen, was hanging up a dish towel. "You're going to be late," she warned Nan.

"Not more than five minutes. It doesn't matter. Thanks for everything, Mom. Sometime maybe I'll be able to talk about this. I just have to handle it by myself right now."

Trudy nodded, uncharacteristic sadness dragging down the corners of her mouth. "Poor dear. I wish I could help, but you're a clever girl and you'll manage, I know. Thanks for making us all so welcome. We must be quite a burden when you're working so hard."

"You know you're never a burden." Nan hugged

her mother warmly. "You've made my holiday wonderful, as you always do. I'll miss you, Mom."

Especially this year, when she'd needed to soak up every bit of that familial affection and support. With a heavy heart, Nan waved to her congregated family as she let herself out the front door and hurried down the stairs.

Chapter Ten

Unbelievably, days went by and Steve caught not so much as a glimpse of Nan. When he worked in the Emergency Department, it was always other neurologists who were on call. Once he heard her name and knew that she was probably in one of the other cubicles, no more than fifty feet from him, but the patient he was working with was in such desperate need that he had to concentrate all his attention there. And by the time he was finished, Nan had long since gone.

Every morning he woke up and thought that this would be the day he would remove the necklace from the coyote. But every day when he saw the chain sparkling there, he couldn't bring himself to do more than touch the arrow like a talisman. It hadn't, obviously, been *her* heart that had been pierced.

For weeks he kept his ears open for gossip

about her, especially about the incident in the clinic. As she had predicted, the fuss had died down as quickly as it had arisen. There had been an undercurrent to her remarks about her department chairman that he hadn't understood. At least she'd assured him that she'd never had an affair with Mark Schneider. Steve thought he could believe her, but hadn't she hinted vaguely that there was something wrong with the situation?

And why was he spending all this time thinking about her when she'd dumped him, anyhow? The last thing he needed in his life was a woman who was there because she felt sorry for him. Steve needed no one's pity. If he was grateful to Nan, it was because she'd pointed out a failing to him. And somehow, in a way he could not quite explain, and not on purpose, of course, she had given him the strength to begin to deal with that failing.

Like it or not, she had caused him pain. His affection for her had been severely reined in, kept on a tight leash. It had not, however, in his case as it had apparently in hers, been only a sexual attraction. From the day they had run together on the path overlooking the Pacific, he had developed an affection for her. Just when she developed her pity for him, he thought sourly. But she had been so matter-of-fact, so straightforward, so honest and wholesome, that she had captured his attention.

He had ignored his growing interest, pretended

it was no more than the circumstance of their both being involved in the malpractice suit that kept him in touch with her. And what about that night in her kitchen? How had he explained it to himself? The truth was that he hadn't. He had simply accepted it, as if it were some preordained behavior. And been grateful that Nan had apparently accepted it in that fashion as well.

A month after his last encounter with her, Steve was still resisting the temptation to call her, or to show up at her office. There was still the malpractice suit. In fact, a court date had been set for early in March. It seemed reasonable to him that they should discuss the case, but his lawyer assured him that it would actually be better if they didn't. The idea seemed to be to let each of them tell their tale in court without any hint of collaboration that might distress the jury.

On a day when he didn't have to work, Steve woke once more to face the bejeweled coyote. He could put the little piece somewhere else. In his proposed office, for instance, the room that he determined at that moment he would paint a burnished red, even though it had already been painted a pure, uninspired white.

He would go down to the hardware store that morning and buy the paint and paint the room himself. And he would move the aqua coyote into the room and stand it in a corner where it would look like no more than a piece of artsy craft. He would put the necklace in a box and tuck it back in a drawer where he was unlikely to come across it for a very long time.

Steve bounded out of bed, full of the energy of purpose. As he drew on shorts and blue jeans, his eyes continued to be held by the coyote. Suddenly he stood frozen across the room, his brows drawn down in a frown. Nan had explained about the coyote, and how it was him, the loner. He saw its image there, as it was at night, like the shadow of some Southwestern butte. And knew it had another meaning as well, one that Nan might not have realized when she gave it to him.

It was Nan, too, howling with the forlorn knowledge of her sexual attraction. Nan, afraid of the depth of that physical need. What had she said? She felt like a lemming, governed by her need, drawn by her attraction, against her will. Steve remembered that haunting cry she gave in her sexual climax. It had shaken him, and made him want to protect her. But she had distracted him with her gift of intense participation, and he had let the disturbing memory slip away.

No, he would leave the coyote in his bedroom. But he would paint his study a burnished red.

Nan watched the weeks go by with a kind of painful resolution. Certainly she had been right to dissolve any connection with Steve Winstead. Not that her body agreed with the decision. At the oddest moments she would feel a sexual tension rising in her, and she would realize that she was thinking of him. At more normal times, lying in bed at night, she would not even try to fight off the desire and the memories. Given time they would dim. Apparently it was going to take a lot of time, she admitted ruefully to herself, but not seeing him certainly helped.

Strange, though, that she wouldn't have caught so much as a glimpse of him in the month and a half since their parting. Even in a medical center the size of Fielding you'd think they'd cross each other's paths from time to time. Nan had made no special effort to stay out of his way, but perhaps he had been more aggressive in his determination not to see her. On at least one occasion, she had known he was in the emergency room when she was there, but she hadn't even heard his voice.

Roger was proving a good distraction. Together they frequently went to movies or played cards late into the evening. Roger was settling down more now, starting to consider moving back into his house. Nan disliked the idea of being alone in the flat when he left, but would do nothing to discourage his efforts to move on with his life. She needed to move on with hers.

But there was still the malpractice suit hanging over her head. The early March date for the trial was inexorably drawing closer. Two weeks, one week. She had been over everything with her attorney. "You have nothing to worry about," he'd told her. But she knew better. Juries weren't always logical. Their sympathies sometimes fell differently than the truth. And it was possible that Steve, in his annoyance over her rejection of him, would purposely or unconsciously give the impression that she was at fault. Just exactly the impression her boss always gave when he mentioned the suit to her.

The situation with Mark Schneider had not improved. Two days before the trial was to begin, he called her into his office again. The modern sculpture seemed more out of place than ever, especially since he'd added an object that sat on the corner of his desk that looked for all the world like a miniature guillotine. He waved her to a chair while he finished dictating an admission summary.

As he released the button on his microphone, he said, "I understand from Janice that you've requested three days off for the trial."

"That's how long the attorney thought he'd need me. I'll be here whenever I'm not at the court."

"Well, you'll have to take them as vacation days. The medical center isn't responsible for your involvement in the lawsuit."

Nan refused to let this egregious falsehood

upset her. "No, they're part of my responsibility to the hospital. They're regular working days."

He narrowed his eyes at her. Today the left eyelid was twitching. "I'm telling you, Nan, that you'll have to take them as vacation days."

"Is this a new policy?"

"This is *my* policy."

Nan flashed a bitter smile at him. "I don't think that's permitted, Mark. You can't change the rules just for me. I'll tell you what. I'll check it out with personnel. If they say I should take them as vacation days, I'll certainly do it."

"You'll take them as vacation days because I've told you to," he snapped. "Your being away is going to put a burden on the department. I'll have to cover for you, just as though you were on vacation."

Her heart was hammering in her chest, but she refused to let him see how distressed she was. "If there's nothing else, Mark?"

"Don't lose the malpractice suit, Nan. There's not likely to be a place at Fielding for someone with that kind of blot on her record."

She rose. "Most people would just have wished me good luck, Mark. You have a really unique way of showing your support." Though she stood for a moment without moving, he merely snapped back on the dictating microphone and began to describe another patient. Dismissed, Nan left his office.

* * *

On the day of the trial Nan dressed in a severe blue suit, with a white silk blouse whose tie flowed only enough to suggest the mildest femininity. She wanted to come off as a doctor, more than as a woman, though the attorney had said a jury would accept her in either or both roles. Nan knew that her choice of suit had as much to do with the knowledge that she would see Steve as it did with the jury's impression of her. She didn't want him to think she had worn something particularly attractive just so he would notice her.

Nan took a briefcase of work with her so that she could occupy her attention when the court itself didn't require her participation. With something to read, or notes to add to an article she was writing, she would not be as likely to let her gaze drift to wherever Steve happened to be sitting. The attorney had told her he would call her first but that she should remain for Steve's testimony, as she would likely be recalled afterward to answer further questions.

The trial was being held in City Hall, a building with a magnificent rotunda that had been endangered by the '89 earthquake and was now marred by bracing beams. As she waited for the elevator, she arched her head back to take in the whole splendor of the glass and steel, the balconies and the spaces above. There was something glorious about the size and detail of public buildings from earlier in the century, she thought. Especially if, unlike hospitals, they didn't have to be modernized to meet new technical necessities. There had been the money to do this marvelous construction, and the talent, and the acceptance of this type of architecture.

"What's so fascinating?" Steve asked, amusement in his voice.

Nan had been expecting to see him. She'd prepared herself, but in her momentary distraction by the architecture, he had caught her off guard. Dizzy from leaning back, she swayed slightly and his hand instantly came to her elbow to steady her. That was the last thing she wanted, for him to touch her in any way. But the dizziness took a moment to resolve, and she could only accept his help.

"I haven't been in here in years," she said. "I'd forgotten how impressive it is."

He glanced up toward the rotunda, but cursorily. "Yes, it's a classic. You okay?"

"I'm fine." Nan moved slightly away from him, and his hand dropped from her arm. "Thanks. Can I ask you a question?"

"Sure."

"Are you taking this time from work as vacation?"

It was obviously not what he'd expected her to say, and a rueful twist twitched his lips. He shrugged. "No. As far as I'm concerned, it's all part of my job. Why?"

"I just wondered." The elevator had arrived, and they both entered, along with half a dozen other waiting people. Nan pressed the button for the third floor and made no attempt to say anything further. She had decided that despite Mark's insistence, she would contact personnel and proceed as they advised, even if it went against his dictates. Though he was her department chair, he was not in a position to make new rules for her alone, just because she'd distressed him.

When the elevator stopped at the third floor, Nan stepped out. She could feel Steve behind her, and she stopped in the hallway to wait for him. No sense antagonizing her codefendant. "My attorney said he feels comfortable with the jury they have selected. No real antagonistic doctor-bashers, just twelve public-spirited citizens." She grinned at him, remembering how comfortable she always felt talking with him. He had fallen into step beside her, and his gaze seemed to penetrate straight into her thoughts. Well, she would keep her mind clear of anything but the trial. Strictly business. That's what she would be. The pulsing in her throat was not something she would acknowledge, and surely he couldn't see it.

"There's nothing like a public-spirited citizen to screw up your day," he said, returning her smile.

Nan realized, with heart-stopping certainty, that

he had forgiven her. Maybe all that meant was that he had moved on with his life and couldn't be bothered with some insensitive woman dumping on him. Probably he had found someone to take her place in his life and had then easily overlooked the harshness of her judgment. What did he care if she had felt sorry for him? Maybe he felt sorry for her now.

She was saved the necessity of saying anything further by the advent of both attorneys as well as a courtroom whose seats were occupied by family members she remembered from the time of the patient's death. Time had not entirely erased those faces, though she hadn't seen them in almost two years now. Nan didn't know whether one was supposed to acknowledge them or not, but it seemed less than human not to, at least from a distance. She smiled and nodded, and received an answering response from most of them. Her heart ached to see that they would not do the same for Steve, and felt the stiffness in him as he sat down beside her in the courtroom.

When the judge brought the day's proceedings to order, Nan, who had never attended a trial before, found herself fascinated by the witnesses and the attorneys. Each time her attorney rose to question a witness, he hiked up his pants for all the world like he was girding his loins to do battle. She shared a loaded look with Steve, but wasn't sure he understood that her amusement was a function of this odd habit and not a concern about the proceedings in general. He sat with his hands on his thighs, ostensibly at ease.

He was wearing a charcoal suit with a yellow shirt and a conservative tie. It wasn't the kind of clothing she'd usually seen him in, and he appeared very professional and reserved. The emergency doctors were often in scrubs, and always in lab coats over their shirts and trousers when they weren't. If she'd ever actually gone out with him, undoubtedly she'd have seen him dressed this way, but it came as almost a surprise to her, and kept her at a distance. A good distance, she assured herself. Anything that helped to separate her from the memory of him making love to her was a very useful thing.

A nurse who no longer worked at Fielding was on the stand. Nan remembered her very well: efficient, helpful, hardworking. The woman managed to hold her own against the plaintiff's attorney. She was able to claim to have done only what was requested of her. She hadn't been in charge of the patient, or made the decisions. Still, Nan was impressed by her self-possession and determined that she would model herself on the stand after that simple dignity, if she were able. Thank God no one from her department was here to witness her performance.

"I call to the stand Dr. Nan LeBaron," her attorney said a short while later.

Nan rose, looked down at Steve, and turned toward the front of the courtroom. "Good luck," she heard him say, and felt again the wild flutter in her throat. "Thanks," she said without turning back. It seemed a rather long walk to the witness chair, where she was required to take an oath as to her telling the truth, the whole truth, and nothing but the truth.

What was the truth? And would it come out here in this courtroom? Nan had read of instances where an attorney had, through the simple use of constantly interrupting a doctor's narrative, caused the story of the patient's treatment to seem disjointed and unacceptable. Her own attorney, of course, kept his questions to matters they'd discussed and elicited the answers he expected. It was the plaintiff's attorney who jumped on any hint of disagreement between the doctors.

This man, Mr. Whiting, was tall and gangly, so loose-jointed Nan could picture him melting into a chair instead of sitting down. He paced before the witness stand, occasionally stopping at his table to pick up and replace notes that he had made to himself. "Tell me, Dr. LeBaron, why in a disagreement between you and Dr. Winstead about treatment of the patient, his authority overrode yours."

"I was a neurology resident at the time," Nan explained. "I was called in as a consultant. Dr. Winstead has years of experience with strokes, and he was in charge of the emergency department at the time. You have to understand that there's no consensus on treatment of strokes. Sometimes even with the aid of a CAT scan and an MRI we aren't able to precisely determine what's going on. In this particular case without the MRI available to us, and the negative evidence of the CAT scan, we had to go by the signs and symptoms and our own judgment of what was going on."

"But you were the expert in strokes, not Dr. Winstead. Wouldn't it have been appropriate for him to follow your recommendations?"

Nan smiled. "I was nominally the expert in strokes, Mr. Whiting. In actual fact, Dr. Winstead has probably seen easily as many as I have, and treated them correctly. He asked my advice because we were in a medical center where a neurology resident is available to him, with the backup of a neurology staff person."

"Was the backup neurology staff person called in to help make a decision on treatment?"

"I phoned the staff doctor on call and described the case. He told me that Dr. Winstead was perfectly capable of assessing a stroke victim correctly."

Mr. Whiting frowned. "But you were on the scene. What did you think Mr. Murphy was suffering from?"

"A small brain-stem parenchymal bleed. He was hypotensive and bradycardic, which indicated a

Cushing response to pressure in the cranium. But he did have the presentation of a crossed syndrome as well, which would have indicated a clot. It was not a clear-cut situation."

"And yet your expertise convinced you it was a bleed. Why didn't Dr. Winstead accept your assessment?"

"The odds were in favor of a clot, and Mr. Murphy had some signs that were consistent with a clot. Dr. Winstead doesn't have to take my advice. Since he was in charge of the Emergency Department, he was ultimately responsible for the patient and had to decide what the treatment would be."

"And did he decide to give heparin, which could cause a further bleed?" the attorney said.

"Dr. Winstead chose to give heparin because it can be of value in limiting or arresting further deterioration in a stroke. You want to limit any neurological deficit, of course. We had obtained a CAT scan because the signs of progressing stroke can be simulated by an intracerebral hematoma, but there was no sign of a bleed. Mr. Murphy had indications that were somewhat contradictory. In other words, he could have been treated in one of several ways that would not have been wrong."

"Tell us what the treatments would have been for the various possibilities."

"He could have been given heparin to prevent

a clot from enlarging, on the one hand. Or we could have controlled his blood pressure and kept his head elevated, and maybe given mannitol and put him on fluid restriction if it was a bleed."

Mr. Whiting stared hard at her. "You would have treated him the latter way, is that correct?"

"Yes, but it's no use second-guessing now. Bleeds are much more likely to be fatal than clots, and there's not that much we can really do for patients other than supportive measures. Stroke is a very serious event, which happens because of a cerebral vascular condition, not because of the medical profession."

"Life and death are often dependent on medical treatment," Mr. Whiting asserted. "In this case Dr. Winstead insisted on treatment that was deleterious to the patient, didn't he?"

"Actually we have no way of knowing whether it was, simply because the patient died. It could have been the proper treatment, and the patient would still have died. Dr. Winstead was well within the community standard of care in his treatment of the patient."

Mr. Whiting's voice took on the tinge of irony. "And yet you would have treated the patient differently, wouldn't you, Dr. LeBaron?"

"Yes, I would have."

"Thank . . ."

"And the patient could just as easily have died with my treatment."

FEVER PITCH

Mr. Whiting, foiled in his attempt to dismiss her at the midpoint of her last statement, said coldly, "You may step down, Dr. LeBaron." And to the judge, "I reserve the right to recall this witness."

Nan felt exhausted. She had barely reclaimed her seat when the judge called for a lunch break. As he rose Steve said, "Come on. I'll buy you lunch."

"No, thank you. I'm not hungry. You go ahead."

"Nan, we need to talk."

She could hardly bring herself to look up at him hovering over her. "Not really. I've finished my testimony, and you already know what you have to say. Steve, I don't actually feel very well. That was more distressing than I expected it would be."

"Of course it was. You shouldn't have tried so hard to protect me."

"It wasn't a matter of protecting you." Her hands twisted nervously in her lap, and she forced them to lie still. "I simply could not bear for that man to distort the situation. God, lawyers must have no nerves at all to be able to twist everything that's said out of all recognition."

"It's not a lack of nerves," Steve grunted, holding out his hand to her. "Come on. We won't talk about the case, and we won't talk about our past, and you can just have a glass of milk if you want. I need you to be around to keep me calm until I have to testify."

"Unfair," she protested. But she stood up, a little unsteadily, and looked past him at the attorneys. "You don't think we should have lunch with them?"

"I've heard far too much from attorneys already today."

He was so brusque and dismissive that Nan, fearing he would do something reckless like tell everyone, including their own attorneys, to go to hell, accepted his genuine need to talk with her, a fellow doctor. She clasped her briefcase sturdily in one hand and followed him out of the courtroom, feeling somewhat reckless herself. Hadn't she managed to stand up to that bully of an attorney and still say pretty much what she'd intended to say? Not bad for her first time on the witness stand. Nan hoped there would never be a second time.

When they found themselves outside City Hall in the weak spring sunshine, Nan frowned at the absence of handy restaurants. But Steve seemed to know precisely where he was going, and she quickened her pace to keep up with him as he headed for the intersection. Once, crossing the street, he absently held his hand out for hers, but she pretended not to notice. The less physical contact she had with him the better.

The restaurant he'd chosen was small and cozy, specializing in food served quickly but attractively for the hurried lunchtime crowd. Steve skimmed the menu as if he'd been there before, and laid it aside. "Their soups are all good, and they come with a chunk of sourdough bread."

Nan told him she'd try the potato and leek soup, and sat back in her chair with a sigh. "How do you know this place?"

"My father used to bring me here sometimes, when he was appearing in court."

"I take it your father's a lawyer and not a criminal."

He shrugged. "Well, with lawyers that's debatable, isn't it?"

"Do you think maybe you're letting this get to you, Steve? They're just doing their job."

"I suppose so, but it's always irritated me. Dad used to bring me along to watch sometimes, thinking I'd be so impressed I'd want to be a lawyer. Hell, sometimes I'd wonder how they could do it—sell themselves to represent any side that paid them. It's a game for them, you know. An intellectual and dramatic game."

"Maybe you wouldn't feel so strongly about it if you weren't being sued," she suggested.

"Oh, I've always felt this way, from the first time I sat in a courtroom. My father must have had some idea that he was showing me justice in action or something. But the first case he brought me to was him defending two kids about my age at the time, teenagers, accused of selling drugs. He badgered an eye witness so badly that she finally couldn't swear she'd seen the two guys, even though she'd known them most of their lives. Dad thought it was just great that he got them off."

Nan could picture the young Steve, probably just as handsome as he was now, and probably rebellious at that age, glowering at the proceedings, slumped on his bench in the courtroom. His father, expecting to be treated like a hero, had probably gotten the sarcastic edge of Steve's tongue instead. And had dismissed it as jealousy, or youthful callousness. Steve was glowering now, at his hands. He looked up at her after a moment, his gaze intense. "You understand what I mean."

It was a statement, and Nan nodded. Steve seemed to assume her mind was on the same wavelength as his, and of course it was. She felt as if she could, right now, read him through and through. But that didn't mean she understood what was happening.

Previously Steve had seemed a rather inaccessible person. Nan knew very little about him, really, other than his medical reputation. In a matter of minutes now he seemed to have transmitted as much information—more—about himself personally than he had in all the time she had known him. And he was telling her something important about himself.

Two bowls of soup appeared on the table. Nan didn't remember his ordering them, but she picked up her spoon and dipped it into the hot, rich potato and leek mixture. Suddenly she felt very hungry. The soup tasted delicious and warmed her all the way down through her body. Steve pushed the basket of sourdough bread over to her, and she lifted out a crusty slice, setting it on her plate for only a moment before slathering a bite with butter and popping it into her mouth.

He smiled at her. "Hungrier than you thought?"

"Yes."

"Good. Maybe I can talk you into their Apple Betty. They serve it with clotted cream."

"Tempter," she accused. "Sounds perfect."

"My dad," he said, resuming his revelation, "is a partner in one of the big law firms in San Francisco. He offered to consult on the malpractice case, but I told him that wouldn't be appropriate. He's good. He would have come up with some exotic line of defense for me that would have sounded great to the jury. It wouldn't have bothered him if it had meant pointing the finger at someone else. That wouldn't be his problem."

"No. But he would have been doing his job."

Steve sipped absently from his cup of coffee. "Right. I'm grateful medicine isn't like that, though. We can be a lot more straightforward about things. Not everyone, I guess. Sometimes I hear people talking about doctors the way I feel about lawyers, you know? They see us as money-grubbers who are out to rip off the system—surgeons who do unnecessary surgery, physicians who charge excessive amounts for simple procedures and send patients to labs that make kickbacks to them. Do you suppose there are a lot of doctors like that?"

"I hope not. I think most people want to trust their doctors, but sometimes they feel disappointed—the outcome is bad, or the doctor was hurried. Sick people, like people caught up in the court system, are vulnerable. And we all have a tendency to want to blame someone when things go wrong." Nan wasn't sure he wanted to be brought back up against their present situation, and she decided to change the subject. "Do we have time for the Apple Betty? I have an aunt who used to make it and serve it heaped with whipped cream flavored with brandy."

Steve looked at his watch and motioned to their waitress. "If we can get it quickly, we'll have the Apple Betty," he told her. "Otherwise just the check."

She was an older woman who regarded him quizzically. "I can have it on the table right away," she said. "You know, Dr. Winstead, you're very like your father."

"Thank you, Gladys," he said gravely, allowing just a quirk at the corner of his mouth to show Nan that this was, for him, a mixed compliment. When the waitress had gone, he leaned slightly toward Nan to say, "I look a lot like Dad. None of his friends ever have trouble recognizing me.

In my parents' circle I'm something of an enigma, though, because I went into emergency medicine. It's too *messy* a field for a real blue blood."

"Is that what you are? A San Francisco blue blood?"

"I suppose. On both sides my parents' families have been in San Francisco for generations. There's a mayor somewhere along the line, and a few judges." His eyes looked troubled. "They're a burden, you know? All those weighty ancestors whose footsteps you're supposed to follow in. My parents look like they tread the straight and narrow, and they certainly wish I would. But it's so confining and so stuffy. Dad has his own ways of escaping that, but they're not . . . Well, let's just say he'll probably never become a judge."

The Apple Betty arrived and was set before them, along with the check. "Thanks," Steve said to the waitress. "You're a wonder, Gladys."

Gladys shook her head with amusement. "*Just* like your dad."

Steve looked chagrined, but said nothing until she was gone. "It's hard sometimes, being compared to him. I worry that I'm like him in more ways than I'd want to admit."

Nan dipped her spoon into the Apple Betty. "Apparently we all turn out like our parents in some ways, even the ones we're most critical of."

"Yeah, that's what I mean."

Steve ate his dessert in silence, apparently lost

in contemplation of the worst aspects of being Steve Winstead III. Nan watched the emotions flicker across his face like cloud shadows scudding across the landscape. She had an overwhelming urge to reach for his hand and hold it, which she steadfastly resisted. These were his problems, and he seemed to be facing them on some level, a level deep enough that it held his attention. He automatically finished the apple concoction and reached for his wallet, almost as though he were alone at the table.

When he saw her reach for her purse, he said, "I'm sorry. My mind wandered there for a moment. No, no, I wanted to take you to lunch. You didn't even want to eat."

"Well, I ate every bite of it," Nan said, allowing her purse to fall back at her side. This was no time to get in a discussion about who was paying. "Thanks. We'd better get moving."

They arrived back at the courtroom as jury members poured into their seats and the attorneys took their places at briefcase-and-paper-strewn tables. The bailiff standing in the entrance blocked for a moment Nan's view of a man waiting just inside the room. She was struck immediately by a sense of familiarity, and knew for certain who it was when she heard Steve behind her say, "Oh, shit."

Chapter Eleven

Steve had purposely not told his father when the trial was to begin, or when he was likely to be called as a witness. Not that he had expected his father to appear in court, exactly. He had simply tried to avoid well-intentioned phone instruction for the preceding week, doubtless filled with good advice, but advice Steve didn't want to hear.

"Dad," he said unenthusiastically, shaking hands. "This probably isn't a good idea, though I appreciate your support."

The elder Winstead gave Nan an appraising, and appreciative, look and returned his attention to his son. "Can't hurt to have family around. And it'll keep your attorney on his toes, knowing I'm here."

Steve thought it more likely that his father hoped to intimidate the opposing attorney. "Did he tell you I was going to be called this afternoon?"

"I asked him to let me know. I'd planned to take you to lunch, but you were gone by the time I got here." Steve's father glanced once again at Nan.

"This is Dr. Nan LeBaron, my codefendant," Steve said by way of introduction. "Nan, my father, also Steve Winstead."

"How do you do, Mr. Winstead?" Nan asked, offering her hand.

Steve's father shook it vigorously. "I hear you performed very well on the stand. Congratulations."

Steve thought his father made her sound like an entertaining seal, but since Nan didn't look offended, he said nothing. The court was being brought to order, and the three of them slipped onto a bench, Steve's father between him and Nan. Steve was called immediately to the witness stand, and as he rose he heard his father say, "Give 'em hell, son" and Nan's quieter "Good luck."

At first it didn't seem like he would need any luck. His own attorney handled him carefully, maybe even exceptionally well. His father might have been right about his presence being a good influence on the man. Steve had no difficulty being clear about the situation and his decisions, and making them sound reasonable. Mr. Rush managed to hint that not calling for an autopsy indicated the family's feeling at the time that there was nothing improper with Mr. Murphy's treatment. And without the results of an autopsy, there was no way to know what had actually transpired medically with the patient.

Steve found his eyes straying frequently to Nan, seated there beside his father. Sometimes, irritatingly, his honored parent was actually talking to her, presumably explaining the relevance of some question or commenting on Steve's performance. Nan looked serious and perhaps even a little worried. Surely she wasn't worried that he would screw things up for her. Not even if it meant shouldering the full blame for any alleged malpractice.

It was when Whiting began to cross-examine him that Steve knew things weren't going to go all his way. The questions were simple at first— when did this happen, why was that a problem?— but they became increasingly pointed, and their point was that Steven P. Winstead, III, M.D., was guilty of malpractice. Steve could feel his temper rising with each subtle inflection and insinuation. He knew it was essential that he maintain control. Again his eyes sought out Nan.

She was taking papers out of a briefcase that she had settled between herself and his father. Had the old goat made a pass at her? Surely not, not here in a courtroom with his son on the witness stand. Then Nan had simply lost interest in the proceedings. Papers from the hospital were more important to her than paying attention to the hot water he was getting into.

Steve felt the necessary emotional shutdown coming to his rescue. Let her do what she wanted. She had already barred him from her life. He could keep things under control now if he maintained the distance he was familiar with, his comfort zone. At lunch he had tried to open up to her, tried to let her into his life. Obviously that had not impressed her. Well, who needed to impress her?

"Perhaps you'd like me to rephrase the question, Dr. Winstead," Mr. Whiting suggested.

He was going to have to pay closer attention to the proceedings himself. "Please do."

"I would like to know how it's possible for you to overrule an expert on stroke, a neurologist, when you yourself are simply an emergency physician."

"Emergency medicine is a specialty, too, for which a doctor does several years of training. Dr. LeBaron was still in training at the time, as a third-year neurology resident. Stroke victims arrive at the hospital continually, and I deal with their treatment."

"But, Dr. Winstead, in the absence of an MRI, wouldn't it have been reasonable to bow to Dr. LeBaron's superior knowledge?"

Nan, though she wasn't looking at him, could not have missed the references to herself. She sat very still, one hand grasping a paper and the other laid possessively on her briefcase, as though she were protecting it from some assailant. Steve was not about to challenge a phrase like "superior knowledge" from the witness box. "In the absence of an MRI, and with the evidence of the CAT scan, I had to use my best judgment, since I was in charge of the Emergency Department at the time. And my best judgment was to give the heparin."

"Which killed Mr. Murphy."

Fillmore Rush was instantly on his feet. "Objection! That was a totally uncalled-for and untrue remark, your honor. It should be struck from the record."

"Sustained." The judge regarded Mr. Whiting with annoyance. "You know better than to make such a statement, counsel. If you have questions to ask of the witness, please do so."

Whiting dropped his head slightly toward the judge's bench, but almost immediately returned to the attack. "Was it the heparin you gave the patient that killed Mr. Murphy, Dr. Winstead?"

"No." Steve said it flatly, biting down the anger that surged up in him.

"Then what did kill the patient?"

"The patient died from a stroke, as a great number of people who have cerebrovascular accidents do."

"And a great number of people who have cerebrovascular accidents," retorted Mr. Whiting, "are saved by the treatment they receive in the emergency room. Why were you unable to save Mr. Murphy?"

"An autopsy might have told us exactly what happened in Mr. Murphy's brain. We are not able to save every stroke victim."

"In retrospect, don't you think it would have been wise to heed the stroke expert's, Dr. LeBaron's, counsel about treatment?"

"If I were in the same position today, under the same set of circumstances, I would treat in precisely the same way I did on that day."

Which was saying a mouthful, and might only be proof of his own rampant belief in himself. But Steve was good, better than most, at diagnosis, and he had treated the patient in the only way that felt proper to him. Unfortunately, there was no real consensus about treatment of stroke victims with the limited knowledge they'd had at the time. Whiting was drawing himself up to sling another arrow, and Steve braced himself.

"If there had been an autopsy, and it had shown that Mr. Murphy had indeed had a bleed from one of the vessels in his brain, would the proper treatment have been to give him heparin?" Mr. Whiting asked.

"No."

"What would the correct treatment have been in those circumstances?"

"If the scan had showed a bleed, the location of the bleed would have determined treatment. In a few cases surgery might be helpful, but for a small brain-stem parenchymal bleed, we would have elevated the head, attempted to control the blood pressure, and restricted fluids. Maybe we'd have given twenty-five grams of mannitol, depending on the circumstances. And then we would have had to wait to see what developed."

"Precisely what Dr. LeBaron suggested."

"Yes." Each time he gave one of these answers that appeared damaging to him, because he feared the jury wouldn't remember the significant "if" clause, Steve wanted to amplify his statement. But he clearly remembered Fillmore Rush's strong advice to answer the question and go no further. It was difficult for him; he suspected it was difficult for any doctor to sit there and not want to clarify the layperson's understanding of a medical situation.

His gaze quickly shifted from the attorney to Nan, whose stiff bearing indicated she was taking in every word, though her eyes were on a paper on her lap. Did she think he was going to sacrifice her to save his skin?

"So it was a mistake to give the heparin?" the attorney was slyly suggesting, perhaps noting Steve's lack of total concentration.

"No, it wasn't a mistake to give the heparin in the circumstances surrounding Mr. Murphy's emergency." Steve cleared his throat. "That wasn't the mistake I made that day."

Mr. Whiting looked like he couldn't believe his good luck, but tried his best to appear as if nothing out of the ordinary was happening. In a sympathetic voice he asked, "What was the mistake you made that day, Dr. Winstead?"

Steve trained his eyes on the opposing attorney. He didn't want to look at his own, or at his father, or even at Nan. "It's always hard to have a patient die, and it happens in the Emergency Department more than most places. You build up a resistance to facing that agony. I should say *I* have built up a resistance to protect myself. I've seen other doctors handle it better. My mistake was in how I dealt with Mr. Murphy's family, not in my medical handling of the situation."

There was an unusual hush in the courtroom and every eye, from wandering about the old-fashioned room with its dark wood furniture and dusty windows, came to rest intently on Steve. He could feel a prickling in his shoulders, a familiar feeling from which he ordinarily tried to escape. Today he forced himself to sit there with it, to take his time in trying to describe what happened at times like this.

"When someone dies," he said, "when a patient like Mr. Murphy dies, there's a family sitting in the waiting room hoping, often praying, for him to live. They invest me, the doctor, with a kind of magical power. If they're good, if I'm good, if the patient is good, then the patient should live. That's not their rational thinking, necessarily, but that's somehow what they expect. And, worse, it's what I expect. I expect myself to be able to save every patient, and of course I don't. So every death is not only a tragedy in terms of a lost life, but a failure on my part. Again, this isn't a rational experience. Doctors are trained to believe they can save lives, and they come to think that means they can save every life."

He couldn't help himself. He had to make sure Nan was listening to him, because he was talking to her. That was the only way he was going to be able to say this. He saw that her arms were around her waist in an almost protective way that looked like she was hugging herself. Her eyes were enormous in her pale face, and they regarded him with something like shock. He returned his gaze to the attorney Whiting.

"In order to protect myself from feeling responsible for each death that occurs, I've learned to put a separation between me and the death. A lot of doctors tell themselves they do that because their judgment would be impaired if they let themselves get emotionally involved with each patient and each patient's family. But it's more than that for me. In actual fact, I feel each death very strongly. I've always been afraid that I feel the deaths too strongly, and that without this emotional distance I create, I'd become . . . emotional and unprofessional."

Steve cleared his throat again, and this time he looked directly at Mrs. Murphy. "When I had to come out to tell Mrs. Murphy that her husband had died, I thought I was presenting her with a cool, rational face that she could rely on to be a pillar of strength at that difficult time." Steve had allowed his voice to take on a trace of irony. "That is, in any case, what I'd always told myself. It wasn't until recently that a colleague explained to me that my approach to bereaved families is . . . less than successful.

"Apparently instead of seeming like someone a family can lean on, I appear cold, and unemotional, and distant. I seem rushed and in a great hurry to be somewhere, anywhere, else. And that's true, of course. I hate having to tell families that someone they love has died. I hate telling people that I've failed to save a life. Their grief makes me uncomfortable; I don't know how to respond to it. Maybe because I feel that they're blaming me, because in some ways I blame myself. But not in a rational, scientific way. In a rational, scientific way, I know I've done my best. I'm just sorry that my personal discomfort has caused families unnecessary sadness and upset."

Steve had nothing more to say. Mr. Whiting didn't seem to have a great deal more to say, either. Though he tried to get back on track by asking Steve a question or two about the technical aspects of Mr. Murphy's illness and death, the power had gone out of his interrogation. Being able to handle emotional crises was perhaps expected of a doctor, but Steve's inability was not grounds for malpractice. It didn't even deviate from the community standard, in reality. Steve wasn't the only doctor he knew who had difficulty handling the emotional aspects of his job.

When Steve was released from the witness stand without any re-direct by his own attorney, he made his way quickly back to his seat. His father clapped him on the shoulder and shook his head wonderingly before whispering roughly in his ear, "Brilliant! I didn't know you had it in you, Stevie. There is nothing you could have done that would have been more effective."

Though he cringed at his father's words, he took his seat without saying anything. It was, after all, just like his dad to think he'd done what he had with the intent of manipulating the jury. Would Nan have understood why he did it? Would she know that he was trying to apologize to the Murphys and to her for the whole messy, unhappy business? Nan was in the process of being recalled to the stand. As she passed him, she smiled and touched his arm lightly. Yes, he thought she understood, a little. There was an openness in her eyes that hadn't been there over lunch. Wasn't there?

Whiting was unsuccessful with her. It was far too late for him to change his tactics and make it appear that Nan was somehow to blame for Mr. Murphy's death. And obviously it never occurred to Whiting that he could question Nan about Steve's confession to learn if she had played any role in that scenario. Perhaps it did occur to him, but looked like a bottomless pit of sympathy for the medical personnel, rather than for the patient's family. In any case, he let her go, grudgingly, and she returned—to sit beside Steve, who reached over to press and release her hand.

They had done what they could, and more than had been expected of them, to defend themselves against the lawsuit. There was no more they could do, and at the break Steve got ready to leave. Fillmore Rush moved to draw him away from his father's tenacious presence. "I won't say I regret what you did," Rush said in his thoughtful way. "But it could have gone wrong for you. It could have made you look like a real loser." He glanced over at the elder Winstead and dropped his voice still further. "It wasn't your father's suggestion, was it?"

Steve grimaced. "No, it was simply something I had to say. Look, Fillmore, I need to get back to work, so if there's nothing further you'll need me for . . ."

"Ordinarily I'd like you here for closing arguments, but in this case it might be just as well if you leave now, both you and Dr. LeBaron." He smiled ruefully. "That way I can concentrate on winning this case without making your admission act as some kind of panacea. It will be a bit of a balancing act. Your father's going to love it, but you might not."

"I'm sure I wouldn't." Steve looked around for Nan and saw her talking with his father. "We'll be off, then. Thanks for your help, Fillmore."

The older man nodded absently and returned his attention to the sheets of notes he'd made on a yellow legal pad. Steve collected Nan, soft-pedaled his father's surprise at his departure, and, with a sigh of relief, left the courtroom.

They stood outside City Hall on the granite stairs leading down to the street and the parking garage across the way. It was already late afternoon, and Nan's head felt ready to burst. Too much was happening, too many stresses were building up in her. Nan, who rarely had had a headache in her life, felt this one throbbing painfully in her frontal lobe.

"What's the matter?" Steve asked, frowning at her obvious distress.

"My head is killing me. I'm sorry. I'd like to say something about what you did in court, but I just can't right now, Steve. I'll talk with you later, okay?"

He shook his head. "If you're feeling that bad, you shouldn't drive. I'll take you home."

Nan had a vision of herself in the MG, the wind smashing against her head, reeling her back against the seat. Or worse, throwing up in his spotless, sporty chariot. "I'll be okay. It's only a few minutes' drive."

They were walking toward the garage as they talked, and she really wasn't sure she should drive. Maybe a cab. She looked around to see if there was one she could simply flag down and be gone in, but the street was cabless. Steve had his hand firmly placed in the center of her back, and she began to feel like it was the only thing holding her up.

This was all psychosomatic, Nan told herself. Outside the building, outside that courtroom, in the fresh air she should be able to pull herself together. She took several deep breaths, but they merely made her feel nauseous. Even swallowing alarmed her, the bile rising in her throat only narrowly seemed to stay where it was. This was stupid. She wasn't going to make it home on her own. She moistened her lips.

"Maybe if you'd just drop me off. I'll get my car tomorrow."

"If we take your car, you can lie down on the backseat," he suggested. "I'll pick mine up later."

Nan was feeling too awful to argue with him. In something of a haze, she led him to her car in the garage and allowed him to open the rear door and help her onto the backseat. Much better lying down, she thought as she felt her head meet the soft fabric of the seat. She drew her knees up and closed her eyes to fight off the feeling of distress in her stomach. She was not going to throw up, not if she had anything to say about it.

What was he doing in the trunk? She could hear things being shifted behind her, but hadn't the energy to lift her head. After a minute or two, he opened the door near her head and placed something on the floor. She could feel his hand then on her forehead and his voice softly near her ear: "If you have to throw up, the tool box will do for a basin. I've put my handkerchief by it, too. I'll try to take it easy on the drive over."

Nan murmured something incoherent by way of thanks. She might have wondered how this had come over her so quickly, except that she realized she'd been fighting it off for some time and only now, when she let her guard down, did it claim her. All those patients who had talked about migraine headaches, was this what they felt like? God, how terrible. And migraines went on, in many cases, for several days.

She felt the car start up, and wind through the garage. The turns and the gasoline fumes both made her feel worse, but after a few minutes they were outside on the street. Steve must have had his window open because a light breeze wafted over her, with that smell of the city after rain. The pounding in her head continued, but the nausea retreated slightly.

The next thing Nan knew Steve was speaking to her gently from right beside her head. "Nan? We're home. I'm going to help you upstairs and into bed."

If it had been possible, she would have managed on her own. But the nauseated feeling returned, and she had to walk carefully. Steve carried her briefcase and kept a hand firmly at her elbow as she climbed the endless stairs to her flat. He unlocked the door with the key she indicated, and followed her inside. Everything was silent, and Roger's jacket was gone from the coatrack in the hall.

"Thanks. I'll do okay now," she said.

Steve set the briefcase on a chair. "Just let me get you in bed, Nan. You're not in any condition to wander around finding aspirin and a bowl to put beside the bed. Hey, I'm a doctor. Let me help you."

She hadn't the energy to refuse. In her bedroom he turned down the covers and plumped up her pillows, which would have made her laugh at any other time. As she began to remove her suit jacket he said, "I'll get the stuff you need. Would you like a cup of tea?"

Nan unfastened the button at her waist and slid

the skirt down to the floor. Maybe tea would help. "Do you know how to make tea?"

"Sure. What kind?"

"I think there's chamomile, with a little honey."

He left and was gone for some time. Nan finished undressing, put on a flannel nightgown and climbed into bed. Her head still ached but the nausea had receded again. Steve came in bearing a tray with a cup, a glass of water, an aspirin bottle, a large mixing bowl and a flower in a finger vase. For no rational reason, Nan felt tears sting at her eyes and abruptly overflow down her cheeks. Oh, just what she needed, to bawl in front of him.

"I'm sorry," she said, wiping furiously at the moisture. "I'm afraid I'm not myself."

"It was in the window box," he said, indicating the flower. "I thought you needed it more in here."

"Thank you." Nan helped herself to the aspirin and took a sip of the water. "I've never had a migraine before."

"It's all the tension, probably. I'm really sorry I got you into this, Nan."

"It's not your fault, Steve. I never meant it was all your fault." Had she? Was it? Nan couldn't think straight. She leaned back against the pillows, trying to ease the pounding in her head. In silence she watched as he placed the vase on her nightstand, and the bowl on the floor beside her bed. He was in her bedroom, being not a doctor but a nurse. Taking care of her. Nan closed her eyes, but a tear nonetheless escaped and coursed down her cheek.

"I'll put the tea here," he said, rattling the cup so she could hear it was descending on her nightstand, too. "And I'll be off unless you need something else."

"No, nothing, thanks." Nan felt his hand on her forehead, and then the brush of his lips in her hair. She kept her eyes firmly closed as he tucked the covers around her. After a moment she heard the bedroom door close, but she was too exhausted to open her eyes, and she almost instantly fell asleep.

Steve found he couldn't leave her alone in the flat. He was not, after all, expected to work, even though he'd planned to head in there to check up on things. Because he'd intended to pick up his car after he got her situated at her place, he'd brought in his briefcase and he sat down now to work on papers at her dining room table.

Her presence only a few rooms away impinged on his consciousness. He hated her being sick, and he felt somehow responsible. He wanted to be there if she woke up feeling wretched. Most of all, though, he wanted her to be well again—and not just so that she could talk with him about the courtroom revelation. But he did want to talk with her about that, and he felt cheated that he hadn't been able to.

Sitting there at the oak table, staring at the stained-glass owl hanging in the window, he realized that this was just another one of his discomforts that he would have to learn to sit with until he could handle it. Nan could not absolve him of the things he'd done wrong. Her approval of what he'd tried to do now, though useful and encouraging, was not the answer to his problems. Nan was not the answer to his difficulties.

But she was the woman he loved.

In his reverie he hadn't paid attention to the clatter on the outside steps, but he was aware of the door being unlocked and opened. Roger erupted into the hall like a genie from a bottle, all energy and promise. Steve didn't know him as anything more than a passing acquaintance, but he felt a stab of jealousy that this man belonged here and Steve didn't. He rose and said, "Roger?"

The other man stopped in his tracks and frowned at Steve, only after two seconds nodding and saying, "Oh, right, Steve Winstead. How's the trial going?"

"Okay, I guess." Steve gathered his papers together while he talked. "The attorneys were about to do closing arguments when Nan and I left. She's sick, a migraine, I think. I didn't want to leave her here alone."

"Sick? Poor kid." Roger tossed his jacket at the

coat rack, where it caught by one sleeve. He didn't bother to adjust it, but turned toward the dining room. "Thanks for staying. I'll take care of her now."

Steve bristled at Roger's unconsciously proprietary air, but he shoved his papers into his briefcase. The man lived here, for God's sake. He was Nan's roommate. He'd lost his wife less than a year ago. There was no sense in Steve's getting irritated with him. Besides, Roger was all eagerness and helpfulness. How could you dislike those puppy-like qualities in any human being?

"I've left her car keys on the table in the living room," he said as he headed for the front door.

"You drove her home? She must have been really sick." Roger tugged at a belt loop. "How are you going to get your car?"

"I'll take the Muni, or a cab if I see one. It's not a problem."

"If you're sure."

Roger seemed to be waiting for him to leave, so Steve let himself out with a final farewell. As he trotted down the stairs he imagined Roger checking up on Nan, making sure her covers hadn't fallen off and that the aspirin and water were within easy reach. Maybe putting a box of tissues near her, something he'd forgotten to do.

Well, the important thing was that she had someone to look after her, wasn't it? Being sick and alone was miserable. He remembered that very well from his youth. Nan would appreciate Roger's ministrations. She'd probably fall in love with him. Maybe already *had* fallen in love with him.

Maybe that was what this whole thing was about—her having fallen in love with her roommate. Who could resist that friendly, needy puppy of a man? Nan's whole family spent their time trying to rescue the weary and downtrodden. What more likely than that she had lost her heart to poor depressed Roger?

Who did not, Steve remembered with a sharp pang, appear at all depressed when he bounced into the flat this evening expecting to see Nan home from court. Steve dispiritedly got on the first bus aimed in the right direction, and found that the long walk on the other end did little to improve his mood.

Chapter Twelve

Nan had been startled to awaken the next morning at seven. At first she was confused about the time, thinking it must be evening of the previous day. But she had woken because she heard Roger's alarm go off, and in a minute she heard a soft tap at her door. "Roger? Is it morning?"

"Yes," he said, sticking his head around the door. "How are you feeling?"

"Fine." Nan checked out her systems—head, stomach, extremities. "It seems to be gone. How did you know I was sick?"

"Steve was here when I came home, working in the dining room."

"Oh."

"And he called later to see how you were. I said you were asleep."

"Yes." Nan draped her legs over the side of the bed and sat up. Still no nausea or head pain.

"Well, it seems to have worked. I just feel a little weak."

"Probably because you haven't eaten. Want me to fix you something?"

"No, thanks. I'll get something before I leave."

His brows drew down. "Do you think it's smart to go out?"

"I'd be bored to tears here." And she'd just have to wait around for the jury verdict. Better to be busy at the clinic, and they were half expecting her. "I'll be fine. Thanks, Roger."

"Hey, I was all set to nurse you, and then you slept through the whole thing." He hesitated in the doorway. "It reminded me a little of Kerri when I saw you sick in bed, but that went away. I'm doing better, you know? Maybe I'll try spending the weekend at home and see how it goes."

"Yes, you've seemed happier. I'm glad, Roger."

He sighed. "Me, too, I guess. Does that sound confused? Jerry says it's okay to be confused."

"I'm sure Jerry's right. Everything takes time, and at every step there must be conflicting feelings." She offered a lopsided grin. "You've been good company, Roger, all this time. I've enjoyed having you here."

He tugged at his left earlobe. "Hey, I'm not going anywhere—yet. Just maybe for the weekend."

"Right."

When he had left, she'd risen to wander into the kitchen for oatmeal and juice. Hunger gnawed at her but she ate slowly, not wishing to bring on the nausea she'd felt the preceding day. But the migraine seemed to be totally gone, and when Roger had finished in the bathroom, she showered and got ready for work.

Though a little shaky, she managed to move right along with her patient load, answering questions from frightened patients about parkinsonism and medulloblastomas and tic douloureux. With a patience bred of understanding, Nan repeated explanations she had given on previous visits, knowing a patient couldn't always grasp the information the first time. She had just finished examining a child with petit mal seizures when she came into the hallway to find Steve hurrying down the corridor toward her.

His appearance there gave her a momentary jolt, remembering what had happened last time. But she couldn't miss the wide grin on his face or the instant gesture he made of victory when he saw her. Nan had not known, until the migraine, how stressed she had been about the malpractice case. Her career had already begun to get off track, and a blot against her record like the loss of the case would have put her in a truly unfortunate position.

"We won," Steve said, loud enough for the nurses and doctors in the vicinity to hear. "Has your attorney called? Rush was delighted. Apparently the jury only took an hour to deliberate. God, what a relief."

Before she could even answer him, Joellen was there thumping her back and congratulating her. One of the nurses stuck a crown of tongue depressors in her hair, and even Mark Schneider, who happened to hear the word in passing, offered his blessing. Steve remained where he was until the brief fuss died down, and then walked with Nan toward the reception area.

"Will you let me take you out to dinner to celebrate?" he asked. When she hesitated, he said, "I really need to talk with you."

"It's not that. I'm still a little weak from the migraine."

"God, yes. I couldn't believe you'd come to work today." He frowned down at her, concern drawing his blond brows together. "What if I brought takeout to your flat? Would that be too much for you?"

Nan thought it would probably be best to talk with him on the phone. "That would be fine. About seven." Treacherous tongue. Oh, well, Roger would be there.

But Roger wasn't. Nan had forgotten that it was Friday, and he had indeed decided to try spending the weekend at his house. The flat was empty when she arrived home at six-thirty, and she automatcially began tidying up the living and dining rooms where both she and Roger were in the habit of sorting out their overdue medical papers, journals, and bills.

There was no need, she assured herself, to clean up her bedroom. But she hadn't had time to remove the tray in the morning, so she got things back to their customary neatness, tossing the flannel nightgown in the laundry basket and returning the aspirin to the medicine cabinet in the bathroom. She stood for a moment in the bedroom doorway, remembering the impression of Steve's kissing her head the previous day. It was probably a figment of her migrainous imagination and the need to be comforted in her illness. Nan shrugged and closed the door.

Steve was ten minutes late, and absurdly Nan had begun to think he'd forgotten, when the bell rang. She set aside the medical journal with which she'd attempted to distract herself and answered the door. Seeing him always affected her physically. He looked so blond and wholesome and athletic that she would have expected to almost dismiss him as another handsome face, without any particular character. But his effect on her was electric, heightening all her senses, causing turmoil in her gut. She could *feel* him when he was near her, like the draw of a magnet.

She flashed a nervous smile. "Come in." Spying the bags of food containers she said guiltily, "I should have offered to make dinner."

"Nonsense." He closed the door behind him

and gestured toward the dining room. "It's hot. Do you want to eat right away?"

"Sure."

Nan had put out plates and flatwear at places across the table from each other. She had also set out wineglasses and a bottle of gewürztraminer. "My latest favorite, but I have chardonnay or zinfandel."

"The gewürztraminer is fine. I brought a split of champagne for afterward."

After what? Nan's capricious mind wondered, knowing full well that he meant after dinner, of course. To celebrate their courtroom victory.

"And Chinese food," he said, looking puzzled. "I don't even know if you like Chinese food. I should have asked."

"I like it." As she watched him efficiently spread out a Styrofoam container of won ton soup and cardboard containers of half a dozen other dishes, she shook her head in amazement. "Did you think I was starving, Steve?"

"No, but I figured if I got enough different kinds of things, there were bound to be some you'd eat. We'll need bowls for the soup."

Nan disappeared into the kitchen and returned with bowls and soupspoons. He stood by a chair, holding it back for her. It was not something her brothers would have thought of doing, certainly not for Chinese takeout. She scooted the chair up to the table and watched as he came around the table to take his seat. Nan was very aware that they were alone and hoped Roger would remember something he'd forgotten and pop up at the front door.

Nan helped herself to the kung pao chicken, the broccoli beef, and the won ton soup to start. She noticed that he took a spoonful of each, like a dutiful child instructed to try a taste of everything. His impeccable manners slightly intimidated her. Did people like Steve notice everyone else's less than perfect adherence to social dictates?

He was watching her. Not so much her manners, Nan thought, as simply studying her face. And she couldn't keep her eyes off him. He looked older to her than he had when she first spoke with him about the malpractice suit. Older, wiser, sexier. And it's all in my mind, she thought. It's all just that I see him differently now, now that I've made love with him.

"My attorney called, too," she said, ladling out some soup for him. "He said, and I quote, that you'd made his job a whole lot easier for him. Steve . . ."

Their fingers touched as he took the bowl from her. "Yes?"

"Your father seemed to think it was a clever gimmick, what you said in court."

Steve grimaced. "I know he did. That's how

cynical practicing law makes you," he grumbled. "My father didn't . . . annoy you, did he?"

Her brow puckered. "Annoy me? I don't understand."

Steve concentrated on cutting a won ton in half with his spoon. "My father's kind of a lady's man. Or he thinks he is. Sometimes he . . . pays too much attention to young women."

Nan giggled. "Does he? How embarrassing for you."

"Well, it is," he insisted, reluctantly matching her grin. "When I saw that you'd put your briefcase between the two of you, I thought that maybe he was, you know, sort of moving into your territory."

"No. He winked at me once, but I thought he had some idea that you and I were involved and it was his way of communicating that information. Actually I put the briefcase there because I was starting to feel sick, and it just gave me a little more distance in case I threw up or something. He was wearing a very expensive suit that I wouldn't have wanted to destroy."

"You seemed to be looking at papers while I testified."

She nodded. "I was trying to distract myself. I thought if I stared at you, you might think I was . . . oh, I don't know . . . trying to get you not to say anything bad about me. I wanted you to feel completely at liberty to say anything you felt you should."

"I said what I did for you, and for the Murphys. I said it because I meant it, and because it needed to be said." He cleared his throat, his eyes almost glaring into hers. "I didn't really understand how much of a problem I had with this until you discussed it with me, Nan. I thought everyone pretty much was in the same boat, and maybe that a few doctors were just slick and handled it better than I did.

"I started to watch other people and how they did it. Maybe I'm learning something. Certainly knowing that it's a problem will make me more careful about how I deal with the families of patients who have died. I appreciate your honesty in telling me about it. And," he added grimly, "I hate your pitying me."

"It was very courageous, and very touching, what you said in court. I wanted to box your father's ears for pretending it was no more than a ploy. Because he knew, Steve. I'd bet my monthly paycheck that he knew how sincere you were."

"And couldn't bear to hear a man expose himself that way." Steve lifted a negligent shoulder. "It was easier for him to fool himself into believing it was just a clever move on his son's part. We Winsteads are good at fooling ourselves."

"Everyone has defense mechanisms," Nan said.

"I didn't mean I don't, Steve. And I shouldn't have said I felt sorry for you. I apologize."

"There's no need," he said a little stiffly. "You were obviously intent on getting rid of me, and telling the truth turned out to be the simplest way."

Nan felt the anguish of being placed in a position to either maintain what she felt to be a proper distance from this man—and hurt him—or to acknowledge that there was more to her complicated feelings for him than she could admit—and possibly hurt both of them. She put down her fork and propped her chin on the shelf she made of her locked hands.

"I don't know what to say to you, Steve. My feelings are so confused. I didn't want to hurt you, but I felt sure you'd pretty quickly tell yourself what a jerk I was to say something like that, and you'd just write me off."

His lips twisted wryly. "I did tell myself that, Nan, but it didn't work. I find it very difficult to think of you as a jerk. On the other hand, I'm not sure I'm the only one here who has a problem."

Nan drew a shaky breath. "Very good. You're right, of course, but that makes me a jerk, doesn't it?"

"Maybe. It depends on what the problem is."

She shook her head. "If I'd been able to tell you that, I would have. It's just something that makes me know it's better if we aren't together. Can you understand that?"

"No." He took a sip of the wine, set his glass back on the table, and stared at it for a long time. "I can't get past the fact that you made love with me, Nan. I don't think you do that lightly. And it was wonderful. I'd stake my own monthly paycheck that you felt that way, too. But you went upstairs afterward and hung the necklace around the coyote's neck because you knew already that you weren't going to see me again. How can I be expected to understand that?"

Nan felt a tightening in her throat that threatened to choke her. This was not a discussion she could embark on with him. "I didn't think you'd mind," she whispered.

"Mind making love to you?" he asked, incredulous. "It was one of the most remarkable experiences I've ever had! You were so exciting and so giving. And so beautiful. And, I swear, it wasn't what I was expecting when I took you there, Nan. I just thought we needed privacy, and it was the easiest place to be sure of having it. Your willingness, your desire blew me away."

"Exactly. And it made you think I wanted a relationship. Or maybe you just naturally assumed that we'd have one. I didn't mean to let the sexual encounter happen. Not because I didn't want it to happen, but because it wasn't right."

"I don't see how you can say that. Why wasn't it right?"

"For all the reasons I gave you then, Steve."

"I didn't hear one reason that even began to balance the scales against the atttraction we have to each other. Except the pity thing." A muscle in his cheek twitched, but he went on. "And that, well, I don't doubt that you've felt sorry for me from time to time. But I do doubt that that was why you didn't want to see me again."

Nan could feel her heart pounding in her chest. Tension flowed through her body like a scalding fluid. Every part of her went on alert. They were on dangerous ground. Not only his probing of her reasons, but her physical reaction to him were filling her with alarm. That urgent quality she'd been unable to resist the night at his house was invading her, making her aware of his intent face, his capable hands, his strong shoulders. She knew a longing for his body which was almost unbearable.

"Maybe you should go, Steve," she whispered.

He looked thoroughly confused. "Go? We were just having a discussion, Nan. I'm not trying to blame you or harass you. I'm just trying to understand."

"I know." She rose from her chair and stood uncertainly by the table. "It's me; it's not you. It would help me if you left."

"Jesus Christ, Nan, what's going on here?" He

was on his feet, too, glaring across the table at her. "Can't we discuss this like rational human beings? If you would just be open with me . . ."

Her hands fluttered at her sides. "I can't really explain. You have quite a strong effect on me."

"Well, I guess I must if you keep wanting to throw me out this way." He moved toward the front door, making no attempt to retrieve any of the parcels he'd brought with him. "I don't understand you at all. If I didn't know you were a perfectly sane woman, I'd wonder if you were having some kind of breakdown. I'm just a guy, Nan. I'm not here to hurt you or upset you, so I'm going to leave. But I think you'd better get some help about whatever it is that's bothering you, because this isn't completely reasonable behavior."

"I know," she admitted. "I'm sorry. I'll be all right after you've gone."

"No, you won't be all right after I'm gone." He already had his hand on the doorknob. "You may calm down, but that's not the same thing as being all right. I haven't done anything to cause this kind of extreme reaction, so something's going on in your head that you'd better pay close attention to."

Nan watched in silence as he opened the door and let himself out. Just before the door closed, she heard him give a tsk of annoyance, and he reappeared, saying, "I forgot my jacket."

He looked astonishingly upset. Even his ears

were flushed with his emotion. He tugged hard at his jacket on the coat tree, and it tilted over, almost falling on him. With a frown so potent the wooden rack should have burst into flames, he righted it. Not bothering to slide his arms into the leather jacket, he retreated toward the door again.

He was going to leave, and she would be left alone to deal with her own emotions, and with her bizarre behavior. No wonder he was so distressed. She had not behaved reasonably. Nan couldn't bear to think that he would leave hating her, thinking her the most obnoxious woman on earth.

"Steve."

He stopped at the door, but only briefly. With a determined move of his hand he twisted the doorknob and pulled open the front door. Well, let him go. It would be much better if he went. Nan did not realize she had moved until she found her hand on his arm, light but urgent. "Don't go. I'll try to explain."

His eyes met hers. The sparkling blue was rich with frustration, anger, disbelief, and just a trace, perhaps, of something more tender. "I feel like I'm being jerked around, Nan, and I don't like it. I wouldn't have thought you'd be that kind of woman. You've always seemed incredibly straightforward. It's one of the things I liked about you from the start."

She motioned him into the living room. With a

certain reluctance he closed the door and followed her, not giving up his leather jacket when he sat down on the sofa. Nan seated herself at a small distance from him and stared for a long moment at her hands.

"We haven't had an ordinary relationship," she began. "I mean, you didn't call me up and ask me out to the movies, or I didn't stop you in the hall and ask if you'd like to go to a play that I had tickets to. We've never been on a date at all, and yet we've been to bed together."

"We could have started seeing each other. I thought we would."

"*After* we slept together. Maybe you thought that was necessary, appropriate."

"Nan, I *wanted* to go out with you. I wanted us to have a relationship. It was you who didn't."

She squeezed her hands tightly together. "I'm not getting my point across. My point is, Steve, that all there was was the sexual attraction. We kissed in my kitchen, and then we kissed all over the hospital. You didn't ask me out."

"I didn't think you'd go with me."

Nan considered this for a moment. "Maybe I wouldn't have. I'm not sure. It was so soon after the disaster with Peter. But the point is, you didn't ask me."

He pursed his lips and shook his head. "It wasn't that. We were playing a game. Both of us. It was different, and exciting, and sort of playful and, as it happens, dangerous. I didn't foresee that. Who could know some patient would walk in the wrong exam room and mistake me for her husband? And that she'd get hysterical about it? That's not something you'd expect to have to take into account. Now, it could have been a nurse or a doctor—and that was part of the spice, wasn't it?"

Nan knew he was right—at least in part. And from his point of view, it must have seemed innocent enough. After all, who really cared if the two of them kissed each other in secret corners? Neither of them were in relationships. They weren't betraying anyone. They were just ... tempting each other. Seeing how far they could go before the relationship took off in a standard, ordinary, uninspired direction—dinner and movies and concerts and spending the night at each other's places.

For Steve it had been just a delightful change of pace.

"It was more than that for me," Nan said.

"I don't understand." Steve leaned back against the sofa and regarded her skeptically. "You're going to have to make this a little clearer to me, Nan. If you wanted something more, you certainly didn't say so. And I trusted you to be open with me. I thought you were enjoying what we were doing as much as I was."

"Yes, of course I was. But I wanted more. I

didn't ask for more because I didn't want to alarm you. My . . . my desire, as you called it, was very strong." Nan swallowed and tried to meet his gaze. "It was consuming."

Steve leaned toward her, his brows drawn down. "Are you trying to tell me that you were sexually attracted to me to an excessive degree?"

"Yes."

He grinned. "Well, hell, Nan, I could have handled that."

"Well, I couldn't."

He straightened. "I see. And so you thought having sex with me once would somehow cure this problem."

"No, I didn't expect that to cure it." She made an awkward gesture with one hand. "I indulged myself, because I didn't think you'd mind."

"I minded that being the end of the relationship."

"I know, but I didn't think that would last long. You're the kind of man who probably doesn't have any trouble meeting women or getting involved with them."

"Why would you think that?"

"Because you're good-looking and smart and rich and personable. And you're not married, and as far as I know never have been."

"What's that got to do with it?"

"Usually it means a man doesn't invest in long-term relationships."

"Where do you come up with all this stuff?

Have you taken to reading those women's magazines that have twenty-point quizzes in them?"

He sounded irritated with her, but Nan only shrugged. "I've been in two relationships that I thought were going somewhere. Neither of them worked out. I've always been a very trusting woman, Steve, but apparently I'm not much of a judge of men. And there you were, far too great a prize for me in the first place, and here I was absolutely consumed with a sexual desire for you, and the two didn't mesh."

"What a load of nonsense! You were afraid. Why don't you admit that to yourself, Nan? You were afraid of how strong your sexual feelings were for me. It didn't have anything to do with whether our relationship would last or not."

She blinked at him, trying to decide whether he was right or not. "That's not how I saw it."

"Look at it that way now," he advised as he laid aside his leather jacket. With an assurance she almost shuddered at, he took her hands and brought them up to his lips. "Let me remind you what that sexual desire feels like, Nan. It doesn't go away just because you try to ignore it."

He turned her hands over and kissed the palms one after the other, nibbling kisses that made her insides grow tense and yearning. His eyes held hers as he sucked on the tip of her thumb, then drew it wholly into his mouth. Already her body felt consumed with the desire she had fought so hard against feeling for the last two months. Away from him it seemed possible to control it; with him she knew better and felt a kind of despair.

"It's not a healthy desire," she said. "It's distorted and excessive."

"Who's to say what's excessive? Maybe you've never felt like this before. That doesn't mean there's something wrong with it."

"You don't feel that way about me."

"How do you know?"

"I can tell. You're attracted to me, but not in this crazy, obsessive way."

"And you think that should scare me off?"

"Of course it should. Who wants a crazy woman as a sex partner."

"You're not a crazy woman, and I want you as a sex partner. I want to make love to you again. I want you to hold me the way you did, and to love me the way you did that night. I'd never had an experience like that before, and if it takes an obsessed woman to treat me like that, I'll take her any day."

Steve moved a finger along the line of her lips, nudging slightly until Nan opened them and drew his finger in. Her eyes pressed shut at the depth of the desire that raged through her. She sucked on his finger as he sucked on hers. Every atom in her body seemed to respond at once. She felt in control of nothing any longer, as though his touch alone were what moved and enticed her.

FEVER PITCH

"Would I be taking advantage of you if I suggested that we go to your bedroom?" he asked, his voice rough with desire.

"I don't know anymore." Nan allowed him to draw her to her feet. "I don't know how to handle this, Steve. I want you. Oh, God, I want you. But I feel as if I should resist the temptation."

His lips were on hers, bringing the sure knowledge that she had to have him. Their touch was like a whole body reminder of the way their lovemaking had been at Christmas. The ache started deep within her and spread to the very tips of her fingers, to the surface of her lips. His tongue entered into her mouth, moving sensuously along her tongue and teeth and the roof of her mouth. She needed him touching her everywhere. She needed him in her *now*.

Clothes had become a barrier. Nan began to shed hers as she walked toward the bedroom. Steve picked them up behind her, saying, "I take it you don't expect Roger home tonight."

"He's spending the weekend at his house." Nan reached behind to unfasten her bra, negligently shrugging out of it as she entered her bedroom. "I'm going too fast for you, aren't I?"

"I'm not sure that's possible," he drawled, pulling her against himself. He lowered his head to take the tip of a breast into his mouth. Nan moaned and released the zipper on her skirt. In moments she was stark naked, pressed against his still-clothed body.

"Undress me," he suggested.

His hands wandered over her body, caressing places that cried out as they passed. She unbuttoned his shirt and tossed it on the floor. She pulled his undershirt out from his pants and tossed it after. His chest felt roughly wiry under her tongue. She caught one of his nipples in her mouth and sucked on it until he groaned. Then she unfastened his belt, unhooked his pants and stripped them off of him. But she left his underpants on, relishing the feel of his throbbing but disguised penis against her groin. She slid her hands inside his jockey shorts and touched him, that urgent, rigid part of him that her body ached to bring inside herself.

He pushed down the shorts, freeing himself from the fabric, but not from her encircling hand. Nan slid down in front of him and took his penis into her mouth. This was not something she'd ever strongly desired to do before. But she wanted him in her mouth, the soft tip tasting of excitement and expectation, the hard length of him filling her in a way she'd never been filled before. Her tongue explored the nooks and crannies of him, her lips rubbed him with her need, her sucking motion drew him to her again and again. This was something she'd needed to do, had dreamed in the long dark nights of doing. Holding him with her mouth, loving him with her tongue. Nothing could possibly be more intimate, or more satisfying to her heated imagination of what would please him.

And she wanted to please him. She wanted to feel his body burst with the wanting of her. Almost as much as she wanted to feel herself explode into ecstasy from having him.

His hands were on her shoulders, massaging her. Her hands stroked the backs of his legs and up onto his buttocks. And her mouth drew him in again, slid along the rough surface of him, and sucked hard to stimulate his release. "Oh, God," he moaned. "I'm going to come, Nan. Is it all right?"

The warmth and stickiness filled her mouth. She had brought him to this, and she reveled in her perverse power. What had seemed so uncomfortable about this other times? She swallowed the semen as though it were a precious treat. And continued to taste him with her tongue and throat and lips. He was stroking her hair, over and over running his fingers through it, his loose-limbed body pressed against hers. At length she released him.

"Jesus Christ, Nan. I can't . . . I thought . . . that was fantastic. And not at all what I expected." He stooped down to put his arms around her and cradle her naked body against his. "Are you all right?"

She nodded her head against his chest but already she could feel the desire beginning to build again. Temporarily, when she was pleasing him, savoring the taste of him, the fires were banked down. But her naked skin against his began to flush with renewed arousal. Her body ached with the need for release. And she wouldn't tell him.

But he had begun to stroke her, gathering her against him and allowing his hands to play down her sides, over her buttocks, down between her legs. Suddenly he scooped her up in his arms and deposited her on the bed as though she weighed nothing. The bed creaked when he laid down beside her, and he smiled. "I like a bed that sings along with you," he said.

He kissed her, as he had kissed her so many times at the hospital. But this time his body pressed against hers, his skin rubbing silently against hers, making her tingle from head to toe. She could feel the urgency of his lips, the hammering of his heart. Her throat ached from the powerful lust that surged through her body.

His lips were on her breasts, caressing, coaxing, teasing. Waves of pleasure flowed down through her body, building in her groin. His hands seemed to follow the pleasure, and to add to it. He was stroking the silky insides of her thighs, separating her legs with a leg of his own. Such a golden body he had. Nan lost her fingers in the disheveled mass of his hair as his head moved lower on her body.

He could have brought her to orgasm with scarcely a touch of his tongue, but he chose to entice her. A lick here, a touch there, building to a crescendo. But then a pause. In the pauses he talked to her. "You're a beautiful woman, Nan. Your body is glorious. Your skin like satin, and electric to my touch. And the taste of you." His mouth on her, almost unbearable in its intensity. The moistness, the drawing on her. Yes, now.

No. Not yet. "You're swollen with desire. Ripe with it. Ready. Oh, I know you're ready, sweetheart. But you can be even more ready." And his tongue, his tongue in her. Oh, God. She would surely die of this desire, of this much pleasure.

And kisses along her thighs, a pattern of them crowded around the site of her greatest pleasure. Kisses, and a tongue that traced her lips, that drew sweetly on her like an insect sipping nectar. Now, surely.

"You taste like heaven. And you're musty like rich old books, spicy as life itself. Can you feel that, Nan?"

His tongue again, in her, on her, this time not stopping. This time urging, fondling, drawing, giving, completing. Nan exploded with the pent-up desire, her body rocked with overwhelming sensation. Still there, his tongue, caressing, extending, lapping. Wild, unbearable pleasure rippling through her body, seventh waves of it. Her heartbeat a wicked flutter. Her whole body flushed with the magnificent release.

Yes, surely this was obsession.

Chapter Thirteen

Nan and Steve lay for some time on her bed, exhausted. His arms were wrapped around her and her head was tucked against his shoulder, her hands lightly resting on his chest. Steve was overwhelmed by the enormity of what had taken place, by the whole revelation and physical encounter. He was, if truth be known, a little scared of what was happening.

Nan's eyes were closed, but he didn't think she was sleeping. Her breathing wasn't regular enough, her fingers occasionally shifted on his chest. Had she been right to try to put a halt to their relationship? Had she been trying to spare him as well as herself?

It was any man's fantasy, having a woman, a beautiful, talented woman, sexually addicted to him. A love slave, of sorts. But in reality, Steve guessed, it was a tremendous responsibility, for a man of any integrity. And he considered himself a man of integrity. He also suspected that he was in love with Nan, and that walking away from the situation was no more an option than callously using her for his pleasure.

Plus, he doubted very much that Nan was actually sexually obsessed with him. A delicious and flattering fancy, but probably far from the whole truth. He was, after all, quite attracted to her himself. Those brief, exciting encounters in the hospital had not been undertaken out of boredom. He had sought her out because just the taste of her lips electrified him. A mad dash to consummate that heady passion would not have been nearly as intriguing as their cat-and-mouse game.

His fingers wandered through her fallen hair. She looked very different when the blond tresses escaped their rigidly controlled French braid. Unrestrained, her hair floated around her face, softening it. She looked young and vulnerable, and about as sexy as a woman could look. Her cheeks were still flushed, her lips full and curved with sultry pleasure. Steve had an overwhelming desire to crush her to him, to protect her from her fears and promise her everything would be all right. As if he could make it so. He tightened his arms around her, and fell asleep.

When he awoke he could tell that it was some time later, though not morning. He was alone in the bed in an inky darkness that suggested the middle of the night. Steve scanned the room until he found a red digital readout of 3:48. Too early for Nan to be up. He stumbled out of bed, naked, and found it icily cold. Stripping the comforter off the bed, he wrapped it around himself and went in search of his elusive lover. In his unfamiliarity with the flat he knocked against the hallway wall, but he chose not to search for a light switch.

Drawn by a flickering light, he made his way to the living room, where he found Nan seated on the sofa, wrapped around with a dark robe, staring at a candle. She looked up and smiled almost shyly at him when she heard him pad into the room.

"I didn't want to wake you, but I couldn't sleep," she said.

"Do you have insomnia often?" he asked sympathetically, dropping onto the sofa beside her.

"Only recently. Sometimes Roger and I run into each other in the middle of the night and play a game of double solitaire."

Steve felt a pang of jealousy, and pushed it away from him. Roger would have seen Nan many times with her hair down, the blue terry cloth robe snugly belted around her waist. And Roger would not have paid the least attention. "Want to talk?"

She nodded. Leaning back against an overstuffed pillow in the corner of the sofa, she drew up her knees, carefully tucking the robe under her feet. "I think we should."

"Tell me what you've been thinking."

She snorted. "A thousand things, all of them contradictory. First I think how great it was, and then I'm ashamed of how I behaved. Then I think there was nothing wrong with it because you enjoyed it, too. Then I think I'm just a crazy person for this obsession. And I don't know how I'll ever get a grip again. Have my life back the way it was, without all these thoughts about you. I go around in a state of suspended arousal. It's been like that for months. It frightens me."

"Couldn't you have told me this in December?"

She shrugged irritably. "Of course not. I'm as proud as the next person."

"What does pride have to do with it, Nan? It's just a physical attraction, after all."

"Oh, it's more than that, and you know it. Even in the dark I can tell you're worried. I can hear it in your voice. You don't know quite what to do with me."

The urge to be flip possessed him momentarily, but he was coming now to recognize that those urges were just attempts to avoid the real emotional issues. Take it one step at a time, he warned himself. She's a very special woman, and a misstep could hurt her. "I don't know what you're going to *let* me do with you," he corrected. "I don't know if you're going to decide you won't see me again because of your confusion. That would be running away, and you've already tried that."

"It almost worked, too," she insisted. "If we just hadn't had the malpractice suit together."

"What about the constant feeling of 'suspended arousal' that bothered you all those weeks?"

"Yeah." Nan offered him a reluctant grin. "Probably some people could get used to it. I found it distracting. I've had neurology patients whose seizures manifested themselves as a feeling of orgasm. They aren't always happy to have them brought under control."

"Who can blame them? Nan, are you going to let us work on a relationship? Are you going to see me after tonight?"

"Do you want to see me?"

"More than anything."

She gave him a wobbly smile. "Then I guess we should try. I'm going to be a big responsibility."

Steve didn't deny it. He opened his arms to her and whispered into her hair as she came to him, "Well worth the effort, sweetheart."

They fell asleep in each other's arms some time later, after a sweet and unhurried joining. Nan had erotic dreams for the rest of the night, but calmed her continually rising desire by assuring herself that in the morning they would make love again. He was too virile, and too curious, to be satiated already. But she feared she could easily frighten him off with her demands, should she let him know how the lust bubbled in her still, undiminished, perhaps heightened.

It was not that each consummation didn't satisfy. Oh, each was glorious in its intensity and in the knowledge that it was really happening, and not just a figment of her imagination, called up to quiet the frantic stirrings in her. She woke with each dream but lulled herself back to sleep by twining her body with Steve's sleeping flesh.

At first light she rubbed against him, sinuously testing the feel of his skin against hers . . . and hoping of course that he would awaken aroused and ready. In the dawn light she traced the curve of his chin with a light finger, thinking that his blond beard would feel delicious against her belly, tickling and brushing her with its rough movement. Though his body responded to her stimulating presence, Steve didn't waken.

In the dimness Nan could see that he was sleeping that heavy slumber of the overworked and sleep-deprived. Probably he had worked nights during the trial and was catching up on the needed refreshment of slumber. Disappointed, but determined to behave like a reasonable human being—though she didn't necessarily feel like one—she turned her back to him and tried once more to find sleep. It wouldn't come.

She remained in bed for the next two hours,

trying to wait for him to awaken. The need had grown in her body to unwieldly proportions. Her breasts tingled and her groin ached. There was that suspiciously awkward tightening of her throat. Maybe it wouldn't be so awful if she just sort of nudged him toward consciousness. She could whisper sweet nothings in his ears, or trail lingering kisses down his body.

Suddenly there was a loud hammering on her front door. Nan shot up in bed and blinked at the clock. Eight-thirty. No one would come to her flat on a Saturday morning at eight-thirty. It must be a mistake. Roger had a key. Anyone else would have called. And yet, muffled by the heavy wood front door and the distance between her and it, she could hear her name being called, by a decidedly male voice that she could not recognize.

Steve, now that it was of no use, awoke and rubbed his face with vigorous hands. "What's happening?" he asked.

"I'm not sure." Nan climbed out of bed and picked her robe up from the floor where she'd dropped it in the middle of the night. "It must be some kind of emergency. No one would just come pounding on my door at a time like this. I'll see who it is. Don't go away."

As she walked she worked long fingers through her disordered hair, pushing it back from her face. At the front door she called out, "Who is it?"

"It's Jim, for God's sake, Nan. Let me in."

Her brother Jim. Absolutely, positively not possible. He should have been in Oklahoma. He should have been sound asleep in Oklahoma. "Go away," she said.

"I'm not going away," he called back, rapping the door with determined knuckles. "I want to talk with you."

"Come back later."

"Don't be ridiculous, Nan. Let me in."

"Why are you here?"

"I'll tell you that when you let me in."

Nan realized they'd never even double-locked the door. The half-eaten Chinese dinner was still on the table. Steve was in her bedroom. Oh, the injustice of life. She opened the door.

She would scarcely have recognized him. Jim ordinarily wore his hair and his clothes in a scruffily disorganized but lovable way. The man who stood before her had had a superior—and doubtless expensive—haircut, and his clothes had probably not been bought off a rack. They looked, in fact, very much like they might have come from Steve's father's wardrobe. "You are not my brother," she informed him, pretending to be about to close the door.

He grinned almost sheepishly. "I look good, don't I? So why the hell is Francine giving me a hard time? I thought she'd like me like this."

"Maybe she liked you the way you were." Nan held the door open and watched as Jim trotted in and aimed directly toward the kitchen, his favorite room in any house. He stopped abruptly at the sight of the open containers on the dining room table.

"Are you having Chinese food for breakfast?"

"No, I'm not having Chinese food for breakfast."

He nodded sagely, and looked around suspiciously. "The only time I ever left food on the table was when a young woman and I were talking and we . . ."

"There's a man in my bedroom," Nan said, feeling the color rise in her cheeks.

"Someone I know?"

"Yes."

"Not Roger!" he protested.

"No, not Roger," she grumbled. "Why does everyone think I'm out to seduce poor Roger?"

"Does everyone?"

"Oh, why don't you go home? And why are you here in the first place?"

"Mind if I help myself to some breakfast while we talk? I'm starving."

"Doesn't Francine feed you?"

"Now, now. Just because you have someone in your bedroom doesn't mean Francine would be so modern."

"So where did you spend the night, Jim?" She followed behind him as he pushed through the door into the kitchen, and took a chair when he opened the refrigerator door.

"At Francine's." He took out a bowl of fruit, a container of 1-percent milk, and a bagel. "Don't you have any butter?"

She pointed to the ceramic cow on the table. "In there. Jim, is this the first time you've been to San Francisco since the holidays?"

"Well, no," he admitted. He sliced the bagel in half and popped it into the toaster. "Did you know that some people eat bagels with cream cheese and salmon?"

"Yes, I knew that. When did you learn?"

"Recently. I've been taking a course."

"In bagel-eating."

He winked at her. "It's not going to do any good to mock me, Sis. One of the things I've learned in the course is to be more sophisticated than to let my sister heckle me."

"Where are you taking this course?"

"In New York."

Nan stared at him. "You wouldn't be caught dead in New York."

"Us sophisticated types don't make judgments like that. New York is the oasis of culture in this country, and if you want to do a quick brush-up on your cultural literacy, you go to New York and hang out there for a few weeks."

"You can't be serious. No one offers a course in instant sophistication. Not even in New York."

"Hell, Nan, people offer courses in just about anything you can imagine. Sophistication is one of them. And New York is where you go to get it. Ask me about opera."

"I wouldn't dare."

"Well, I don't know much yet, but I've learned a few things to say, like 'Opera is the greatest of the arts—music and drama combined, surrounded by magnificent set design and costumes.' I went to one, though, and I didn't much care for it."

"Too bad."

"I thought so, especially since Francine is rather fond of it, you know?"

"I didn't know. Jim, is this all on Francine's account?"

"Well, what could she see in a hick like me?" He buttered the bagel and took a bite. "Garlic? You eat garlic bagels for breakfast?"

"You don't see me eating one, do you? They're Roger's."

"So he still lives here."

"Yes, but he's spending the weekend at his house."

"So you can spend it here with what's-his-face."

"Roger doesn't know anything about that."

Jim poured himself a glass of milk and chose a cold pear. "Did you know sophisticated people never drink milk in public?"

"I think they're kidding you about that one."

"No, no, it's true. Look around you at any good restaurant. They've taken us to several very good restaurants."

"This course must cost a fortune."

"It does." Jim frowned at the glass of milk. "And it would be well worth it if Francine appreciated my remarkable progress."

"But she doesn't."

"She just won't admit it," he protested. "I mean, how could she help but feel more comfortable with me when we go out if she knows I'm not going to order a glass of milk at Ernie's?"

"How indeed?" Nan asked rhetorically. She noticed a movement in the doorway off the hall and found Steve standing there, fully dressed. She waved him into the room. "Jim, you remember my friend Steve Winstead."

Steve did a double take at Jim's transformation. He entered the room with his hand out to Jim, who glared briefly at him before accepting it. A master at the socially awkward situation, if not the emotionally fraught one, Steve smiled ruefully at Jim's patently protective bristling. "I have honorable intentions," he said.

Jim laughed and shrugged and sat back down to his breakfast. "They all say that. Want a bagel?"

"Not a garlic one." He regarded Nan circumspectly, and she lifted her shoulders in an "I don't know any more than you do" gesture. "What brings you to San Francisco?"

"I came to show off my new sophistication to Francine," the younger man admitted. "And she kicked me out."

"*After* you spent the night there," Nan said.

"Well, yes, but it's discouraging all the same. She told me she had to work for a few hours today, and that I should ask you why the whole thing pissed her off. Do you know?" he asked Nan hopefully.

"You mean like it's a girl thing and naturally I'd understand it? I think, Jim, it's because you didn't have enough faith in her to think she'd accept you the way you were."

He looked dubious. "She said something like that. But isn't it better if I don't embarrass her? Besides, it's kind of fun to learn how the nobs behave."

Steve looked questioningly at Nan, and she said, "He's taking a course in sophistication in New York."

"Probably I could just hang around Steve for a few days," Jim said thoughtfully. "He knows all about this stuff, doesn't he?" An expression of enlightenment suddenly enveloped his cherubic features. "*That's* why you talked to Mom and Dad at Christmas, isn't it?"

"I don't know why I let you in," Nan grumbled, her color high again.

"I won't ask," Steve said, though his eyes sparkled. "At least not now. Maybe I should leave the two of you alone to catch up."

Jim looked relieved at this, but Nan felt both frustrated and disappointed. Not that she didn't want to visit with her brother, but there was so much to get sorted out with Steve. "Will I see you later?" she asked diffidently.

With his back turned to Jim, he gave her a slow, insinuating smile. "Around three?" he suggested. "I need you to look at some furniture with me."

Nan pictured his empty house, and the featherbed-type pillows in front of the fireplace. Her color deepened. "Haven't you made any progress on that?"

"Some. Will you come?"

Jim, apparently thinking her decision waited on him, said, "Francine will be finished by noon. We thought we'd take you out to lunch, but we'd be back by three."

Nan thought of saying something pert to him like "It would have been nice if you'd mentioned this earlier," but she merely said, "That will be fine. Won't you have some breakfast before you leave, Steve?"

He looked longingly at the refrigerator but shook his head. "I'll pick something up on my way home. Nice to see you again, Jim." As he passed Nan, he allowed his hand to rest briefly on her shoulder. "See you later."

Though Steve arrived shortly after she returned from lunch with her brother and Francine, Nan had had enough time to wonder whether she could talk him into bed first thing. When she opened the door, he grinned and said, "Thank God! I was afraid you'd be in Saran Wrap—and we've got an appointment to keep."

"Oh, hell," she muttered, almost with good grace. "I can see you're going to be a very slippery customer."

He dared, nevertheless, to kiss her—a long, passionate kiss that left her protesting, "Unfair. Where are we going?"

"To see some furniture."

"Now, there's a life-threatening emergency."

"This is a private transaction and relatively important." He helped her on with her jacket, brushing his lips against the top of her head. "It's a bed we're looking at."

She laughed. "In that case . . ."

As they drove to a house in Noe Valley, he explained that he'd been accumulating furniture through a variety of sources, ads and woodworkers, and interior designers and estate sales. "It's mostly modern, but craftsman modern. Greene and Greene type stuff. It's been fun tracking it down. One of the things that's helped distract me," he said, eyeing her significantly. "When you were at my house, you mentioned it was craftsman style."

"Did I?"

"Yep, and I decided to investigate that. I discovered that my house was designed by a disciple of the Greene brothers, and it occurred to me that

I should try to furnish it in keeping with that style. I've commissioned stained glass for several of the doors and windows from the Little-Raidl Studio. They've come up with some great designs. And I've found an architect who will try to modernize the kitchen in keeping with the style, too. So I owe it all to you, Nan."

"Glad to have been of some use."

"My house didn't have a lot of the built-in furniture real Greene and Greene places did, and it's a lot smaller than most of those. But I've been able to find a lot of stuff that works really well on the smaller scale. You should see the polished wood put together with polished dowels. It's gorgeous."

"I hope I will see it," she said, "very soon."

He winked at her. "I promise. Now this piece we're going to see I've only heard described, but it sounds perfect."

When Nan stood before the extraordinary craftsmanship of the bed, she felt a thrill of delight race through her. She ran her hand along the smooth surface of the beautiful dark-grained wood, understanding the skill and devotion that had gone into its creation. The headboard was actually a whole wall of bookshelves and intricately designed drawers and lighting, the footboard a statement of simple elegance.

The owner, who had acquired the bed with his house, obviously found it more a nuisance than a work of art. He assured them that the bed could be taken apart to be moved, though it would require someone knowledgeable.

"I have someone," Steve assured him. Then he turned to Nan and asked, "What do you think?"

"It's a very handsome piece," she said, her eyes telling him a great deal more. "Will it fit in the room?"

He shrugged slightly. "By its measurements, yes. There would still be room for the coyote, with its necklace."

Nan flushed, but felt a stirring deep inside her, sexual and yet more. She slipped her hand into his. "Well, then, if the price is reasonable, perhaps you should buy it."

And he did.

Without discussion they returned to her flat, where they stood for a long time in the hall merely holding onto one another. Steve could feel the tension build in himself as he knew it rose in her. He was aware of her breasts pressing against his chest and his own rigidity, the straining of his desire. "If this is obsession, it's perfectly acceptable to me," he whispered against her hair. "I seem to have caught it from you, like a fever. Just looking at you, just hearing your voice, makes it race through my body."

Her eyes, a clear, rich hazel, were alive with desire. Steve knew that his own burned with the need to join with her, to fill the part of her that ached for him, to merge with her flesh and be a part of her. His lips found hers, velvet and eager. His hands stroked her back, running down over her buttocks. He felt the shudder of her longing against his heart as her body rippled against his. Odd, to have this instant arousal with no need for foreplay. Puzzling, and exciting, and challenging. Steve locked fingers with her and drew her into the living room. "Would you put on some music?" he asked.

She cocked her head in a lazy, approving way and with scarcely a pause slipped a loose cassette into a tape deck. The strains of a Don Williams ballad flowed into the room. "Roger and I are fond of country music," she said.

"It'll be a new experience for me," he admitted, taking her into his arms and moving slowly around the room with her. Their bodies swayed tightly together, already feeling meshed in a subtle, appealing way. Steve could feel the arousal grow in himself, heightening gradually to a level of urgency where he suggested that they might want to go to the bedroom.

"I have a better idea," Nan responded, backing slightly away from him. She began to remove her clothes, her eyes steadily on him, and he followed suit. Her sweater, his shirt. Her bra, his undershirt. Her slacks, and his cords. Her panties and his shorts. And then she moved back into his arms, her flesh from head to toe pressed against his.

He was on fire at every point where they touched, his skin like a supersensitive conductor of sensation from her to him, deep, deep into the core of him. He could hardly bear the pleasure and the anticipation. She rubbed against him in a laughingly exaggerated attempt to tease him. He moaned deep in his throat. "You're killing me," he protested. "The bedroom?"

"Soon."

Obviously she could take more of this than he could, Steve thought ruefully. And so, all being fair in love and war, he danced her up against the archway into the hall and dropped his head to her breast. That delicious, tempting breast that had for too long escaped his attention. That firm, soft treasure that came so easily to his bidding. His lips drew the nipple in, already stiff with desire and yet still the soft tempter of his tongue. He could feel her moan in his mouth.

"The bedroom?" he suggested.

"The bedroom."

She was not restrained in her passion. He loved to hear the gurgling sounds of excitement she made in her throat and feel the urgency of her hands. He loved her touch on him, her sure, eager fingers stroking him, drawing him toward release. Her body was open to him, vulnerable and tense with excitement. He ached with the pleasure she gave him and with the unbearable sweetness of her body. She tasted of summer sunshine and autumn breezes and winter icy sharpness and spring renewal.

He led her and she followed. She guided him and he understood. This kind of unity was previously unknown to him. She drew him to her and he thrust inward and against the bud that awaited his stimulation. She came to him and he came to her, joined, rocking, urgent. Nothing was so sweet as her crying out, her intense release. His own came crashing after hers, like a wave of rocks, spattering everywhere, satisfying the smallest aroused atom of him.

Steve brushed the damp hair back from her forehead and kissed her closed eyes. "You are one sexy, delightful woman, Nan. Mind if I keep you?"

Her eyes blinked open and regarded him with cautious intensity. "We don't know if this is more than sex, Steve."

"I do know, and it is. For me, at least."

As if he hadn't answered, she said, "And you don't know what it's like to be the object of someone's sexual obsession. It's new, and intriguing to you, but if you stopped caring about me, it could be awful for you."

"I don't understand."

"No, of course you don't." She closed her eyes and turned her head away from him. He could feel a shudder run through her body. In a whisper she

FEVER PITCH

added, "If things were different, and they could easily change, I might make you very uncomfortable."

"I don't think things will change."

"Things always change. Let's just enjoy this for now, okay, Steve?" she said with finality.

He kissed the spot where a tendril of hair curled next to her ear. "Okay," he agreed, even as his mind raced to conclusions that disturbed and alarmed him. Had she just told him she was the object of someone's sexual obsession? And what did that mean—to her, and for them?

Chapter Fourteen

Nan's office mate, Joellen, had already left when Steve arrived to take Nan for a quick lunch in the cafeteria. "I don't know that I want them to see us together," she had protested that morning when he was leaving.

He had considered her thoughtfully. "I do. And I think you should get used to it, because I intend to become a fixture in your life."

Nan had reluctantly agreed but she hadn't quite come to terms with the idea. Though she had let herself enjoy every minute of the weekend with Steve, she had refused to look ahead, even as far as the next day. Matters were a little more complicated than Steve realized, but why wonder or worry about what would come next until it was absolutely necessary? Apparently Steve was intent on making it necessary.

It was slowly dawning on Nan that what she

felt for Steve was indeed more than a mere sexual obsession. And that it had been from the start. It was not simply Steve's Greek-god good looks and his casual virility that had attracted her. Right from their run together, she had felt an edgy involvement with him. She had, without quite intending to, made an investment in his life that had changed him.

His emotional distress at the time had moved her. In addition to feeling sorry for him, she had admired his lack of defensiveness and his willingness to come to terms with his newly identified problem. Nan was aware that he had originally run with her in order to prepare *her* for the malpractice case. His ability to shift gears, to look at the situation from another point of view, and to be honest with himself were capacities she had recognized instantly.

Certainly he had shown no interest in her then. Except that he had driven her to get her family at the airport, and he had come to dinner with them, and he had given her a Christmas present that had indicated there was more to his attachment than a few stolen kisses at the hospital. Why hadn't she been able to recognize that?

Steve appeared in the open doorway of her office, his golden head tilted slightly to the right, as thought he weren't quite sure of his reception. Nan was in the process of dictating notes to the local medical doctors of patients who had been hospitalized over the weekend. She gestured Steve into the room and switched off the button on the dictating microphone. "We could grab a sandwich from the catering truck and find an empty lecture hall," she said.

"Nope. Together, in the cafeteria, looking at each other with passionate gazes."

"In an empty lecture hall we could fool around a little," she tempted.

"Yeah, but not enough." He ran a finger sensuously along her lips, his back blocking them from view outside her office. "In the cafeteria we can start gossip about us. *Much* more fun than starting a riot in your neurology clinic, which we've already done, anyhow."

Nan sighed dramatically and pushed a batch of papers away from her. "All right. I'm trusting you on this, Steve. It doesn't feel like the right thing to do—yet."

His brows went up. "Yet? Is there something we need to do first? Like what?"

As if in answer to this question, Mark Schneider appeared in the doorway and cleared his throat. "Do you have a moment, Nan?" he asked, staring pointedly at Steve's back.

Steve turned around slowly, his hands still jammed in his lab coat pockets. He nodded to the department chairman with a courteous movement of his head.

"I'm just off to lunch," Nan said, feeling herself stiffen.

"A celebratory one, no doubt, with Dr. Winstead." Mark smiled benevolently on Steve, adding, "We're all very relieved that the lawsuit is so satisfactorily resolved."

"Thanks."

Schneider had moved into the office and now placed a piece of paper facedown on Nan's desk. "My secretary called my attention to this. No need to worry about it now, but it should be corrected and returned to my office by the end of the day."

Nan could see that he expected her not to make a fuss with Steve there, but she knew what the paper was, and she turned it over. "I checked with personnel, and they told me to do it this way."

"They must have misunderstood," Mark said coldly. "You took time away from work, and you should use vacation time to cover it."

Steve was frowning. "For the trial?" he asked Nan. "I remember you brought that up."

At the same time Nan said yes, Schneider picked up the paper and returned it to a file he held in his hand. The skin over one of his cheekbones seemed to twitch. "We'll discuss it later, Nan."

Nan said, "Fine," but Steve was not to be deterred from his understanding of the situation. "You expect her to use vacation time to cover the trial?" he asked Mark directly.

"This is a departmental matter," Schneider replied with a curt nod as he spun around on his heel and left the room.

Nan instantly rose and grabbed her purse from the floor. "Okay, let's go."

"Not so fast! Something is going on here, and I don't like the sound of it." Steve waved her back to her chair and drew up one on the opposite side of her desk. "Your department chairman is insisting that you take vacation time for the days you missed because of the malpractice trial, right?"

"Yes." Nan fingered the button on the dictating machine, turning it on and off several times.

"And personnel told you, and rightly so, that it was legitimate working time, right?"

"Right."

"But he still insists that you take it as vacation time, because he told you to." This time it wasn't even a question. Steve regarded her with pursed lips. "Tell me what's going on."

"It would be hard to explain."

"Try."

"How about tonight, when we have more time?"

"How about now, when you can't distract me with your feminine wiles?"

Nan sat staring for a long time at the dictating machine. How could she explain this? She'd never told anyone, not Angel and not Peter. Because she knew what their reactions would have been, that this was sexual harassment. And it wasn't, exactly. After asking her out a few times and being turned down, Mark Schneider had not asked again.

Nan finally said, "He thinks he treats me just like every other resident and fellow, but it's not really true. Enough people have remarked on how hard he is on me that I know I'm not imagining it."

"And why is he hard on you, Nan?"

"According to him it's for my own good, and because I have a lot to learn."

Steve reached across the desk and grasped her restless hands. "Look at me, Nan. Do you want me to tell you why?"

"You don't know why," she said softly, barely making eye contact.

"I think I do. I can put two and two together as well as anyone."

"I haven't had an affair with him, Steve. I told you that at Christmastime."

"I remember."

"And it isn't sexual harassment. I could have handled sexual harassment. I've managed to educate several members of my department about their behavior when it was out of line."

Steve nodded and locked his fingers with hers. "I can believe that. You're a very determined woman, and you know what's appropriate. But you couldn't fight Mark Schneider."

Nan was afraid he misunderstood. "Not because he's chairman of my department. That wouldn't have made any difference."

"No." Steve held tight to her cold fingers. "I watched him just now. At first I didn't see, or hear, anything remarkable. But I saw you stiffen and I paid more attention. It wasn't just a battle of wills, or an authoritative power play. There was something about the way he looked at you."

Nan dropped her eyes to their linked hands. "He watches me. His eyes follow me whenever we're in the same room. And he always seems to know where I am and what I'm doing."

"When did he ask you out?"

"Oh, right at the beginning, when I came here as an intern. But as I said, I wouldn't go, and he stopped asking. He didn't harass me, Steve."

"Just overcompensated for his *interest* by treating you more rigorously than others in your position."

Nan could feel tears stinging behind her eyes, but she refused to give in to them. "He took it on himself to make me work harder than the others, generally acting as though he were a well-meaning uncle."

Steve grimaced. "But there was that burning desire beneath a very thin veneer of studied helpfulness. As chairman of your department, he was in a unique position with regard to your situation. Holy hell, Nan."

"He's never handled it well, but he's tried, Steve. I've watched him struggle with it. I thought in time he'd get over it, but it hasn't happened." She bit her lip. "I've thought of leaving Fielding, as much as I love it here. Underneath the excitement of the medical center, there's always been this . . . discomfort dragging me down. Four years is a long time. So now, when I should be thinking about next year and where I'm going to be, I'm torn. He sort of threatens not to keep me on staff, but, in a funny way of course, he almost has to, for his own sake. It's an ugly situation, for both of us."

"And what will he do when he sees that you're involved with me?"

"I don't know. Nothing, I should think." She smiled sadly. "I haven't known what to do, Steve. There hasn't really been anything I could do. I can't actually talk about it with him because he denies it. I've asked him to talk with Jerry Stoner, but he acts as though I were the one who had a problem."

"What happened when you went out with what's-his-name?"

"Peter. He never came to the medical center, and I never took him to department functions, but Mark knew I was seeing someone. It didn't change things for me, for better or worse."

"An interesting allusion." With their linked hands, he drew her to her feet. "Let's go to lunch.

I'd like to think about this for a while. We can talk more later, okay?"

When Nan had developed her sexual attachment to Steve, she had not been able to erase the image of Mark Schneider from her mind—staring at her, obsessed with her. It was how she felt about Steve. She wanted to touch him. She wanted him to touch her. She felt aroused just thinking of him, and that was not a state she was accustomed to, even in sexual relationships. In addition, of course, Nan and Steve had *had* no relationship, not really. So Nan had seen herself, as she allowed the secret kissing to continue, as indulging in an obsession that had no foundation in a real tie to Steve.

With her body in a constant state of arousal, she had been able to think of little else. Which was very distracting. Nan had hoped that making love with him would satisfy that unfortunate craving of hers. It had only whetted her appetite. And made her grateful that she hadn't agreed to continue seeing him, because her obsession would surely have been as distasteful to poor Steve, who scarcely knew her, as Mark Schneider's was to her. Nan would not let Steve see her behaving that way. It was embarrassing and shameful. Much rather he be briefly annoyed with her fickleness than discover the depth of her depravity.

Or so her reasoning had gone. Nan realized now

FEVER PITCH

as she drove with Steve across the Golden Gate Bridge that it sounded melodramatic, but the intensity of her sexual feelings had been and still was alarming to her. Even now, knowing she had other strong feelings for Steve, she could believe that the sexual feelings overshadowed all the others. Which didn't seem a particularly healthy state of affairs to her.

"Are you warm enough?" he asked, reaching over to lay the backs of his fingers gently against her cheek. "I can put the top up if you like."

The fresh spring air sped past her, releasing tendrils from her French braid and tossing them about her face. Nan felt exhilarated by the openness of the car and the immediacy of the March night. "This is great. I keep the top down ninety percent of the time on the LeBaron."

"Speaking of LeBarons, will your brother tell your family about us?"

"Undoubtedly. Though maybe not quite the situation he found when he arrived." She grinned ruefully. "That's why I didn't want to go home to change. I knew the phone would ring or the answering machine would be blinking message lights at me. I'll talk with them soon."

"What are you going to tell them?"

"That depends on what kind arrangement we come to."

"Arrangement?" His eyes looked amused. "Very good, Nan. This sounds serious."

"I'll bet you haven't said anything to your family about me."

"No, the longer I can keep you my secret, the better. With the best intentions in the world, they'll only manage to make things more difficult for me, and you, and us. I moved across the bridge to put some distance between me and them. They keep wanting to drag me into their social world, and I'm just not interested."

"Why not?"

"Because it feels so artificial to me. Who cares about wearing the right clothes and going to the right restaurants and having the right family background? Medicine is different. Everything about it is real, at least in my job. People hurt and you try to heal them. You don't care if they're rich or poor, black or white, gay or heterosexual. You just try to find out what's wrong with them and make it right—or as right as you can. That seems so much more important to me than all this social snobbery and financial righteousness. I guess there's an element of all that in medicine—the arrogance and the monetary concerns. But I won't play that kind of game. It leads nowhere."

He shrugged and looked embarrassed. "Sorry. I didn't mean to make a lecture of it."

"I don't mind. I need to know that kind of thing about you." Nan watched lights coming on in houses on a distant hillside. They looked welcoming in the dark of evening. "I'm greedy, Steve. I want to know everything about you, and you don't talk about yourself as much as most people."

"Don't I?" His brows came down slightly, and he looked thoughtful. "I suppose I don't. I was taught that you shouldn't talk too much about yourself; that it's bad manners. And the kind of talk I'd hear in my parents' set was annoying to me—where people had gone skiing, or how much they'd spent on their houses, or the kinds of cars they drove. Doctors do it, too, and lawyers and businesspeople. But to me it's like advertising how well-off I am, or how I know the right places to go because I'm with the in-group. You know what I mean?"

Nan laughed. "I'm nouveau riche, remember? We're better at it than anyone. We may go to the wrong places and buy the wrong stuff, but we talk about it all the time."

"You've never done any such thing."

"Just because I'm careful, and I keep my eyes open. Look at Jim. He's determined to polish himself up because he thinks that stuff is important. And it is, in a way. Your parents would be appalled by mine."

A wide grin spread across his face. "Oh, I can hardly wait! Your dad and mine. Your mom and mine. Talk about infusing old blood with new spirit! Remind me to get a video camera before they all meet. I want it on film."

"It would be embarrassing for my folks."

"Nonsense. Sincerity will win out over smooth manners every time. At least that's how I see it."

"They may not see it that way."

"Sweetheart, by then your brother will have primed them for the whole social scene here. I have the utmost faith in Jim's ability to point out the ludicrous side of it and your tact in helping them feel comfortable." He glanced over at her as they drove toward the Belvedere road that led up toward his house. "Was Jim hinting that you had already tried that at Christmas?"

"I thought you weren't going to bring that up."

"I only promised not to say anything right then."

Nan frowned at the dashboard, thinking how to explain. "My folks were upset that I wouldn't tell them who gave me the necklace. To them it meant that I was ashamed of you, or I was ashamed of them. Since I wasn't going to discuss you, and I didn't want them to think I was ashamed of them, we kind of got into a discussion of their social polish, first my dad and then my mom. I'm surprised they said anything about it to Jim. Maybe they did because he got this thing into his head about getting some social polish of his own for Francine."

Steve reached over to squeeze her hand. "I like your folks, Nan. They're great people."

"Yes," she agreed, and fell silent again.

They drove for some time before he said, "Nan,

FEVER PITCH

I talked with Jerry Stoner this afternoon. Just gave him a hypothetical case, you know, without mentioning Mark's name, or yours. He said he'd be perfectly willing to broach the subject with Mark if you wanted him to. He thought he might be of some help, and that it wouldn't be the first case of its kind that he's seen. So you can think about whether you want to do that."

She stared at him, openmouthed. "You don't waste any time, do you?"

"Not where you're concerned. Are you sorry I did it?"

"No. I would have done it years ago but I didn't want to get Mark in trouble, and he's always been so adamant that he didn't have a problem."

"Jerry had no difficulty believing my anonymous department chairman could have a problem. He was very matter-of-fact about the whole thing. He even said it would be a mercy to get some help for the guy, who's probably been suffering torments about it."

"I think he has been," Nan said. "He just thought he could handle it by himself."

"And he hasn't been able to. Well, he'll need help now when he sees you with me at the medical center. That's going to make things even more difficult for him. So do you think you'd like to talk with Jerry?"

"Maybe." Nan tried to picture Mark being exposed to her own particular passion for Steve, and added, "Probably. But I may look for a job outside Fielding."

"That's entirely up to you. I just want you to do what will make you most comfortable," he said as they pulled into his garage.

It had been so long since the first time she'd been there. Nan could clearly remember how she'd felt that first time, and what she had intended to do. She had been filled with the need for physical contact with him, and the need had made her tense and anxious. Once again she could feel the rising tide of desire in her body, but this time the tension was replaced by anticipation, and the anxiety by a warm vulnerability. Her body felt open to him already, simply awaiting his touch.

Steve led her into the house with her hand clasped in his. The simple connection was almost enough to distract her from what he was showing her—but not quite. The kitchen he dismissed as "not tackled yet" but the rest of the place had been transformed. The wood paneling in the dining room and living room were now matched by a smattering of crafted furniture that fit perfectly into the setting. The fireplace alcove had built-in seating—wooden benches with tufted pillows—that had the feel of window seats. There were bright Navajo rugs on the polished hardwood floors and books on the bookshelves behind leaded-glass doors. There was a wonderful old rocker and an end table of intricately put-together wood with a marble center surface.

Nan shook her head wonderingly. "You've made it something special. I can't believe you found all this stuff in just a couple months."

"I had help," he admitted. "And the stained glass for the windows and the landing won't be done for another six weeks. But it's great, isn't it? It's just how I pictured it, completely different from the antique furniture I grew up with. It's not too dark for you, is it?"

All the dark paneling and the wood floors might have seemed oppressive to some people. Nan ran her fingers along the wood of the dining table. "No, I love all this wood. It feels warm and alive to me. The copper and tile on the fireplace, the white surface between the beams and above the paneling, all of it seems perfect. Everything *glows*."

His smile was mischievous. "And I kept the feather bed handy," he explained, lifting the lid of a bench to reveal the goose down pillow stuffed within. "We can pull it out any time for in front of the fireplace."

"The perfect host," she said, but she felt a tightening in her throat. "Show me upstairs."

"I haven't had time to get the bed moved over yet," he said when he led her into what was obviously his bedroom, where the cot still stood, and little else. Except the coyote. "I've kept this here for you."

He lifted the gold necklace with its arrow and diamond from the folds of the red neckerchief. "Every morning I woke up and saw it there. At first it made me angry and kept me forcused on how you'd behaved so badly. But I couldn't stay mad at you, as hard as I tried. Before I would realize it, my mind would be making excuses for you, and remembering how special you seemed to me. I'd remember our run, and the trip to the airport, and doing dishes at your flat, and kissing you. Kissing you all over the medical center, like two teenagers in the first throes of passion. And then the magic of making love to you here."

Steve pulled her against him, hugging her tightly. "I wanted you back here. I wanted you wearing the necklace again. May I put it on you?"

Nan read his intention in those overpowering blue eyes. He was asking her to make a commitment. Not just of her body, but of all of her. She swallowed painfully against a constricted throat. "Tell me what it would mean. Tell me what you'd expect of me."

"Basically, everything," he said, touching his lips to her forehead. "Let me show you something."

Off of the smallest room on the second floor, which he was in the process of making into a study, there was a tiny balcony. He opened the door and ushered her out onto a space that barely held the two of them. Its view was of San Francisco across the bay, but it was a very different view than the one from the living room. This view was partially obscured by feathery branches of a cypress tree that swayed in the slightest breeze. The lights of the city disappeared and reappeared in varying configurations, always magical and always elusive.

"That's what love is like, I think," he murmured against her hair. His arm tightened around her shoulder. "It's mystical, and concrete, and constantly shifting, and wondrous. Now you see it, now you don't, but you always know it's there. It's just that things get in the way sometimes that make it harder to see the whole picture for a while."

"Like sexual obsession?"

"You'd probably have seen the whole picture a lot sooner if you hadn't thought your physical attraction to me was an obsession like Mark Schneider's. I grant you," he said seriously, "that it's a strong attraction, and that makes you uncomfortable. But my guess is that it will calm down in time. Not too much, I hope. I'm delighted by it. But I think there's something strong underpinning it that's a lot more than sex."

The cypress tree branch swayed so they could briefly see the moon shining down on San Francisco. But even when the branch covered the moon again, they could see the moonlight bathing the city. Nan felt herself gripped by strong emotion. "I was so frightened when I didn't seem to have any control over my desire. You would kiss me, and my body turned to liquid fire. I felt addicted to that pleasure, and I lusted for more. But we didn't have any kind of relationship. And that seemed very much like Mark's obsession. I simply couldn't let that happen to me, or to you."

"Well, I was afraid, too," Steve admitted. "It was easier to play games with you, thinking they were games you were happy to play, than to face what was happening to me. To realize that I was falling in love with you. I've been afraid I couldn't fall in love that way, that deeply, because of my father."

Nan turned to look up at his shadowed face. "But why?"

"He's a philanderer. Most of their life together, he's had affairs with other women, and my mother tolerates it. But I'm like him in a lot of ways, and I've had trouble in the past with women, with how I treated them."

Nan stood very still. The branch swept across the city view again and shuddered in a scented breeze. "How have you treated them?"

"I think I may have used them. I could always tell myself I wasn't, that this was something they wanted. And they said they did." He frowned, the fingers of his right hand unconsciously stroking her shoulder. "But I felt like I was imitating Dad. I felt like I wasn't *giving* anything. If a woman offered something, I took it, and tired to justify doing it. I didn't know until you how much I *wanted* to give."

"But you played a game with me."

"Yes, but that was different. Actually, that game was to tempt you, and to keep me from taking something from you before you were ready. I was afraid if we just acted like any couple starting to date we'd—oh, I don't know—go to bed together without it meaning anything, for either of us. I didn't know then that you were afraid of being obsessed with me. And when you finally admitted that, I had the most wonderful realization that I wasn't like my father at all."

"Because you didn't want to take advantage of it?"

"That, but more. I found I liked being responsible for you. It wasn't a burden to know you were vulnerable about your attraction to me. It was an opportunity to give you something only I could give you. You ran away from me earlier because you didn't think I could give you that."

"I had no right to ask it of you."

"And you had no reason to trust me."

Nan leaned her head against his shoulder. "I used to be a very trusting person, but I'm not as much anymore. I wanted to trust you. But I couldn't even seem to trust myself."

"Do you think you could trust me now?"

"Yes. I seem to have entrusted you with this

crazy problem of mine, and you manage to make me feel normal. And cared for."

He encircled her waist with his arms. "Loved, Nan. I want you to feel loved. And I think you love me, too. That's not just wishful projection, is it?"

Nan met his intent gaze steadily. "I don't know how long I've loved you. I don't know when I started loving you. I just know that I do. When you kissed me in my kitchen, all sorts of things changed forever, but I didn't know it then. It was almost as if my body had to teach my heart what was happening. I've never felt like this about anyone before."

"No, neither have I. We're quite a pair, aren't we?"

She nodded and raised her face for his kiss. It was like one of their early kisses, full of promise and startling in its effect. Sensations cascaded through her. But alarm had turned to acceptance, and fear to trust. She was incredibly vulnerable, but he loved her. And her overwhelming desire was rooted in her love for him. Together they would make a remarkable team.

"Shall I put this on you?" he asked, holding out the necklace.

"As long as you remove my clothes at the same time."

"I can handle that, but maybe we should go inside."

"Whatever."

DON'T MISS THE FIRST TWO
EXCITING NOVELS IN THE FIELDING
MEDICAL CENTER SERIES
BY ELIZABETH NEFF WALKER

WHEN OPPOSITES ATTRACT

Dr. Angel Crawford and Dr. Cliff Lenzini were both dedicated doctors. Angel was the most promising new resident at San Francisco's prestigious Fielding Medical Center. Cliff was the Center's most brilliant surgeon. When these two talented physicians worked together, even though their concern was the same, sparks flew as their views clashed. But when they came together after hospital hours, a different kind of heat was generated.

Angel respected Cliff as a doctor and as a man, and she expected equal treatment. How could she keep going back into his arms when he persisted in patronizing her as a person? She had no answer until she discovered the real man behind Dr. Cliff Lenzini's surgical mask ... until she discovered her true feelings ... and what it was she so deeply hungered for ...

HEART CONDITIONS

"NOT ONLY WILL YOU GET TO ENTER THE SOPHISTICATED WORLD OF MEDICINE, YOU'LL GET TREATED TO A WONDERFUL ROMANCE BETWEEN TWO VERY CAPTIVATING PEOPLE. DON'T MISS THIS KICK-OFF NOVEL."—CATHERINE COULTER

FRIENDS

When Rachel Weis became medical ethics consultant at San Francisco's prestigious Fielding Medical Center, she knew she could depend on Dr. Jerry Stoner for support. She and the brilliant psychiatrist had been friends long before Rachel was tragically widowed—and now she needed his strength and insight as she battled for patients' rights.

AND LOVERS

But when Jerry began to play a growing part in her personal life, Rachel felt the chill of panic. In the past, passion had only caused her pain she didn't want to risk again. How could Jerry, who had been her friend for so long, now become her lover? How could she again make herself vulnerable to a man ... vulnerable to loss? Rachel recited this litany to herself over and over ... but she couldn't quiet her hungry heart....

◐ SIGNET   **◼ ONYX**

PASSIONATE SECRETS, SCANDALOUS SINS

- ☐ **BLISS by Claudia Crawford.** Rachel Lawrence seeks to mold her beautiful great-granddaughter Bliss in her image despite the objections of her entire family. Then comes the riveting revelation of the shocking deception that Bliss's mother and aunt can no longer hide ... as four generations of women come together to relive their lives and love, and face the truth that will shatter their illusions and threaten to doom their dreams for the future. (179374—$5.50)

- ☐ **NOW AND FOREVER by Claudia Crawford.** Nick Albert was the type of man no woman could resist. Georgina, Mona, and Amy were all caught in a web of deceit and betrayal—and their irresistible passion for that man that only one of them could have—for better or for worse. (175212—$5.50)

- ☐ **NIGHT SHALL OVERTAKE US by Kate Saunders.** Four young girls make a blood vow of eternal friendship at an English boarding school. Through all the time and distance that separates them, they are bound together by a shared past ... until one of them betrays their secret vow. "A triumph."—*People* (179773—$5.99)

- ☐ **WORLD TO WIN, HEART TO LOSE by Netta Martin.** Alexandra Meldrum stormed the male bastions of oil and property, using anything—and anyone—to win back her family's honor. Now she has it all. There's only one thing more she desires. Revenge. Revenge on the one man who is her match in business and master in bed. (176863—$4.99)

*Prices slightly higher in Canada

Buy them at your local bookstore or use this convenient coupon for ordering.

PENGUIN USA
P.O. Box 999 — Dept. #17109
Bergenfield, New Jersey 07621

Please send me the books I have checked above.
I am enclosing $_____ (please add $2.00 to cover postage and handling). Send check or money order (no cash or C.O.D.'s) or charge by Mastercard or VISA (with a $15.00 minimum). Prices and numbers are subject to change without notice.

Card #_____ Exp. Date _____
Signature_____
Name_____
Address_____
City _____ State _____ Zip Code _____

For faster service when ordering by credit card call **1-800-253-6476**

Allow a minimum of 4-6 weeks for delivery. This offer is subject to change without notice.

① SIGNET

ROMANTIC ENCOUNTERS

☐ **LAURA by Hilary Norman.** Laura's idyllic girlhood was shattered by an unspeakable act that made her fear she could never be happy or normal again. Her erotic initiation came in the arms of a man nearly twice her age, a master manipulator who knew all her secrets and used them to bend her to his will. Now Laura realized she had made the deadliest mistake a woman in love could make. (180127—$5.99)

☐ **FASCINATION by Hilary Norman.** A beautiful woman, a dazzling jewel, and three generations of family secrets ... "A winner all the way!"—*Atlanta Journal and Constitution* (403789—$5.99)

☐ **RIVERBEND by Marcia Martin.** As a dedicated young doctor, Samantha Kelly was ready to battle all the superstitions and prejudices of a Southern town seething with secrets and simmering with distrust of an outsider. But as a passionate woman she found herself struggling against her own needs when Matt Tyler, the town's too handsome, too arrogant, unoffical leader, decided to make her his. (180534—$4.99)

☐ **BELOVED STRANGER/SUMMER STORM by Joan Wolf. With an Introduction by Catherine Coulter.** Bestselling author Joan Wolf has received both critical and popular acclaim for her compelling romances many of which have become collectors' items. Now, this exclusive dual collection brings back two of her long out of print contemporary love stories. (182510—$3.99)

*Prices slightly higher in Canada

Buy them at your local bookstore or use this convenient coupon for ordering.

PENGUIN USA
P.O. Box 999 — Dept. #17109
Bergenfield, New Jersey 07621

Please send me the books I have checked above.
I am enclosing $_____ (please add $2.00 to cover postage and handling). Send check or money order (no cash or C.O.D.'s) or charge by Mastercard or VISA (with a $15.00 minimum). Prices and numbers are subject to change without notice.

Card #_____ Exp. Date _____
Signature_____
Name_____
Address_____
City _____ State _____ Zip Code _____

For faster service when ordering by credit card call **1-800-253-6476**

Allow a minimum of 4-6 weeks for delivery. This offer is subject to change without notice.